Franklin Horton

Copyright © 2018 by Franklin Horton

Cover by Deranged Doctor Design

Editing by Felicia Sullivan

ISBN: 9781723880940

All rights reserved.

No part of this book may be reproduced in any form or by any electronic or mechanical means, including information storage and retrieval systems, without written permission from the author, except for the use of brief quotations in a book review.

❀ Created with Vellum

ACKNOWLEDGMENTS

This book is dedicated to the people that make books happen. To the readers, the writers, the friends, and the family.

Writers, particularly this one, are a contrary bunch. It takes a patient and supportive tribe to keep them on track and productive. Thanks for your comments and encouragement. Thanks for the reviews you leave on Amazon and for the stories you share.

In particular I'd like to thank my author buddies Steven Bird and Chris Weatherman, with whom I've spent many hours over many drinks discussing writing, guns, and the decline of Western civilization. One day we actually need to write the ridiculous books we've brainstormed on those late nights.

I'd like to thank Kevin Pierce, the narrator of all my audiobooks, for his professionalism, his wisdom, and for what we've done together.

I'd like to thank esteemed gun writer Van Harl for his encouragement and Henry Rifles for their technical support.

I'd like to thank my good friend "Richard" for the hundreds of hours of inspiring conversation and correspondence that helped me to distill this book to its essence. I appreciate the friendship and support.

Finally, thanks to the Mad Mick himself. You know who you are and I hope I've done you proud.

1

It was early fall and the nights were becoming cool in the mountains. Eleven tired women walked through dew-soaked grass, their wet feet cold nearly to the point of numbness. It was a small blessing. Beyond the grassy field lay the steep trail of jagged shale leading to the grow houses. That shale sliced at their bare feet like razors.

The men who accompanied them, their kidnappers, did not give them shoes, hoping bare feet would slow the women if they tried to escape. The women did not know what they'd do when winter came. They expected they'd still be working but would they be given shoes? They were certain the men would come up with something to keep them occupied. Better they be given some useful labor than to be left at the mercy of bored men, for there was indeed *no* mercy at the hands of bored men.

The women were escorted by a team of two heavily-armed men. Each carried an AR-15 and wore a handgun. Enough people had been shot at the camp that the women knew the presence of the armed guards was not an idle threat. They would not hesitate to shoot if they had to.

Kellen was at the head of the line, walking behind a guard they called Buster. She couldn't help but notice that Buster allowed his rifle to dangle freely from its sling as he mumbled curses and furiously scratched his body with both hands. Kellen saw redness and an oozing rash creeping up the back of Buster's neck. The same rash covered both his arms and she could only assume it covered the rest of his body. His misery brought a smile to her face.

For three weeks, Kellen and her crew had discreetly collected poison ivy and poison oak during their work at the grow houses. During their bathroom breaks, they wrapped sandwich baggies around their hands, grabbing handfuls of poison ivy leaves and then folding the baggie down to encapsulate the leaves like a doctor peeling exam gloves from their hands. Before the terror attacks came and the country fell apart, one of the women in the camp had supplemented her income by selling essential oils. With a basic understanding of the chemistry behind extracting oils, they'd come up with a plan to extract urushiol, the chemical irritant present in the plants, by boiling it.

Kellen turned to the woman behind her in line and made some pointless comment, using the ruse to check out the guard behind them. She was pleased to find him in distress also, clawing at his neck with his fingernails, trying to find some relief to the rash clearly overtaking his body. The only thing these men were concerned with was their personal suffering. It was fair justice for them, considering the suffering they doled out on a regular basis.

After the women had extracted a quantity of the oil, they began adding it to the laundry. They were required to wash the men's clothing several times a week, doing the washing in tubs and drying the clothes on a clothesline. Over the course of two weeks they had hit nearly every man's underwear and t-shirts with the oil. Now they were beginning to see signs of progress. The women knew the oil would not be debilitating, but at least hoped the itching would be distracting. This was the very moment when Kellen would find out if that was so.

She tightened her grip on the hoe she was carrying and threw a quick glance behind her. The rear guard was staring off in discomfort as he shoved a hand into his pants to dig at his blistered and chafing crotch. Kellen coughed, the signal for the women to prepare to fight. The women readied themselves, gripping their weapons and hardening their resolve.

At the rear of the line, the woman immediately in front of the guard drove the handle of her hoe into the guard's already irritated groin. He doubled over in pain, gasping for breath. Following through with the movement she'd practiced hundreds of times, the woman spun the implement around and used both hands to bring the sharp end of the hoe down on the man's head. He dropped like a rock.

The man at the head of the line turned lazily to see what was going on, his rifle dangling as he scratched and scraped at the inflamed skin beneath his shirt. Kellen was already in full swing, aiming at his head like it was a fleshy piñata. He barely had time to register surprise before the thick hoe handle connected and there was a crack like a home run being knocked from the park. The guard nose-dived into the hard dirt.

Kellen rushed forward and stripped the forward guard of his rifle. She straightened, switched off the safety, and fired a single round into the air. The shot echoed and reverberated, filling the valley and rolling across the mist-covered lake. Another woman rushed by Kellen and removed the guard's handgun from a black nylon holster. Other women took the guns from the rear guard. One of them, clearly harboring a grudge for some indiscretion, paused long enough to repeatedly bash the downed man in the head with the buttstock of the rifle. If he was not dead, he would likely be impaired by a lifelong brain injury.

At the sound of the gunshot, women throughout the camp mobilized and fell into the plan they'd been hatching for weeks. They turned on their blistered and oozing abductors. Women with knives rushed from the kitchen, slashing at guards and plunging their butcher knives deep into the bellies of the men who had taken them from their homes. The laundresses weaponized the cudgels with which they stirred the tubs of soaking laundry. The women of the gardens rose to brandish their hoes and pointy trowels.

The men of the camp did not stand idly by and allow this to happen. The armed men had a distinct advantage and they used it, whipping up their rifles and snapping off shots, trying to drop the army of wailing banshees streaking through the camp toward their freedom. In the infirmary, a kidnapped nurse had worked for two weeks to treat the unidentified rash that was debilitating the men of the camp. Of course, she hadn't worked too hard at easing their pain since she was in on the scheme. The vile-smelling unguents that she so diligently applied to the worst of the cases was actually not a medicine at all, but a solution of animal feces and petroleum jelly that encouraged infection.

At the sound of the gunshot, the nurse took up a scalpel and went to check on her first patient. He lay in a cot separated from the others by an old bed sheet draped over a string. When he opened his eyes and smiled at his angel of mercy, she plunged the scalpel into his neck and twisted it, boring a wound from which he would be unable to staunch the flow of blood. She worked quickly to dispatch her other two patients, both of them sleeping peacefully.

After the way in which she'd been treated in the camp, she had no remorse for their misery and deaths. With her work complete, she grabbed a hidden pack containing bottled water and rations she had stolen from those designated for her patients. She threw it over her shoulder and ran from the building. She made it only fifty yards before she was spotted. When she failed to comply with an order to halt, a guard shot her in the back. She died in the wet field, tiny seeds from the tall grass clinging to her damp pink cheeks.

Kellen and the other armed women from her work party streamed back into camp. They hoped to find a full-fledged revolt underway with all of the brutal men dead or dying. Instead, they found more fallen women than men. In fact, the fighting appeared to be mostly over. Men were no longer shooting, but standing around looking at the bodies of dead women and trying to figure out what the hell had happened.

This changed things. There were women who needed to be freed but could they even get to them? Kellen and her accomplices conferred. They could open fire at the assembled men but more men were pouring onto the grounds now. They had neither enough weapons nor ammunition to drop all of them.

And what would happen if they opened fire and gave away their position? The men would surely mount horses and chase them deep into the hills where they would be killed, or worse. If they were going to get away, they had to leave now. Those women who didn't get away would have to find another opportunity.

Kellen was uncomfortable having to make decisions for a group of people. "What do we do?" she hissed.

"We shouldn't go together," one of the women spoke up. "We'll leave a track like a herd of cattle."

Kellen nodded vigorously. "You're right. Two groups?"

She looked around the group and found nodding heads, scared faces.

"They're talking on their radios," one of the women said. "When they can't reach our guards, they'll come looking for us."

"Then let's go," Kellen said. "Enough talk. Let's get what gear we can off the two guards, then we split up and disappear."

The women ran back to their fallen escorts, falling upon the unconscious and injured men like a flock of buzzards. Each of the two groups took one man's pack. They turned out the guards' pockets and took lighters, knives, and anything else they found. There were quick hugs and whispered encouragement, then the groups split off. Each ran as fast as their bare feet would carry them over the sharp paths of rotting shale and limestone.

BRYAN WAS asleep when the first shot was fired. He'd stayed up too late and drank too much last night. Gunshots themselves were not that unusual. Sometimes the men dropped deer to add variety to the meals or fired to deter pesky bears. When the shots continued it became clear something more was going on. Bryan's foggy mind immediately raced to invasion, a result of his persistent fear that someone would try to steal what he was building here.

He scrambled out of bed, disoriented and wobbly. He didn't know whether to go for a rifle, his clothes, or try to make an escape into the hills. He had a plan for that, with gear cached in a waterproof blue barrel. Then it occurred to him he should probably go for his radio. He turned it off at night because he didn't want to be bothered with the chatter of sentries and early morning work crews. He picked up the black Motorola from his nightstand, turned it on, and listened for a moment, hoping to glean some insight. Men were barking at each other, shouting instructions across the radio to each other. He couldn't make heads or tails of it. After a few moments of this he became frustrated and hit the transmit button.

"Everybody just shut the fuck up. What the hell is going on?"

The radio traffic fell silent. Everyone on the channel knew who the irate voice belonged to and no one wanted to deliver the bad news. Bryan assumed they were trying to outwait each other, to see who drew the short straw and had to start talking.

"Jefferson, this is Top Cat. It looks like we had a little escape attempt."

Jefferson was the radio call sign Bryan had assigned to himself. It originated with his obsession with Thomas Jefferson, the founding father and gentleman farmer after whom he modeled himself. Top Cat was the farm manager.

"Top Cat, you said *attempt*. Am I to take it their effort to escape was unsuccessful?"

There was enough of a delay that Jefferson knew he was not going to like the answer.

"I don't have a full count yet but I'd say I've at least got twelve to fifteen escapees. Maybe a dozen or more dead. There are several unaccounted for."

"What about our people? Did we lose anybody?"

"I got six not responding to their radios," Top Cat replied. *"I would assume those are either dead or in pursuit of escapees. I've got men out there trying to run down those six right now and figure out why they're not answering."*

Bryan looked for something to throw but the only thing convenient was the radio and he needed that. "Dammit! Get a team on horseback after those escapees. And listen, I know the men are going to be pissed off but I don't want those women harmed. If anyone leaves one of the women unable to work, they've got to cover all their duties. Is that clear?"

"Do you want me on the search party?" Top Cat asked.

"No," Bryan snapped. "I want you and Lester in my office in fifteen minutes. I want a full report on what you know."

"Got it," Top Cat replied, his voice sagging, indicating how little he relished that meeting.

Bryan's radio clattered onto his nightstand and he flopped backward on the bed. He rubbed the sleep from his eyes and sighed heavily. The burden of being a landowner in hostile times was weighing on him. There was more work needed done than he had people to perform it.

They had a marijuana crop to harvest. They had poppy seeds that would soon be ready for harvesting opium. This first batch of opium would be traded and sold in its unrefined form but Bryan had hopes that by next year, if the world didn't get back to normal, he might be able to produce heroin. He had a rough idea of how to do it and was going to spend the winter reading up on the process.

They also had food crops that need to be preserved and firewood that needed to be processed for the winter. There were literally hundreds of jobs needing to be done and, without fuel and electrical power, they all required manpower to accomplish. Nothing was easy anymore. Counting both his voluntary and involuntary workforce, Douthat Farms had over one hundred mouths to feed. That number was regretfully smaller now thanks to the dead bodies currently scattered around the property.

Bryan Padowicz had been a history professor at a small liberal arts college in central Virginia. He was in his late-forties, his thick beard and hipster man-bun beginning to show traces of gray. The collapse of the nation had both disrupted and inconvenienced Bryan. His summer days usually revolved around the same routine. He would smoke some pot and then hang out in Main Street coffeehouses, philosophizing and trying to impress young female students. Most evenings there was a party somewhere, and those also provided him with an ample opportunity to dazzle young women with his wit and intellect.

While Bryan certainly had the trappings of a socialist professor, and often pretended to be one, it was just for show. He was purely a capitalist. He'd been growing marijuana since his own college days and had gotten damn good at it. While he told folks he had installed solar panels and rain barrels on his quaint Victorian home to help the environment, he actually used his solar array to provide unmonitored water and electricity to his basement grow rooms.

Since liberal arts professors were paid a paltry sum, the marijuana operation helped him live the lifestyle he felt he deserved. He did not deal with ounces and quarter-ounces of pot as he had in his college days. He only dealt in pounds and quarter-pounds, and the proceeds from that allowed him to travel when the mood struck him. It allowed him to buy expensive pieces of art from obscure galleries. Always having top-notch pot also provided him with yet another way to meet and woo young women.

As a history professor, Bryan had enough experience with collapsing civilizations to read the writing on the wall. After the terror attacks rocked the nation, he knew it was going to take a while for the United States to get back on its feet. It was a small attack but well-planned. The terrorists had hit just the right spots in the infrastructure that they swept the legs right out from under modern society. There was a domino effect, technically called a *cascading systems failure*, which caused other systems to fail as a result of losing fuel, power, and communications. Now they were little more than pioneers living among the useless trappings of modern society.

Bryan also understood there was a possibility the country might reemerge from this disaster as a nation that held little resemblance to the earlier United States. He wanted to be ready for any contingency. His understanding of history told him men who controlled trade and commerce prospered, while those who isolated themselves and hid out in bunkers would remain isolated and poor. He wanted to establish himself, to put himself in a position where he might be one of the financial powerhouses of the re-emerging world. Padowicz might one day be mentioned with the same reverence as Carnegie, Vanderbilt, DuPont, Westinghouse, and a long line of others.

He'd lived in the same college neighborhood for years, a place where he could walk to class and to the local bars. It was also close enough to the core of the college community that young women could come by and visit him. Though information was sparse in the early days of the collapse, there was no panic and unrest in Bryan's community. He sat around each evening with his friends, smoking weed and discussing the state of things. It was during one of those bull sessions that Bryan hatched the plan that would lead him to seize Douthat State Park and re-christen it Douthat Farms.

Nestled in the mountains of Virginia, Douthat State Park was a product of the Works Project Administration, a depression-era program that put Americans back to work building infrastructure projects. Between the WPA and the Civilian Conservation Corps, several rustic state parks were built across Virginia. Bryan had visited Douthat State Park since he was a child, camping there with his parents. It was one of his favorite places in the world. He would hike the winding trails, observe the wildlife, fish and kayak the lake, and lie on the swimming beach in the warm afternoon sand.

Bryan hatched his original plan over many stoned afternoons, laying out how he could become a colonial-era gentleman farmer if he could find the appropriate place to do so. His companions, mostly impressionable young men, were enthralled with his plan. He explained the ideal location would be remote and have a portion of the infrastructure already in place.

One afternoon, the random act of stumbling over a mountain bike helmet in his junk room reminded him of riding at Douthat State Park and he instantly knew it would be the ideal location. He understood it was too early in the collapse to act on his plan immediately but he knew how to make it happen. He'd give things a month. When employees at the camp knew they weren't getting paid anymore, and no more guests were coming, the place would be ripe for the taking. Most of the staff would be gone. What few remained could be easily driven out. Or killed.

He understood he couldn't do it alone. He would need an armed force both to *take* the facility and to *keep* the facility. He would also need a labor force, though he was entirely ambivalent as to whether this force would be volunteer labor or forced labor. As a student of history, he was aware that slave labor was frowned upon but may be necessary to implement his plan.

Adhering to the Latin proverb that fortune favors the bold, Bryan began the process of assembling a team. To each potential member, he made clear they would not merely be a collective of farmers but potentially an army of conquerors. This was a time their descendants would tell stories about. They would become legend.

BRYAN SAT at his desk facing Top Cat and Lester. His office was a meticulously staged scene that conveyed power and authority. He wanted there to be no doubt as to who was in charge. No doubt of who was the mastermind behind what they were carving from the land.

Rather than opulence, the look Bryan was going for was rustic pioneer crossed with reluctant warrior. He tried to imagine if an early colonial landowner had an office on the far reaches of their property, a place he may only use once a month, how that office would be decorated. To that end, the seating was overstuffed leather for himself and crude, uncomfortable ladder back chairs for his guests. The walls were decorated with pioneer implements like early agricultural tools, broad axes, and crosscut saws. There was a pair of rustic oil lamps on his desk, and even a candlestick. A rifle rack on the wall held a small selection of rifles, from an AR-15 to a selection of lever-actions.

The only special touch he was missing, and one he had always wanted, was a genuine human skull. He imagined it sitting on a short stack of books, perhaps volumes by Jefferson. He hoped one day he might make a trip to the University of Virginia and steal some of Jefferson's personal possessions for the desk. An inkwell and fountain pen would be delightful.

Sitting at his desk, Bryan knew Lester and Top Cat were waiting for permission to be seated, but he had no intention of granting it. He wanted them uncomfortable. Sometimes a leader had to assert his authority and this was one of those situations. Bryan let out a dramatic sigh. He wanted his frustration to be evident.

"Just what the fuck happened out there?"

Top Cat had difficulty focusing on his boss, although not because of fear. He was fairly certain the poison ivy had spread to his eyes. They itched furiously and they were burning. Just thinking about it made his underarms start itching again and he slid a hand into his shirt to scratch. He found the skin open, bleeding, and painful to touch. It was miserable. The worst suffering he'd ever experienced.

"Can you at least stop scratching long enough to tell me what happened? You look like an orangutan picking at fleas."

"Sorry," Top Cat mumbled. "It just itches *so* bad."

At the mention of itching, Lester slipped a hand into his pants and began digging at his inflamed groin. His facial expression conveyed apology and embarrassment, but also desperation.

Bryan stared at the man with disgust. "What the fuck is going on with all this scratching and these oozing sores? Is there some kind of disease going around? A syphilis outbreak?" Bryan fought the urge to begin scratching his belly. He had the rash too and had taken most of the camp's limited supply of anti-itch medication for his own use. Had the camp known he had it, there may well have been a riot.

"We just found out they put something in the laundry," Lester said. "We think it was part of this whole escape plan. We were able to extract that information from one of the laundresses."

Bryan let out a long breath and stared at his desk. "Did all the women escape?"

"Not all of them," Top Cat answered.

Bryan cut his lead man a sharp look. "Did you kill the rest?"

Lester shook his head. "No, there's nine or ten left alive and uninjured," Lester said. "There may be twenty or so dead but they were all shot because they had improvised weapons. All the rest of the women disappeared into the hills."

Bryan ran his tongue over his teeth, aware at that moment he'd failed to brush his teeth that morning. "I trust you are pursuing them?"

Top Cat nodded. "Of course. We've got men on foot and horseback all over these hills but I don't know how effective they'll be. This damn rash is so bad a lot of folks can barely walk or ride horseback. It's definitely slowing us down."

"That leaves about ten women to do the work of what ten times that number were doing before," Bryan said. "We have food that needs to be harvested and processed. We need firewood cut and stacked for winter. Not to mention we have grow houses full of marijuana and poppies that need to be tended."

The farm grew more food than they could eat. They used the surplus as commodities to be sold and traded off in the neighboring communities. It built goodwill with the neighbors and Bryan hoped it would encourage them to turn a blind eye if there were questions about what went on at the farm. Not every community wanted dope-growing slavers in their midst, but it was surprising how much forgiveness a bushel of beans could purchase.

Besides raising potatoes, corn, and beans for trade purposes, they also bartered marijuana. Certainly, people who had become accustomed to smoking marijuana every day did not want to stop just because the world collapsed. He hadn't had their grow house arrangement long enough to pull in a full crop yet but Bryan traded off some of the pot he'd brought with him to get guns, ammunition, tools, and even diesel fuel.

As he reminded himself many times, those who prospered in the world were those who took advantage of opportunities. When something came along that allowed you to leapfrog ahead of your fellow men, it would behoove you to grasp it. Bryan understood that things may one day go back to normal. He may even have to let Virginia have its precious Douthat State Park back, but by then he hoped to be a wealthy man.

"We have men who can pitch in and help," Lester offered. "We'll just have to pull them off other jobs."

Bryan looked at him like he was idiot. "Every man we put on crops is one less I have providing security for this community. I need every available man patrolling trails, guarding roads, and manning outposts. Do you like what we have here?"

Lester pointed at himself, questioning.

"Yes you!" Bryan said. "Do you like what we have here?"

"Yes. Of course."

Bryan looked at the other man. "And you, Top Cat?"

Top Cat nodded.

"Then remember we may have to fight to keep it," Bryan said. "The best way to defend it is to engage any force before they get this far. That depends on manpower."

"We could try a recruitment push in the neighboring communities," Top Cat suggested.

Bryan shook his head. "Absolutely not. I don't want locals in here seeing the food and resources we have. I don't want word to get out that we have an involuntary labor force. I don't want them thinking they have to drive us out so we don't steal their women too."

Top Cat understood his boss was right. The guy was always thinking ahead a couple of steps. "Then what do you suggest?"

Bryan looked from one man to the other. He'd already decided on a plan even before the men showed up in his office. "I want a raiding party. Perhaps twenty or twenty-five men, whatever we can spare from here. Each man with two pack horses. You bring back women and anything else you can find, but *especially* women."

"That would leave us undermanned," Top Cat pointed out.

Bryan smiled. "Not your concern. You're not going to be here. I want you and Lester both on the road. You guys were supposed to be running the day-to-day operation of this place. You were supposed to be on top of things. If you hadn't gotten lax, today's fuckup wouldn't have happened. I hold both of you responsible. I need you to get out there and fix this. To prove to me that you deserve to be here."

The men shifted on their feet, wanting to defend themselves but not wanting to be booted out of the community. This was not a democracy and their opinions meant nothing, even if they were requested.

"You don't want any local women?" Lester clarified.

"No," Bryan said. "I've been clear about this. You go a hundred miles from here before you even start looking. And make sure you don't lead anybody back here. The last thing we need is some posse riding in here to hang us for kidnapping."

Lester asked, "When should we leave?"

Bryan frowned at Lester with disappointment. He thought the answer should have been evident. "Don't let the door hit you in the ass on your way out. Which means *now*."

2

Conor Maguire felt the approach of colder weather in the morning air. He wore short sleeves but caught a slight chill on his front porch until the sunlight hit him and warmed his skin. He sipped coffee from a large mug, his favorite, embossed with *Coffee Makes Me Poop*. It had been a Father's Day present from his daughter Barb, who really knew how to pick a gift.

There had been no frost yet, but that would come soon. The previous night had probably gone as low as the upper forties, but if the recent weather pattern held they should see upper sixties to lower seventies by the end of the day. It kind of sucked to not have a goofy weatherman updating them each evening on what to expect. It sucked not having an app on his phone that would allow him to see a current weather radar. All that technology had disappeared with the nationwide collapse.

Goats and hair sheep wandered the fenced compound nibbling at clusters of grass poking through crumbling fissures in the asphalt, dry leaves crackling beneath their hooves. Chickens trailed the goats, searching for bugs, worms, or anything unfamiliar to eat. Crows cawed in the distance, making their plans for the day. Conor dreaded the winter. He dreaded the cold and the inevitable discomfort winter brought. He dreaded the misery and suffering. Not so much for himself, as he was well-provisioned and had wood heat, but studies both public and private had shown that the first winter with no power would result in a massive loss of life.

As a statistic, those lives meant little to him. He was a solitary person. But when you zoomed in on them, those lives were neighbors, they were kids he saw playing in the yards of homes he used to drive by; and elderly folks who waved to him from the porches of humble houses with white aluminum siding and cast iron eagles over the garage door. When spring came, when the crocuses pushed through the cool, damp earth, the world would be a changed place. Conor could not help but be very concerned about what stood between the world he looked at now and that future world he could not even imagine. Between those two bookends lay volumes of death, sickness, suffering, and unthinkable pain.

Conor's friends called him "the Mad Mick," and if you knew him long enough you would understand why. He walked to the beat of his own deranged and drunken drummer. He had his own code of morality with zero fucks given as to what others thought of it. He lived with his daughter Barb in what he referred to as a *homey cottage* on top of a mountain in Jewell Ridge, Virginia. His cottage had once been the headquarters of a now-defunct coal company. It was a massive, sprawling facility where there had once been both underground and longwall mines. Numerous buildings scattered around the property held repair shops and offices.

When Conor first looked at the property he thought it was absolutely ridiculous that a man might be so fortunate as to live there. It reminded him of the lair of some evil genius in an old James Bond movie. It was surrounded by an eight-foot high chain-link fence and topped with barbed wire. There was a helipad and more space than he could ever use. There was even an elevator that would take him to an underground shop the coal company had used to repair their mining equipment.

The ridiculous part was that the facility, which had cost the coal company millions of dollars to build out, was selling for just a fraction of that because it was in such a remote location no one wanted it. In the end Conor came to own the facility and it did not even cost him a penny. His grateful employer had purchased the property for him. It was not an entirely charitable gesture, though. Conor was a very specialized type of contractor and his employer would do nearly anything to keep him at their beck and call.

In an effort to make the place more like a home, Conor had taken one of the steel-skinned office buildings and built a long wooden porch on it, then added a wooden screen door in front of the heavy steel door. Going in and out now produced a satisfying *thwack* as the wooden door smacked shut.

Conor placed his coffee cup on a table made from an old cable spool and sat in a creaking wicker chair. Barb backed out the door with two plates.

"I hope you've been to the fecking Bojangles," Conor said. "I could use a biscuit and a big honking cup of sweet tea."

Barb frowned at him. "You're an Irishman, born in the old country no less, and you call that syrupy crap *tea*?"

"Bo knows biscuits. Bo knows sweet tea."

"Bo is why you had to take to wearing sweatpants all the time too," Barb said. "You couldn't squeeze that big old biscuit of yours into a pair of jeans anymore." She handed her dad a plate of onions and canned ham scrambled into a couple of fresh eggs.

Conor frowned at the insinuation but the frown turned to a smile as his eyes took in the sprinkling of goat cheese that topped off the breakfast. "Damn, that smells delicious."

"Barb knows eggs," his daughter quipped.

"Barb *does* know eggs," Conor agreed, shoveling a forkful into his mouth.

Conor was born in Ireland and came to the U.S. with his mom as a young man. Back in Ireland, the family business was bomb-making and the family business led to a lot of family enemies, especially among the police and the military. After his father and grandfather were arrested in *the troubles*, Conor's mom decided that changing countries might be the only way to keep what was left of her family alive. She didn't realize Conor had already learned the rudiments of the trade while watching the men of his family build bombs. Assuming Conor would one day be engaged to carry on the fight, the men of the family maintained a running narrative, explaining each detail of what they were doing. Conor learned later, in a dramatic and deadly fashion, that he was able to retain a surprising amount of those early childhood lessons.

He and his mother settled first in Boston, then in North Carolina where Conor attended school. In high school, Conor chose vocational school and went on to a technical school after graduation. He loved working with his hands to create precise mechanisms from raw materials, which led him to becoming a skilled machinist and fabricator.

Conor was well-behaved for most of his life, flying under the radar and avoiding any legal entanglements. Then he was married, and the highest and lowest points of his life quickly showed up at his doorstep. He and his wife had a baby girl. A year later a drunk driver killed his wife and nearly killed Barb too. Something snapped in Conor and the affable Irishman became weaponized. He combined his childhood bomb-making lessons with the machinist skills he'd obtained in technical school and sought vengeance.

How could he not? Justice had not been served. There was also something deep within Conor that told him you didn't just accept such things. You continued the fight. There was the law of books and there was the law of man. The law of man required Conor seek true justice for his dead wife.

When the drunk driver was released from jail in what the Mad Mick felt was a laughably short amount of time, the reformed drunk was given special court permission to drive to work. Conor took matters into his own hands. He obtained a duplicate of the headrest in the man's truck from a junkyard and built a bomb inside it. While the man was at his job, Conor switched out the headrest. A proximity switch in the bomb was triggered by a transmitter hidden along his route home. One moment he was singing along to Journey on the radio and enjoying his new freedom. The next, his head was vaporized to an aerosol mist by the exploding headrest.

No one was able to pin the death on Conor despite a lack of other suspects. He had a rock-solid alibi. The proximity trigger detonated the bomb because the man drove within its range. No manual detonation was required on Conor's part at all. After putting everything in place, Conor took his young daughter to the mall to get a few items. Dozens of security cameras picked up the widower and his daughter.

Oddly enough, his handiwork resulted in a job offer from an alphabet agency within the United States government. A team of men who made their living doing such things were impressed with Conor's technique. They recognized him as one of their own and wanted to give him a position among their very unique department. He would work as a contractor, he would be well paid, and he would be provided with a shop in which do to his work. There were no papers to sign but it was made quite clear that any discussion of his work with civilians would result in his death.

Conor knew a good opportunity when he saw it. He accepted the offer and, as he proved his worth, his employer decided it was worthwhile to set Conor up in his deep-cover facility in Jewell Ridge, Virginia. On the surface, Conor presented himself to the local community as a semi-retired machinist who'd moved to the mountains to get away from the city. Mostly as a hobby and to help establish his cover, he took in some machining and fabrication work from the local coal and natural gas industry. Behind that façade, Conor was *the guy* that certain agencies and contractors came to for explosives and unique custom weapons for specialized operations.

Over his career, Conor created pool cue rifles that were accurate to 250 yards with a 6.5 Creedmoor cartridge. A rifle scope was integrated into a second pool cue and the matched set was used for a wet work operation in Houston that never made any newspapers. He once made a music stand for a clarinetist turned assassin that transformed into a combat tomahawk. It was used for an especially brutal assassination in Eastern Europe.

He turned automotive airbags into shrapnel-filled claymore

mines that replaced standard air bags in most vehicles and could be triggered remotely or by a blow to the front bumper. For another job, he'd created a pickup truck that appeared to have standard dual exhausts from the rear. In reality, one exhaust pipe was normal while the other was a rear-facing 40mm grenade launcher.

He routinely created untraceable firearms, suppressors, and unique explosive devices. His explosives contained components sourced from around the world which made it difficult to ascertain the bomber's country of origin. It gave his employer plausible deniability. He had resources in every shadowy crevice of the world and they were always good to send Conor the odd bit of wire, circuitry, and foreign fasteners to include in his handiwork.

Like many bomb makers, Conor was fastidious in his level of organization and preparation. That carried over to his home life. His compound on the mountain had backup solar, available spring water, and food enough to last him for years. Even with those food stores, he maintained a little livestock just to freshen up the stew pot.

"What's on the agenda today, Barb?" he asked. "What do you have planned for yourself?"

"There's a girl at the bottom of the mountain, JoAnn, who I've become halfway acquainted with. It's just her and her dad. Kind of like us. I ran into her yesterday and she said she was going to be doing some late-season canning so I offered to help. She's canning things I've never done before, like French fries."

"Canned French fries. That sounds bloody magical," Conor said. "Plus I'm sure it would be nice to get some girl time, huh?"

Barb smiled back at her dad, a wee drop of mischievous venom in the expression, and yet another demonstration she'd been aptly named. "Actually, it would just be nice to be around somebody who's not telling the same old tired jokes and boring stories all day long. Somebody who doesn't think they're God's gift to humor and storytelling."

Conor faked offense. "I always thought you liked my stories. I thought they were part of our familial bonding. Those stories are your heritage."

"You need new stories, Dad. I don't know if you've noticed or not but, when you tell a story, I'm usually sitting there beside you mouthing the words along with you. I know exactly how they all go. But I guess sitting there making fun of you also counts as bonding."

Conor looked smugly at his daughter. "I had a new story for you when I went over to Damascus and helped that girl Grace and her family. You were on the edge of your seat."

"Yes, but as much as I'm tired of the old stories I don't want you putting yourself at risk just to bring home new material. Besides, you're getting too long in the tooth for those kinds of adventures. You're not an operator anymore. Your days would be better spent puttering around the garden in a cardigan, half-drunk on Guinness, cursing at the beetles and weeds."

"Don't be so quick to put your old dad out to pasture, Barb. I've got plenty of good years left in me. And plenty of good fights."

Barb raised her cup of tea toward him in a conciliatory toast. "Well, here's to hoping those fights die on the vine. I hope you never have to use them."

"I'll toast to that," Conor said, raising his coffee mug.

"So what's on *your* agenda today, dear father?"

"I spoke to a man the other day who lives down in the valley near the Buchanan County line. Since the shit hit the fan he's been taking in horses people could no longer feed. Now he's got more than he wants to take care of over the winter. I told him I might be willing to trade for a few so I'm going to go look at them."

"Ah, a horse would be nice. It could take me an hour to walk to JoAnn's house this morning. It would be half of that on a horse and a lot less effort."

"It will damn sure be easier to carry a load on a horse than on a bicycle," Conor added.

"So you've given up on your bicycles, have you? I'm shocked. I thought you were training for the Tour de Bojangles, twenty-one days of bicycles and biscuits?"

Conor shook his head. "I've not given up on bicycles but my tender arse has. It's become *delicate* in my golden years."

Barb smiled at that. Despite her banter with her father, she loved him dearly. It was just the two of them in the world and that was fine with her. One day she may have room for a husband and children but she was in no hurry. She would try to wait the world out and see if things got back to normal one day.

"An hour is still a long walk," Conor said. "Take your full load-out."

Barb rolled her eyes. "You know I don't go out without my gear."

"It doesn't hurt to remind you. We check and we double check. That's what we do and that's how we stay alive. Not just your rifle and your pistol, but your go bag and your radio."

She gave her dad a thumbs up. "Got it, Dad."

"You better," he warned. "Some things are joking and bullshit. This is not. This is life and death. Every single day."

"Roger that."

"Plates too," he insisted. "Plate carrier and armor plates."

Barb groaned. "It's too hot, and it's heavy."

Conor gave a conciliatory smile. "Well, if you're too weak to carry the weight…"

"I'll take them," Barb said, getting up from her seat. "You're driving me nuts with this." She went into the house to get her gear together. She had no intention of carrying those heavy plates. She would have to find a way to slip out without him seeing her.

3

An hour later Barb was halfway down the mountain, the road changing from steep switchbacks to a gentler winding course. She was headed in the opposite direction of her father, and he'd insisted on knowing exactly where she was going and when she'd be back. He'd been that kind of dad before the collapse and he was even more safety conscious now. She tried to comply as best she could but there was a streak of defiance in her. She was extremely capable and she wasn't certain he always acknowledged that. She was proficient in martial arts and could outshoot most anyone. He'd raised her that way and she had no issues with it. She just wished he would recognize her abilities a little more, but perhaps that was all daughters complaining about all dads.

She encountered a man walking in the road toward her and froze. Her first reaction was to throw her rifle up to a ready position until she determined if he was a threat or not. She quickly identified the young man as Ragus, a regular on the porch of their compound. Her dad had a tradition of taking in strays and defending the underdog. This boy was both and she had no need for him. Although she didn't dislike him, he'd done nothing to earn special favor from her either.

The oddly-named boy broke into a large grin at finding Barb on the road with him. The boy made no secret of the fact that he was enamored with her and considered himself a worthy suitor. At her age, the couple of years between them seemed more significant than that same number of years might at a later point in her life. To the young man, Barb was beautiful, dangerous, and the woman he loved, at least as much as a boy his age understood love.

"You're a pretty sight to come up on," Ragus said. "For a moment I thought the sun was rising a second time on this beautiful morning." He was a little shy and found it hard to say things like this to her but nothing else he'd tried had worked. He was running out of options.

"You're nearly as full of shit as my dad. No wonder you two get along so well." Barb was not swayed by flattery. "What are you doing out this morning? Did you forget your daycare was closed and walk all the way to town?"

The boy was not deterred in the slightest. Barb could abuse him all day and the dazed smile he wore in her presence would never leave his face. "Going fishing with a friend. Why are you out wandering around the mountain by yourself?"

"By *myself*? Just who should I have with me?"

"Why, a man, of course. I'd be glad to be that man and escort you wherever you're going."

Barb couldn't stop herself from bursting into laughter. "I haven't seen a man this morning. All I've seen is squirrels and boys, both full of nothing but chatter and concerned with nothing but their nuts."

Ragus blushed at that and lost some of the wind in his sails. "You're welcome to come fishing if you want."

Barb looked around the boy, examining his hands and seeing only a rifle. "I see no tackle. You plan on shooting them with that Henry rifle?"

"No, I've got a hand line in my pocket. The Mad Mick showed me how to use it."

Barb snorted. "The Mad Mick. He been filling your ears with stories of his adventures?"

"Maybe."

Barb started to give the boy a lecture about how her dad's stories got bigger with each telling. She started to tell him her dad had had some wild adventures over the years but he needed to slow down and take life easier. She started to say all those things but stopped herself. Conor, her dad, the Mad Mick—whatever you wanted to call him—had saved this boy's life, and if that boy wanted to put him on a pedestal she should probably just leave it alone. The boy needed someone to believe in and her dad was as good a vessel for that belief as any.

"Where you going fishing?" she asked, softening her tone.

"There's a boy I know back at the next intersection and I'm going to see if he wants to go with me. If you want us to walk with you, it will only take me about ten minutes to run and get him. Then we can walk you wherever you want to go."

"I appreciate your concern but the only thing worse than having one awkward teenage boy around is having two. And I say again I don't need an escort. If we ran into trouble, I'd just end up having to save the two of you."

The boy didn't argue, but hung his head in defeat. He'd struck out. Again. "Maybe I'll see you later."

Seeing him so dejected, and knowing what he'd been through, Barb almost felt a glimmer of guilt at being so hard on him. Almost. "You wouldn't want to come with me anyway. I'm going to a friend's house to do some canning. Unless you're interested in peeling and slicing vegetables, you should probably just stick with your plans."

As soon as the words were out of her mouth, she could see him processing this information. He was trying to determine if getting to spend the day with her was worth the boredom of having to process vegetables. "I think I'll just go fishing, but thanks anyway."

She was relieved. "Well, then I'm going on my way. Stop by the house one day. My dad don't mind you nearly as much as I do."

That remark brought a smile to the boy's face. He could not help but be entertained by her brutally sharp wit. She could spew venom at him all day and he would sit and take it. He waved as she walked away.

She'd taken no more than twenty steps when she felt like she was being watched. She stopped in her tracks and looked back over her shoulder to find Ragus staring at her. She was immediately aware this was not so much out of concern for her safety as out of concern for the movement of her backside.

Only mildly embarrassed at having been caught, the boy threw up his hand in an awkward wave. Barb began to raise her rifle. The boy's eyes went wide and he took off running like a scalded dog. That brought a smile to Barb's face. She wouldn't have shot him, though. Perhaps she might have shot *at* him, but she certainly wouldn't have intentionally hit him. She couldn't rightly kill someone her dad had put so much effort into saving.

Ragus probably owed Conor his life. They first met the kid when he slipped into their compound to steal a chicken. The dogs alerted on him and cornered him in the henhouse, snarling and growling. Conor would have been within his rights to shoot the lad, especially with times being what they were, but it was evident the young man was starving.

Conor stared down the iron sights of his rifle at the boy. A flashlight mounted to the rifle illuminated the boy in a blinding circle of light that forced the kid to shield his eyes. "Did your old man send you here to steal from me?"

The boy shook his head slightly. "I ain't got no old man."

"Your mother then? You trying to feed your mother? Tell me the truth, boy, or I'll kill you and boil your meat for my dogs."

There was no defiance in the boy. Only defeat. Conor sensed the boy would have found it a relief if he pulled the trigger and killed him.

"She died a couple of days ago."

That admission hit Conor hard. He'd been raised by his mother and lost her too. "Have you eaten since then?" he asked.

The boy shook his head. "I didn't eat for the last couple of days before she...before it happened. I'm not sure of the last time."

Conor led the young man into their home and fed him leftovers from their dinner. The boy ate ravenously, like a dog left to starve at the dump. Conor had to tell him to slow down for fear he would choke. At that point, it had only been about five or six weeks since the collapse, but the boy ate like he had not eaten in that whole time.

"So, why are you all alone, boy?" Conor asked.

The boy wiped his mouth with a hand, ignoring the napkin Barb had set out for him. He took a drink to wash down a large mouthful of food. "My daddy left when I was a kid."

"You're still a kid," Barb pointed out.

The boy scowled at her, apparently not fond of being called a kid. "I'm seventeen."

"You don't look it," Barb said.

Conor held a hand up to his daughter. He wanted to handle this. Her badgering wasn't helping anything. "And your mother?" he pressed.

"She passed a couple of days ago. She had cancer real bad before all this happened. She lost her job because she couldn't go anymore. Without doctors and medicine the end came quicker than they said it would. It was...bad. It was awful."

It appeared the boy had more on his mind, like there were more words wanting to come out, but the memory of what he'd been through was blocking them. Conor, and even the sharp-tongued Barb, let it rest. The demons would come out of their own accord when the time was right. No use forcing it.

"So how are you taking care of yourself?" Conor asked.

"He's clearly not," Barb noted, gesturing at the boy as if his presence proved her point. "He's a wastrel."

Part of Conor wondered where she'd learned such a word. "How are you planning to get by, boy? You keep stealing from people, you're going to get killed. That's not a feasible plan for survival."

The boy did not respond. The answer was obvious enough he felt no need to state it.

"How are you going to defend yourself?" Conor asked.

Again, no response.

"Do you even own a weapon?"

"I got this," the boy said, reaching into his pocket and withdrawing a small revolver. Lacking experience and training with firearms, he waved the pistol around, sweeping everyone with the barrel.

Conor's hand lashed out and grabbed the revolver, twisting it from the boy's frail grip. "Easy there, cowboy. We need to go over some basics before you get this thing back." Conor dumped the cylinder of mismatched ammunition onto the table. The pistol was a cheap .38 with a two-inch barrel. The sights were no more than grooves in the frame of the handgun. It wouldn't be accurate beyond a couple of yards.

"Please don't take that," the boy begged. "I might need it."

"This may be decent for self-defense but only at fistfight distances. You have anything you can hunt with?"

The boy shook his head, looking down at the table and at the revolver. Conor shot his daughter a pleading glance, frustrated at the boy's predicament and not sure what to do. When Barb was no help, offered no answers, Conor again addressed the boy.

"I'll give you a rifle," he said. "Nothing fancy, but something that will put meat on the table."

The boy's eyes got wide. "One of those fancy army rifles like you got?"

"Oh no. I give you something with a thirty-round magazine and you'll be blowing off shots with no regard for aim. I'm going to give you a lever-action, something that will force you to pay a little more attention to what you're doing."

"But you said I may need to defend myself," the boy said. "Don't I need something that holds a lot of bullets?"

"No. Most days, if you need thirty rounds to get yourself out of the shit, you might as well kiss your ass goodbye. A decent lever-action or bolt gun will hold off the bad guys until help arrives. That's all you need to buy yourself some time."

"Can I have it now?"

"You come back tomorrow, lad. You come early and we'll put a meal in your belly. Then I'll show you how to shoot a rifle and take care of one. When I'm comfortable you're safe, I'll send you home with the rifle and a box of shells."

"How long is one box going to last me?"

"When it's empty, you come back and tell me what that box of shells put in the stew pot. I'll refill you. Don't you worry about that."

4

The morning had warmed considerably by the time Barb reached the base of Jewell Ridge. JoAnn, lived on a small family farm with her father, who was in poor health and couldn't do many chores around the place anymore. Most of the work fell to JoAnn. Barb didn't know the girl well. She didn't know anyone here very well since she and her father kept mostly to themselves. She'd met the girl collecting firewood not long after the collapse.

Barb happened to be walking by on the road and heard the solid *thunk* of an ax in wood. She'd looked in the direction of the sound and saw a thin girl, exhausted and frustrated, trying to section a tree so she could carry pieces home. Barb, who like her father was usually willing to help those who were trying to help themselves, offered to lend a hand. JoAnn gladly took the help, figuring a girl of around her own age couldn't be any threat. Had it been a man asking her the same question, JoAnn would have run for the house and hidden while her father threatened him with a shotgun.

Most of the houses in this the area of central Appalachia were built right on the road because there was such a shortage of flat land. The farms were nothing like the rolling pastures of North Carolina where Barb had been born. Farms here were often straight up and down the hillsides. Cattle created switchback trails for moving up and down the hills. JoAnn's farm was the same way. The house was immediately off the side of the road with acres of wooded mountain land stretching out behind it.

Barb was just around the corner from JoAnn's home when she heard a gunshot and a bloodcurdling scream. It was the voice of a young woman. JoAnn's voice.

Barb bolted toward the scream, unslinging her rifle. She flew around the bend of the road without regard for what might be waiting on her. There, the tree-lined road opened up around JoAnn's family home. She flicked off her safety and scanned as she moved, not seeing anything that concerned her, though the screams and yelling had not stopped.

The gate at the driveway was hanging open, which was unusual, and she went through it, running up the gravel drive. She was constantly scanning for cover, looking for a place to hide if she came under fire. The scream had turned to sobs and wailing. It was tortuous, listening to that, wanting to make it stop. It was all she could do not to burst around the house at full speed and try to fix whatever the situation was but she couldn't get herself killed. That would help no one.

She flattened herself against the house and forced herself to slow down. She took several quick, deep breaths to calm her breathing. The cries of anguish were coming from behind the house, which Barb knew held the garden and a few outbuildings. She moved to the corner of the house, peered around a loose downspout, and saw a man struggling to pull JoAnn away from her father's body. Her dad lay collapsed in late-season beans, gangly limbs sprawling from a blood-soaked torso. Even if her dad was still alive, he wouldn't be for long with the quantity of blood he was losing.

A second man stood among the dying tomato plants, a rifle dangling from his hand, while the other man attempted to subdue JoAnn. He was not paying any attention to his surroundings, apparently unconcerned that the gunshots and the girl's screams might draw attention. He would not have a chance to learn from his mistake. Without any hesitation, Barb put the illuminated chevron of her rifle optic on the man's center mass and sent two quick rounds into his body. He fell into a heap, arched, and died.

The crack of the gunshots startled both JoAnn and her attacker. His grip on JoAnn's arms slipped and he backpedaled a couple of steps before falling on his ass. He landed on his slung rifle and was struggling to get it into firing position when Barb's rifle cracked again, the shot shattering his upper left arm. He cried out and tried to staunch the flow of blood but barely got a hand over the wound before another round caught him beneath the left eye. His head snapped backwards and he sagged into the soft dirt of the garden, a surprised look on his face.

JoAnn took this opportunity to scramble on all fours to her collapsed father. She cradled his head in her hands and repeated his name over and over, beseeching the creator to bring him back, but he was dead. Barb ran to the garden and checked both of the men she'd shot. They were dead as disco. She didn't recognize either of them.

She moved to the sobbing girl, placing a gentle hand on her shoulder. "Get up, JoAnn. We have to go. There could be others."

JoAnn's dirty face was streaked from tears. Her expression said it all. She wondered how she could leave this man who had meant so much to her. How could she leave her dad laying there in the garden?

"He's dead," Barb said. "There's nothing you can do for him now. He wouldn't want you to die too. You know that."

When JoAnn didn't immediately get to her feet, Barb hooked an arm beneath JoAnn's, hoisting her to her feet. "We have to go. *Now!*"

Barb tugged at the stumbling girl, trying to get her moving in the right direction. In trying to save her new friend, Barb failed to maintain awareness of her surroundings. She held her rifle in her weak hand, pointed uselessly upward as she used her stronger arm to tug at the grief-stricken JoAnn. When Barb's eyes finally went back to the road in front of her, she found a line of armed men waiting on them.

Her heart sank, but she was a fighter. She did not weigh odds. She fought out of reaction, out of pure instinct. She released JoAnn, the girl falling into the tall grass, and shifted the rifle back to her strong hand. Before she could get it shouldered, a blow like she had never felt before struck her in the center of her chest. Barb collapsed forward onto her face, gasping for breath. She was certain she now knew what it felt like to die. What it felt like to take a bullet to the chest and bleed to death with your face in the dirt.

It was agonizing.

There was a flicker of thought, the awareness that her dad might never know what happened to her. There was an awareness of how sad that would make him. Then rough hands grabbed her shirt and she was flipped over onto her back. Her hands were gathered in front of her and zip-tied together. Part of her wondered why they were bothering to bind her after inflicting what was surely a mortal wound. Then she noticed a man retrieving something from the ground beside her. It was an arrow with a round steel tip. A blunt arrow for hunting small game.

It was the last thing she saw before a hood was drawn over her head and cinched a little too tight around her neck.

5

Ragus walked backed down the paved mountain road with his fishing buddy, Dakota. Dakota had complained the entire time because Ragus insisted on walking so fast. Each time Dakota brought it up Ragus insisted he was in no hurry, but in truth, Ragus hoped to catch up with Barb again. He was certain if he had enough time with the woman he could win her over. Ragus had heard women jokingly say they wouldn't go out with someone if he was the last man on Earth. He wondered if Barb felt the same way about him. If times continued to get worse and the death toll mounted, perhaps Ragus *would* be one of the few men remaining in *her* world. Surely that would improve his odds.

Ragus and Dakota were nearly to the bottom of the ridge when the gunfire broke out. At the first shot, Ragus was unconcerned, assuming a hunter must have shot at an animal. The next shots came in rapid pairs and Ragus immediately become more concerned. Conor taught Barb to shoot in double taps when killing mattered and time permitted. When it clicked in his brain that those shots must be Barb firing defensively, he bolted down the road without saying a word to his friend.

"Hey, wait up! Where are you going?" Dakota shouted after him.

When Ragus didn't answer, Dakota picked up the pace. He couldn't catch up to Ragus, though, who was in an all-out sprint to find the source of the shots.

Ragus knew which house Barb was headed to and slowed before he got there, knowing it lay around a blind corner. He eased around the bend, not wanting to run full tilt into the midst of a gunfight. He hugged the ditch line at the tight corner, which kept him closer to the concealment of the woods. He moved quickly but cautiously, more of the landscape opening up before him with each step. He raised his rifle and verified there was indeed a round in the chamber

He saw the horses first. Perhaps as many as a dozen. A single man leaned against a fencepost in the midst of the tied horses. Ragus raised his rifle and aligned his scope on the man. It was purely a reaction but his brain overruled acting on it. He hesitated. If there was a man for each of these horses, the shot Ragus fired would draw them back to him. He couldn't fight off a dozen men, especially with a lever-action rifle. He needed to wait and see what was happening. He forced himself to retreat, backing away from the scene and receding into the shadows like smoke rising into a forest canopy.

In his retreat, Ragus heard flapping sneakers approaching on the road. He realized Dakota may not have understood to stop and wait. He was just trying to catch up with his fishing buddy. As quietly as possible, Ragus moved to intercept his friend before the man at the fence heard his flapping feet.

Dakota flew around the corner and was startled to find Ragus coming toward him. He started to cry out but Ragus intercepted the boy, clapping a hand over his mouth and muting him. Dakota tried to suck air, winded from running. He tugged at the hand over his mouth. Ragus shushed him with a finger raised to his lips. The gasping boy didn't have the breath to put together a question but his expression made it clear he did not understand what was taking place.

Ragus pulled the confused boy from the road into the concealment of the woods, then leaned to his ear and whispered, "I think my friend Barb is in trouble. I think this is where those gunshots came from. I need to check on her. You stay here and don't move."

His eyes wide with fear, the boy nodded quickly. Ragus left him, scrambling through a dense underbrush of blackberry vines, tall pokeberry plants, and poplar saplings. He followed the fence line of the property, trying to make as little noise as possible. He looked where he put his feet with each step, trying not to step on anything that would announce his presence. While he wasn't a warrior, he was a hunter. Moving through the woods stealthily, trying to keep yourself hidden, was a basic hunting skill. When he reached a point where he could see into the backyard, he found Barb bound and hooded. A man stood over her with a bow in his hands, inserting an arrow into a quiver.

Ragus felt a surge of panic. Had Barb been shot with the bow? If so, would she even survive without access to medical care? Seeing Barb in such a helpless state infuriated him. There were only two people he cared about in the world anymore and this indignity injured both of them. He clenched his hand tightly around the stock of the Henry rifle.

Despite the small caliber, carefully placed shots might still drop their targets. But how many carefully placed shots could he even take before those men were shredding the woods around him with their weapons? These men carried an assortment of weapons. There were a couple of bolt action rifles, but there were also modern military-looking rifles. He had no doubt that by the time he got off two or three shots, the remaining men would be laying down a shower of lead in his direction.

The men surrounding Barb slid hands under her bound arms and yanked her to her feet. She supported herself unsteadily but the two men did not take their hands from her. Ragus noticed a second hooded girl who must've been the friend Barb was visiting. He also saw several dead men he'd somehow missed. It would not surprise him to learn Barb might have killed them. It would certainly explain why they were treating her so harshly.

In his struggle to come up with a plan of action, Ragus recalled what Conor said when he gave him the rifle. He explained that some situations were not resolved by blindly throwing yourself into battle at the risk of your own life. Sometimes battles were won by delaying the worst outcomes until help could arrive. If he couldn't immediately win this battle, perhaps he could at least pursue these men and leave a trail for Conor to follow. Then, together, they could wade in and take heads.

The assembly of men moved from the back of the house to the front, where Ragus could see them securing gear on horses. They hoisted Barb into a saddle and lashed her hands to the saddle horn. Ragus could not hear what was being said but saw a single man giving out orders. He had to be the leader of this group. On his word, they mounted up and plodded off in no great hurry, as if this were simply another routine stop on a long list of stops.

Knowing he had no time to waste, Ragus hurried back to Dakota, less concerned about stealth on the return trip. Branches and berry vines tore at his skin and clothes. Usually wary of snakes, he paid the ground no heed this time. He found his friend waiting on him, wide-eyed and terrified.

"What is it? What's going on?"

"Kidnappers. They've taken Barb and the girl who lives at this house. There's dead men back there too."

"Who is Barb, anyway? Why do you care?"

"Barb is Conor's daughter. The Mad Mick. The Irish guy who lives at the top of the hill in the old coal company headquarters. He's my friend."

Dakota's look of confusion vanished. The boy didn't recognize the name but everyone on the ridge knew the wacky old Irish guy who lived in the coal company headquarters. Ragus took his arm and spoke to him intently.

"Listen, Barb said her dad was going to Johnny Jacks' house looking for horses. You need to head over there and tell Conor what happened. Tell him I'm in pursuit and I'll leave him a trail. You got it?"

Dakota frowned. "I'm not supposed to go anywhere but fishing. I'll have to go by my house and ask my mother."

Ragus lashed out and clubbed the boy on the side of the head. He grabbed him by the collar and pulled him close, leaning in. His words came through clenched teeth. "You go now and you go as fast as you can. Don't stop anywhere until you find him. If something happens to her or if he doesn't get the message, I'll kill you *and* your mother when I get back. I am not joking."

Ragus shoved the younger boy away. The kid scrambled to his feet and took off running, his face red, tears pouring down his face. Ragus felt bad about hitting him but knew of no other way to convey the urgency of the moment. Relieved at getting the boy on the road, Ragus was overpowered by the urgency of Barb's situation. There was no time to think, organize, or plan. He just had to go. He slung his pack on his back, took his rifle in his hand, and loped off in the direction the horses had gone.

6

Conor McGuire was a man of contrast. While his bread and butter was violence and mayhem, he also loved the peaceful life of the country. He built bombs. He built assassination weapons. He was likely responsible for hundreds of deaths around the world. He also loved walking on a wooded road on a beautiful morning. It was, as he said, when his Irish came out.

He would let his guard down as much as a man of his background could and he would sing the ballads of his childhood and his homeland if he could remember the words. If he couldn't scratch the lyrics from memory, he would hum the tune to keep it alive. It was like blowing on an ember to keep a fire going. The fire, in this case, was the memory of Ireland. When the English, the Irish, the Scots, and the Welsh came to America in the eighteenth and nineteenth centuries, this was where they settled. West Virginia and Southwest Virginia reminded them of home. It did the same for Conor.

The morning warmed as the sun rose, arranging shimmering pockets of dappled light on the dirty roadway. With no traffic and no highway department, debris was building up. The ditches beside the road had filled with silt and rain, and now washed gravel and dirt into the pavement with each storm. Such impediments could cause a nasty wreck on a bicycle as Conor had learned on his last long trip. In the early days after the collapse he'd taken a multi-day bike trip to help the friend of a friend, and on his way home he'd hit a rock with his front tire, taking a nasty fall. Horses would be unconcerned with such debris. They could step over an obstacle in the same way Conor could.

Johnny Jacks was a local farmer who raised cattle and had a fondness for horses. He was in his mid-seventies now but, as Conor heard it, for the last forty years he was the guy who took in neglected and unwanted horses. A lot of people loved the *idea* of having a horse, but they needed things, and could be expensive to feed and care for. When horse owners hit hard times, horses were often one of the first things to suffer. Responsible horse owners recognized this and found people like Johnny Jacks to take the horse and care for it. Irresponsible horse owners often waited until neighbors complained to the police or animal control, often ending up charged with animal cruelty. Then they were forced by the court to get rid of their horse and they ended up with folks like Johnny Jacks.

Johnny never paid for horses. The deal was if he was going to take your horse and care for it, then you gave him the horse and all the tack for free. Johnny had plenty of land and he sowed several pastures in grass that made good horse hay, so feeding the horses had never been an issue for him. That summer, when society collapsed, farmers were in the same boat as everyone else. They might have livestock they could eat or barter but they had no fuel for the tractors. That made it a lot harder to take care of their farms.

Johnny had been able to get two cuttings of hay before things went south. If it was a mild winter he figured he could get his cattle and a small herd of horses through the winter. A rough winter would wipe him out. He had over thirty horses now and he decided the responsible thing to do was downsize.

He'd spread word through the community he was willing to trade horses for any type of supplies he might be able to use. Conor heard word of this through a neighbor and decided he would walk the seven miles to Johnny's house and discuss a trade with him. In better times, Conor would have picked up the phone and called but that was not a possibility now. He had to walk. He considered a bike ride but had no interest in pushing the contraption all the way back up the steep road home. If things went as planned this could be his last seven mile walk. He could ride back home on his horse leading a string of other horses. That was the plan.

The farm he was looking for was in the Whitewood area, all downhill from Conor's house. For most of the morning walk, he didn't see a solitary thing to concern him. He saw squirrels and songbirds. Once he thought he heard a deer but he never saw it. As enjoyable as the walk was, he was pleased when the land began to flatten out. He was close to his destination.

Conor found the mailbox with the last name Jacks on it exactly where he was told he would. He turned off the main road and walked up a gravel road to a cluster of barns, a riding rink, and a small frame house covered in white aluminum siding. An ornamental gate blocked the entrance to the narrow sidewalk leading to the house. Here in America, as in his own native country, he didn't approach a country house without hailing from the road. This was especially important now that people were on guard.

"Hello inside. My name is Conor. I'm a neighbor come to talk to Mr. Jacks about some horses."

Conor unslung his rifle and leaned it against the fence, not wanting to appear threatening. He could see curtains moving in the gentle breeze through open windows. Certainly he'd been heard. He was preparing to repeat himself when the front door opened and a diminutive older lady in quaint clothing swung the door open and stepped onto the porch. She wore a denim skirt and a high-collared white shirt. An apron was tied around her waist. She carried a shotgun in her hand but held it to the side in the manner of the cautious but polite. Under current circumstances it was as customary a greeting as anyone might expect and Conor was not put off by it. He would have been more concerned for any elderly lady who opened the door to a stranger without a weapon.

"What did you say you name was?"

" Conor Maguire, ma'am."

"Whereabouts you from, Conor?"

Conor nodded in the direction from which he'd come. "The top of Jewell Ridge there. I live in the old coal company headquarters."

The lady he assumed to be Mrs. Jacks nodded. "I heard tell of you. No offense but you talk a little queer. That ain't a Jewell Ridge accent I be hearing."

Conor laughed. A lot of the country folk around here, especially those who had lived most of their life without television and outside influences, spoke in the odd manner more traditional and similar to that of their forbearers. Their phrasing and word choice was not contemporary but likely as ancient as his own.

"I'm not a native of Jewell Ridge. I came here by way of North Carolina, and before that, Ireland."

Mrs. Jacks furrowed her brow and nodded, filing away the information. Over the course of her life she'd seen an albino deer once. She thought she'd seen UFOs on two different occasions and had seen a Bigfoot-type creature carry off one of their goats tucked under a hairy arm. This was her first Irishman. "That a fact."

"It is," Conor said agreeably. "I heard tell Mr. Jacks was hoping to trade off some horses. I'm in need of some."

"You'd have to talk to him about that."

"Hence my appearance on your doorstep, good lady. I was hoping to do so. Might he be around somewhere?"

Mrs. Jacks shook her head and Conor's heart sank. "Somebody cut the fence in one of our pastures last night to steal cattle. Every critter we owned walked off through the downed fence. Johnny is out with our two sons trying to round them up. They're all we got. I have no idea when he'll be back but I don't expect him soon. They have to track down the livestock and then repair the fence. Best come back another day."

Conor understood she was right but hated that he'd walked all this way for nothing. Of course it hadn't been completely for nothing. It was good exercise and he got to witness a beautiful morning. It wasn't like he had anything else to do.

He smiled at the woman. "I appreciate your time, Mrs. Jacks. Please tell your husband of my interest in the horses. I'm wanting four of them and I've got things to trade I'm certain he'd be interested in."

The lady nodded and smiled at him, raising a hand in a departing wave. "I'll pass it on. Are you agreeable for him to come calling on you? It's a far bit easier for him to ride to you than for you to walk back down here again."

"Oh, I'd appreciate that very much," Conor said. "It's a half-day's walk."

Conor was disappointed that he was unable to get his horses but he was determined not to let it spoil his day. There was nothing that could be done about the turn of events. He threw a wave to Mrs. Jacks, shot her a smile, and exited out the gate. At least on the return journey he would get to see the backside of everything he missed on the way over.

The walk back home was entirely uphill and Conor was intent on showing it who was boss. He fought constantly in his daily life against aging and weakness. He pushed himself whenever he could, trying to stay as strong and sharp as he could. He set out at a brisk walk, wanting to get a good workout since his other goal, that of getting horses, had fallen flat.

He was a little over halfway home when he encountered a crying boy coming toward him on the road. The boy ignored Conor at first and didn't make eye contact. The kid looked around twelve or thirteen, possibly even a little younger. Conor couldn't exactly walk by without asking him what was going on.

"Stop your crying, my boy. What's the matter with you? What's wrong?"

At the sound of Conor's accent the boy's eyes widened. "Are you Mr. Conor?"

Conor smiled. "I am he. You can call me Conor. What's up with the squalling and snotting?"

"I was supposed to come find you. Ragus sent me."

Conor's brow furrowed. His mind raced. "Is Ragus okay?"

The boy bobbed his head to the affirmative.

"Then what's wrong, lad? Out with it."

"He told me to tell you they kidnapped the girl, Barb. She's his friend."

Conor's focus instantly narrowed to a single point on this boy's face. "Who kidnapped Barb? Tell me exactly what happened."

"Ragus and I were going fishing. We heard gunshots and something about it must not have sounded right because Ragus took off running. He ran to this house where he said his friend Barb was going. There were men there and they took her."

The boy got himself worked up again, starting to cry. Conor wanted to slap him across the face to sober him but he needed to be gentle here. It was the fastest way to get the information he needed and speed was critical.

"Did you know these men? Had you or Ragus ever seen them before?"

The boy shook his head.

"How many men?"

"I-I don't k-know," the boy stammered. "I didn't actually see them. Ragus made me hide in the woods. Then he came back and told me what was going on."

"Where's Ragus now?" Conor was becoming a little angry Ragus had sent this kid back to relay this story to him. If Ragus had seen the kidnappers, he should have been the one back here relaying the information. Where the hell was the boy?

"Ragus went after them," the kid said.

That revelation shocked Conor for a moment, then he realized he probably shouldn't have been surprised at all. Ragus was that way. That was the type of person he was. Of course he went after them. The boy was untrained and had minimal firepower but still he pursued. He would have done it because it was the right thing to do.

"When Ragus came back to you in the woods, what exactly did he say?"

"He told me Barb had been kidnapped by a group of men and he was going after them. He said he would leave a trail for you, and he told me to go straight to you and tell you."

Conor clapped the boy on the shoulder. "Thank you, son. You did a fine job. If you ever need anything, I'm in your debt. You know where to find me right?"

The boy nodded, backhanding his snotty nose.

Conor gave the boy another pat and took off running as hard as he could.

7

Conor was fortunate he had to pass his compound on his way across the mountain. He was already armed, of course, and he had a pack with gear, but he was not dressed for battle. Most days he entered his property by means of gate in the eight-foot tall chain link fence. When he reached the gate, he leaned over and removed a necklace containing several keys. He opened the padlock, hung it back in the hasp, and burst through the gate. He was sweat-soaked and breathing hard but focused with laser intensity.

Another key from the necklace let him into the main living quarters. As he ran through the entryway he began stripping off everything but the keys he carried around his neck. There was a welded steel cage in one part of the main living quarters. It had been a tool cage in one of the shops and Conor moved it in here as his primary weapons locker. In that cage, his full load-out from socks to helmet was ready to go.

He opened the lock and threw back the heavy door, hearing it rebound as it slammed loudly into the side of the cage. He gave himself a cursory drying with a t-shirt he yanked from a hanger. Throwing the damp t-shirt to the floor, he yanked on a pair of Under Armour underwear that came nearly to his knees. They were skin-tight, knee-length, and would prevent chafing from his sweat-soaked gear if this turned into a long slog.

He sat down on a stool and yanked on a pair of high merino wool socks, followed by a pair of multicam BDU pants. They were expensive Crye Precision gear, a gift from a friend who owed him a favor. He tugged on Reebok combat boots with zipper sides. His t-shirt was a moisture-wicking synthetic. He tucked it into his pants before fastening them and latching the buckle on the cobra belt.

The BDU shirt was also Crye Precision. When he slipped it on, he wrapped his battle belt around his waist. It was High Speed Gear and already loaded with magazine pouches, full magazines, an individual first-aid kit, a multitool, a fixed blade combat knife, and a Safariland holster with a Glock 17 riding in it. The plate carrier was also High Speed Gear and also completely ready to go. He dropped it over his head, latched the side buckles, fastened all the Velcro straps, and then attached it to his battle belt. Though he sometimes trained with an empty plate carrier, this one was ready to go with level IV ceramic plates.

He unhooked an Eberlestock Gunslinger backpack from the wall. It was fully loaded with everything he needed for exactly this situation. He'd always hoped this day would never come but that didn't mean it wouldn't, so he chose to be ready. He grabbed a bump helmet off a hook with a PVS-14 night vision device mounted and ready to go. Conor wasn't wearing the helmet now so he hooked it to the pack and then stood in front of the rifle rack. He kept three weapons ready to go at all times. There was a suppressed submachine gun in 9 mm, a medium-range AR with an illuminated low-power scope, and a precision sniper rifle.

Conor had no idea how far he would have to go or how long he'd be on the road. Medium-range seemed the way to go. He clipped the rifle to his single-point sling and slipped on the pack. It already contained everything he'd need. It was set up for just such an emergency as this–grab and go. There was food, water, shelter, and ammunition.

He backed out of the cage and locked the door behind him. He ran to the front door and locked it also, sprinting across the yard. He went through the chain-link gate and replaced the padlock, then set out at the fastest run he could manage in full gear. He couldn't remember how many miles it was to JoAnn's house. Six? Seven? That would be two 5k runs done back to back. Best not to think about it.

Just run.

Despite frequent training, Conor could not recall having done anything like this run in a long time. He trained with sandbags, with cinderblocks, he sparred with his daughter, and he did all manner of cross-training, but running down a paved road with a full pack was an animal unto itself. His feet pounded the pavement, jarring his old knees and reminding him of every ache, every pain, the years had inflicted on him. Every old injury reared its ugly head and reminded him of its existence. But pain didn't mean stop. It meant dig in. It meant focus.

Although the fact he was running downhill worked to his benefit, it amplified the bone-jarring shock his body experienced with each step. It took him exactly an hour and thirteen minutes to reach JoAnn's house. He slowed at the wide cattle gate that opened onto the road. It was never left open like this. A glance at the ground showed him the hoof prints of an entire herd of horses. It was impossible to tell how many riders there'd been. Some of the prints revealed odd shoes that appeared to be homemade. He crouched and touched one. It was scored like rebar. Perhaps these men were having to make their own horseshoes.

He slung his weapon back to high-ready and moved efficiently through the gate. He trained his gun on the house but heard nothing. Flattening himself against the wall, he moved as quickly as he could to the rear of the house and popped his head around the corner. There were bodies in the garden. His heart sank.

Conor raced to the garden and saw the first body. It was an old man. He was fairly certain this was JoAnn's father. He thought he recognized the man from seeing him in the yard or sitting on the front porch in better times. He had taken a gunshot to the chest and was dead.

There were two more men lying in a different part of the garden whom Conor had never seen. They wore clean, fairly expensive outdoor clothing, had good hygiene, and clearly bathed regularly. Wherever they'd come from, they had the resources to care for themselves. While not fat, they were well-fed, which was a rarity these days. Both men had multiple gunshot wounds, including one to the head. Their manner of death had Barb written all over it. She always liked to add that last, Mozambique-style shot to the head before calling the job done.

He scoured the ground frantically. It had been trampled by many feet. It was hard to decipher the scene. One possibility was that she'd engaged the two men after catching them in the act of killing JoAnn's father, then was overpowered and taken prisoner. The most important information gleaned from the scene was there was no blood spilled that was not attributable to the three corpses. He hoped that meant she was uninjured.

Before fleeing the scene, Conor made a quick pass through the dwelling. The back porch and kitchen were covered, prepared for canning, which was consistent with Barb's plans. Inside, Conor found a neat home that was well cared for despite current conditions. There was no one inside.

Conor burst through the front door, crossed the yard, and ran down to the road. He took a moment to confirm the direction he thought the kidnappers had taken, then started running. He pushed the bite valve of his hydration bladder into his mouth, feeling like he should take a drink. The idea of drinking made him nauseous. He rinsed his mouth and spat to avoid swallowing the water. He returned his focus to his breathing and ran as hard as he could. It was true. Someone had taken his baby girl.

8

Ragus fell into a steady running pace on the trail of the horses. He held no illusion that he would outrun and overtake the horses. It wasn't even likely he could rescue Barb unless something just short of a miracle occurred. His plan was to try to stay on their trail and mark it for Conor. If he could find a way to slow the kidnappers down it would be even better.

The boy was no stranger to running and working out. This past school year had been his first as a wrestler. He'd started the year with a lot of anger bottled up inside of him after his mother's cancer diagnosis. It left him with a hair trigger temper and a chip on his shoulder.

One day at school a kid named Eustis pulled his trigger by making fun of his name and he got in a fight. That happened a lot, kids making run of his name because it was unfamiliar to them. This particular kid seemed to know where it came from and he insisted on making an issue of it. Ragus wanted to end the fight before the loudmouth spread the word from one of the schools to the other.

Eustis may have been full of testosterone but Ragus was full of hate. He wanted to shut that kid's mouth and he wanted him to be scared to open it again. Ragus threw the first punch, catching the kid totally by surprise. He'd expected Ragus to be scared, but he held so much hate anymore that he had no room for fear. He dominated the fight until they were separated.

The teacher who pulled him to the office was also the wrestling coach and during that short trip to the office convinced Ragus he should join the team. The coach admitted he'd probably allowed the fight go on a little longer than he should have because he was so impressed by Ragus' natural ability. He wanted to see what he was capable of.

Once on the wrestling team, Ragus started working out in the mornings and evenings with the team, which included long runs to increase their stamina and endurance. A friend of his mother's was driving her to her treatments so Ragus was home for long periods of time by himself. The workouts gave him something to focus on, a much-needed distraction. It gave him an outlet for the anger and frustration.

Once the world fell apart, Ragus had no way to get to summer practices. He had no idea if they were going on or not. They took wrestling pretty serious at his high school and he could easily imagine the coach telling the wrestlers that the collapse of modern civilization was no reason for not showing up to practice. It was also harder to eat well so he'd lost some of the bulk gained from weightlifting. His stamina and his ability to run had not been impaired, though, and it was a damn good thing.

After what he figured to be a half-hour of running, and perhaps three miles of distance, Ragus allowed himself to stop on the bridge over Busthead Creek and take a break. Oddly-shaped scuff marks in the hot asphalt told him he was headed in the right direction. It was like some of the horses had irregular shoes that were homemade or something. He didn't know much about horses but he recognized a horse shoe when he saw it and these didn't look like proper ones.

He took off his pack and retrieved a water bottle, dropping the pack on the ground. His t-shirt was soaked with sweat. He pulled it off, mopped his face and hair with it, then tucked it under a strap in his pack, hoping it would dry while he was running. He saw some pink blotches on the t-shirt and realized the pack was chafing blisters on his skin that had popped already.

The pack wasn't loaded for fast and light travel. Following Conor's advice, the pack was set up so Ragus could survive in the woods for a night or two if he didn't make it back home. There were things in there that would be useful in that scenario, but perhaps not so helpful in the one he found himself in at the moment.

He flipped open the pack lid and scanned for the heaviest items. There were a few cans of soup, a hatchet, and the hydration bladder full of water. It was immediately obvious he could lose a couple of pounds of pack weight just by ditching some of the cans of food and the hatchet. As he drank the water in the hydration bladder, he would stick with the smaller water bottle he carried and not refill the heavier bladder. He had a few small cans of tuna and chicken and he planned to eat those next to lighten his load. Every ounce would help. He didn't know how far he had to run. Hell, he didn't know how many days he might have to run.

If three miles felt like this what would thirty miles feel like? A hundred? Yet if that was how far he had to run, he would do it. He would stay on the trail until he could not lift his legs to move another step.

Not wanting to leave his excess gear there to be stolen, Ragus hurried around the corner of the bridge and stashed the gear in a narrow recess where it met the bank. He could retrieve it at a future date if nobody else found it first. There may be more he could get rid of but he'd wasted enough time taking a break. The urgency of the situation was pulling at him again.

"Don't be weak," he scolded himself. "If you stop or slow down, you better have a damn good reason for it."

He fastened the pack shut, then slung it over his bare back, the raw, blistered skin burning as it made contact with the pack. He picked up the Henry rifle and started running again.

His muscles had stiffened up during the break but they also welcomed the exertion. The sensation was familiar and comforting. It cleared his head and gave him something to focus on. It helped him to forget some of what went on in his life. It helped him forget some of what he'd seen his mother go through as she died. It seemed odd to him that the pain of running, the suffering it inflicted, gave him some of the only peace he'd experienced in a long time.

His mother's last days were awful. She'd run out of pain medication and he'd made several trips to town to try to find more but it wasn't easy. Pharmacies weren't open and they weren't going to let a kid refill an opiate prescription even if they were. Because of the opioid epidemic, pain pills were among the most regulated medications available.

Desperate, he'd even raided his mother's emergency money, kept in the family bible, and gone to the home of a man he'd heard was a drug dealer. There were indeed men there and they looked like they were of the type who would be hanging out at a drug dealer's house. They said they could help him and showed him into the house. Once there, they beat him up and robbed him, then laughed when he explained he needed the pills for his mother.

"I heard that before," one of the men said.

"Hell, I've used that story before," the other man said, both of them breaking into laughter.

"She's dying," Ragus pleaded. "Help me."

"Then why waste good dope on her?" one of the men said. "It ain't going to do her a damn bit of good."

They let him go and Ragus limped off, bruised and bleeding. His eye was swollen shut for days and his jaw hurt when he moved it. Ragus made a pledge on his painful walk home. Before this disaster was over, while there was still no law in place, he intended to go back there and take his revenge on those men. He would make them beg for their lives and he would kill them anyway.

When he reached home, he could hear his mother's screams from the yard. It was hard to force himself to go back inside but what could he do? She had no one else. He had no one else.

He didn't understand the details of what inside her was causing the pain. He didn't understand how the cancer worked, how it was killing her, but it caused her great pain. At times he suspected she was sending him on pointless errands just to get him out of the house, knowing her cries of pain were upsetting him. He didn't want to leave her side though. As much as he wanted the suffering to be over, he didn't want to lose her. He didn't want to be gone when she died. He was all she had and he couldn't abandon her, no matter how much she asked.

He could tell something was changing within her when the long bouts of screaming and crying began to be replaced by periods of unconsciousness. Those periods of unconsciousness became longer and longer. One day she woke with utter lucidity for the first time in weeks. She did not cry or scream. She did not arch and writhe in discomfort.

She looked around the dark room, the bedsheet curtains pulled to aid her sleep, until she found her son in the dark interior of the bedroom. He sat in a chair against the wall, his knees drawn up to his chest and his arms wrapped around his legs, like a child hiding in the closet. When she found his familiar shape it took her a moment to focus. She extended her hand and beckoned him to her side. He moved to the bed and knelt there, taking his mother's hand in both of his.

"Is it over?" he asked. The naïve intention of his question was to determine whether she had defeated the cancer and whether the sickness was over. Her cancer was serious, but Ragus assumed it could be overcome in the way pneumonia or the flu could be.

When she nodded, his heart soared. He thought it was finally over and she would get back to being herself again. She would start taking care of him the way it was supposed to be, instead of him having to take care of her.

"It *is* almost over," she agreed. "I can feel it."

The overwhelming sadness with which she said those words made him realize this was not a triumph but a goodbye. His face ran through a range of emotions and finally to an unbearable anguish that erupted from him in violent sobs. She tried to pull him to her in a hug but didn't have the strength. She barely got a frail arm to his shoulder. She rested the hand there, unable to even orient the hand in a way that would allow her to comfort him. It didn't matter though. Ragus was so blinded by tears he didn't even notice the gesture.

When she next entered sleep, she never regained consciousness. There were several times he thought she was dead but discovered she was still breathing when he held a hand mirror over her mouth. It was something he'd seen on a TV show. When finally her body began to cool to the touch, he knew she was gone. He hadn't even been aware of the moment of her passing.

He buried her underneath the tree where they played so often. When the yard wasn't overgrown, it was a pretty spot and they had good times there. The digging was hard, with tree roots crossing like steel reinforcement embedded in concrete. He had to use a shovel as often as an axe to get the hole deep enough. When it was complete, he wrapped her in a blanket and carried her outside, shocked at how little she weighed. It felt like he was carrying a child.

Her loss left him in a dark place. He brooded in the stale house, unable to find even a candle or flashlight with which to cut the darkness. Instead he sat there in the floor, listening to his stomach growl and rodents scratch inside the walls. In the daylight, he tore through every inch of the home trying to find any morsel of something he might eat. He ate ketchup packets, old Halloween candy, and a few packets of sugar. He even found a package of crackers that had come with a fast food salad in the sticky filth beneath the car seat. A devoted hater of salads and other "rabbit food," Ragus would have killed for a salad at the moment.

He eventually realized there was nothing at the house that would keep him alive. In a few weeks he would end up as weak as his mother. Shortly after, he would end up just as dead. So while he was still able to walk, he took the pistol from his mother's nightstand and went looking for food, ending up in the Irishman's chicken house. Part of him hoped the man would shoot him. He was that far beyond caring.

Instead, the family, or at least Conor, had taken him under their wing. He'd given the boy a way to take care of himself. He taught him about channeling his anger and preventing it from consuming him, something Conor said he knew a lot about. Ragus owed him his life. If he lost his trying to save Barb that was okay, because he'd have been dead anyway if the family hadn't saved him. If it hurt pursuing her, that was fine too, because he knew about pain now as well. There was nothing the road could throw at him that he hadn't suffered already.

He ran harder, sweat starting to pour again. He clenched his jaw, pumped his arms, and pushed himself harder, making it hurt. "Bring it," he hissed.

He was speaking to the road, to the men, and to the very world itself.

"Bring it!" he bellowed.

9

Along the highway outside of Tazewell, Virginia, the party from Douthat Farms gathered in the parking lot of an eating establishment in the middle of nowhere. The men were ravenous and they knew their growing collection of prisoners had to be hungry too. Not that their comfort was of any concern.

While they'd been successful in their effort to gather a new female labor force for the farm, they'd been less successful at finding food. They'd brought little with them, counting on their looting to feed them. The problem was they were trying to steal from folks who had nothing to steal. Blinded by their own abundance, they'd greatly overestimated the resources of the population at large.

When they came across the abandoned barbecue joint located in a garishly painted barn miles from any town, they were all overcome with memories of what a roadside barbecue place smelled like with its roasting meats and spicy sauces. They could have continued on, stopping someplace with fewer epicurean associations with which to torture them, but this was the first good spot they'd come across.

"Break the fucking door down," Top Cat ordered, scratching at the rash around his raw neck. "The place is empty. Maybe they left some canned food behind."

Lester took a small group of men, kicked out a kitchen door, and rooted around. The rest of the men kept an eye on the hooded and bound prisoners, balanced uneasily atop their tired mounts. At Top Cat's urging, they'd sought to kidnap women in pairs–mothers and daughters, sisters, friends. They knew from experience women were less likely to run away if they were leaving someone behind that they cared about. They felt an obligation to stay together, even if that meant suffering and dying together.

"Nothing in there except barbecue sauce and spices," Lester reported back, digging at his oozing armpit.

Just the thought of meat cooked in that sauce and those spices made Top Cat's mouth water. He was sure the other men felt the same. He'd kill for a plate of ribs, baked beans, coleslaw, and a hot buttered roll. And some pie for dessert. A couple of nice cold beers to wash it all down with.

"They've got a hell of a smoker though," Lester said. "We kill a cow and we'd have the makings of a mighty nice cookout. There's even a spring coming off the mountain for cool, clean water."

"Yeah, well, I didn't see any cattle," Top Cat grumbled. "So I guess we might as well stop slobbering over it."

Lester grinned. "I did."

"Where?"

Lester pointed. Top Cat wheeled in his saddle and squinted toward the distant field behind the restaurant. Sure enough, a couple of red and white cows grazed peacefully in the distance.

"Those are Herefords," Lester said. "We could cook steaks for everyone here and smoke the rest for the trip back."

"How long would smoking take?"

Lester shrugged. "Overnight probably. The thinner you cut it, the faster it dries. We get a bed of coals going and we could be eating steak in an hour or two."

"Let's do it," Top Cat said. "See any place to stash the prisoners?"

"There's a cinderblock building around back near the smoker. An old garage or something. Only got one door and no windows. It'll be perfect."

A few minutes later, Top Cat was personally overseeing that the prisoners were properly secured in the garage when he heard a shot ring out, then a second. It was Lester dropping one of the steers. The women were hooded with their hands bound in front of them. They were paralyzed with fear, some of them crying, others too scared to even utter a sound. An empty five-gallon bucket was brought from the restaurant and placed in the cinderblock building for a toilet. A roll of toilet paper chewed full of holes from mice was found in a public restroom and tossed in with them.

"Cut'em loose," Top Cat ordered, digging at his inflamed groin.

One of the men flicked open a folding knife, pausing to scratch his itching forearm with it, then carefully removed the zip ties. They needed each woman to be capable of work so it was worthwhile to protect them. It had been made clear to each and every man on this mission that no abuse of their precious cargo would be tolerated.

"You can take off your hoods for now but they go back on in the morning," Top Cat said. "Don't lose them or you'll be wearing somebody's drawers on your head for the rest of the trip."

Taking permission to remove their hoods as permission to begin talking, some of the women bombarded Top Cat with questions, begging for freedom for themselves or another of their party. Some made promises, others threats. The chorus of desperate chatter overwhelmed him.

He drew his weapon and fired a round into the air to silence them. The women flinched at the eruption of deafening noise in the confined space, some yelping or screaming, but it had the desired effect. The women backed away, retreating to the most distant recess of the shadowy building.

Top Cat stood in the shaft of light coming through the open door, his pistol smoking in his hand. "Do not mistake me freeing you for the night as weakness. No one is going back home. No one is being released. You will never see your family or your home ever again so you better start accepting that. If you try to escape, I'll kill you and whoever we picked you up with. We'll bring you water in a moment and food when we have it. Until then, shut the fuck up and mind your manners."

Top Cat backed out the single door to the structure and it was barricaded behind him. He holstered his pistol and checked Lester's progress. In the distance, he could see him working on the downed steer with a large knife taken from the restaurant kitchen. "Anybody have firewood ready?"

A nearby member of his crew, formerly an assistant manager at Radio Shack, nodded. The poison ivy had spread to his face, covering it in crusty yellow sores. "There's a shed piled full."

"Get fires going," Top Cat ordered. "One in the smoker, one in the grill beside it. We're going to need lots of coals. We got a lot of food to cook."

The man looked like a deer in the headlights.

"What?" Top Cat growled.

"I've never built a fire before."

"Then find someone who can, dumbass."

The man hurried off.

"Get the prisoners a bucket of drinking water," Top Cat told another man. "See if there are any cups in the restaurant."

He nodded and disappeared. Lester was soon back leading a horse with half a small steer draped over its back.

"Jesus, that's a lot of meat," Top Cat said.

"Steaks for all of us," Lester said. "We can smoke more for tomorrow and make jerky for the rest of the trip."

"I guess we're spending the night here," Top Cat said. "I'd like to have put a little more distance between us and the towns where we gathered these women."

Lester shrugged. "We're armed. Let them catch up with us. We'll send them running home with their tails between their legs."

∽

BARB SLOWLY PACED the interior of the cinderblock building, trying to assess her situation. JoAnn sat in the floor, desperately hugging another crying woman. JoAnn mourned her father but she didn't know if the other woman cried from loss, fear, or anticipation of what their future was to be.

The pain of the ride had been exhausting. Barb thought she might have a few cracked ribs, perhaps a broken sternum, from the blunt arrow they'd hit her with. It hurt to move. It hurt to breathe. If she'd worn that damn body armor her father went on about the arrow wouldn't have dropped her. But then there was no telling how it might have gone if the arrow hadn't stopped the fight. She would probably have fought to the death. So maybe the lack of body armor actually saved her life, though it hurt like a bitch at the moment.

Part of her, the wounded child, wanted to curl up in a ball and cry, but that wasn't who she was. She wasn't one to lie on the floor and take the role of victim. She was an alpha. She would prefer to use her time trying to figure a way out of this situation. She would prefer to plot the deaths of her enemies.

"Where are they taking us?" someone asked.

Barb looked in the direction of the speaker but couldn't see well in the gloom. Only small pinpricks of light came in around the door. It was enough to see a gritty patch of concrete in the center of the floor and little pockets of illumination around the room but that was all.

"Do you know, Barb?" JoAnn asked.

"Possibly slavers of some sort," Barb replied. "They don't seem to want to hurt us. We must be more valuable to them undamaged. That makes me think we're the cargo."

"They killed my dad," JoAnn moaned, starting to cry again.

"That's why you need to stay strong," Barb said. "Dwelling on what you've lost won't help anyone. It doesn't help you, your father, or anyone here. Everyone needs to be strong, both for themselves and for everyone else. That's the only way we have a fighting chance."

"What good is that going to do?" asked a woman. Barb couldn't get a good look at her in this light but remembered her from when their hoods were removed. She looked to be in her mid-forties with bad teeth. She wore a tank top that revealed old tattoos with crude lines and misspelled words. Her skin had looked like leather in need of some saddle soap.

"We can better support each other if we stay strong," Barb explained. "We'll be in a better position to take advantage of any opportunities that might present themselves."

The woman gave a dismissive laugh that turned into a smoker's cough. "I don't know what the fuck you're talking about. I was out of food and only had one thing left to trade. My body. If that's what these guys want they're welcome to it as long as they keep me fed."

Barb stared in the direction of the woman. "I'm not so easily won over. Anything they want from me, they'll have to fight to take."

"They'll get what they want in the end. There's more of them than there is of you," the woman said. "Might as well give it up and take what enjoyment you can. Ain't no use getting beat up over it."

While the woman was outnumbered in her opinion, there were others who agreed with her. Barb didn't approve of the woman's attitude but she bit her tongue. It was easy to be judgmental when you had a bunker full of food. Barb was not in the same situation as most of these other women. If she were, perhaps her view would be different. Especially if she had kids to feed.

It was on the tip of her tongue to express her defiance, to tell these women that she would not be taken so easily, but she quickly realized she needed to keep any plans she made secret. It was possible one of these women might offer to trade information about her for special treatment. Maybe they would whisper her plans into a guard's ear while she was sleeping. Another prisoner could give her up for as little as a solitary cigarette or a swig from a bottle of liquor.

Barb needed a moment to herself. She walked to a distant corner and slid down the wall, her legs stretched out in front of her. The movement hurt and she realized she'd need to be more careful until she healed up. JoAnn came and sat beside her.

"What are we going to do?" JoAnn whispered. "How are we going to get out of here?"

Barb shook her head but that movement hurt too. She was getting a headache from dehydration. She needed to remind herself to drink as much as she could when water was available to them. "I don't know. I don't want to say too much in front of the other women until we know who we can trust. Some of them I'm not so sure about."

"Me neither," JoAnn agreed.

"My dad will come for us," Barb whispered. "As long as he can find us, he'll take us home."

"I hope you're right, but he better be bringing more than just himself. There are a lot of men out there."

Barb smiled in the darkness. "You don't know my dad. Twice this many would not stop him. Three times this many. He's a very determined man. And a very dangerous one."

10

In the Appalachian Mountains of Virginia, fall often brought cool nights but the daytime temperatures could be quite warm. Shirtless, Ragus felt the sun burning his skin, the padded straps of his pack gnawing into his shoulders, but he did not want to stop moving. His jeans were sodden and rivulets of sweat were running down his legs. He'd been forced to cinch his belt tighter, trying to keep the wet jeans in place. Like the pack, they rubbed and abraded his skin yet the pain only urged him forward.

His water was gone, the empty bottle clipped to his belt beating a cadence against his thigh as he chugged steadily onward. He thought he recalled a stream running close to the road a short distance ahead of him. He would stop there and use the mini Sawyer filter Conor had given him to refill his bottle. He'd once fished the river for horny heads and smallmouth bass with his uncle Orbie just a week before Orbie was crushed to death in the mines.

Before reaching the stream, he was forced to slow to a walk when he was stricken with a cramp in his hamstring that refused to go away. When he could not walk it out, he stopped and desperately massaged the muscle, so taut and painful it felt as if a rod were being threaded through the meat of him, like a hunk of chicken being shoved onto a skewer. From being on the wrestling team he understood what was happening. He had sweated the salt from his body and needed to replenish it.

If this was wrestling practice he would simply go to the cooler and filled a paper cup with a sports drink, but he didn't have any, nor did he have any salt pills. He walked in agony for twenty minutes before the cramp began to ease. By that time he was passing the Gas & Guzzle, a local convenience store. He eyed the shell of the store, the windows broken out and discarded packaging littering the parking lot.

His leg ached from the cramp and he didn't know what lay ahead of him. He could be running for hours or days so he decided to make a quick pass through the store to see if he could find anything of use. The store smelled of mildew, sour milk, and rotted food. Broken glass ground beneath his shoes, gouging the narrow oak planks on the floor, dark as ebony from decades of traffic. Ragus started with the drink coolers and found them looted of nearly everything. There was not a single can, bottle, or quart of beer anywhere. In fact, everything alcoholic in the entire store was gone. Ragus wondered if the alcohol had been purchased in the days after the collapse or stolen after the store was abandoned.

Every soft drink, every sports drink, and every bottle of water was also missing. Only the spoiled containers of milk were left behind, many of them intentionally busted against the wall in what passed for lowbrow entertainment. The food shelves had been ransacked and nothing remained there except for plastic bags hiding bread and hamburger buns beneath dense wigs of powdery green mold.

Checking for nuts and beef jerky, foods easily eaten on the run, Ragus was disappointed to find the racks empty. He tilted the displays carefully and looked beneath them. He managed to find a half-dozen beef sticks and a pack of peanuts that had been lost in the looting. The find brought a smile to Ragus' face. He picked the bounty up and shoved it in his pocket.

Walking toward the counter he saw that every tobacco product, whether intended for smoking, dipping, or chewing, was absent from the shelves. Near the counter he found a half-pot of desiccated coffee sitting on the burner of a Bunn coffee maker. Beside it, mold filled the transparent vat of a slushy machine, ready upon the restoration of power to dispense an especially vile concoction.

Ragus studied the condiment center, looking at napkins, straws, and seasoning packets that had been passed over by looters. Then he was struck with an idea. Rifling through the packets, he found plenty of sugar and salt. They had apparently been of little use to anyone but they would be to him. They should allow him to make a passable sports drink from his next water refill. It would be without the artificial flavoring and coloring he was used to but should prove sufficient to make his muscles stop locking up on him.

He took as many of the packets as he could find, putting them in his pack. His clothes were already so saturated with sweat they wouldn't survive in a pocket. Deciding he'd wasted enough time there, he gave in to the pull of the road, the pull of his responsibility. He stepped back on the road and forced his tired muscles to resume plodding along the pavement. Every few minutes he would veer off the shoulder of the road and find a prominent branch clearly visible from the road. He snapped the tip of it but left it dangling in place, a marker he hoped would show Conor he was headed in the right direction.

As for his own certainty that he was headed in the right direction, Ragus was relying on the scuff marks of homemade horse shoes on the paved road and the trail of horse manure littering the highway. Certainly there had been other people on horses who'd come this way but Ragus was certain he was on the correct path. The horse manure was so abundant it was like following a small town parade.

Sore and nearly exhausted, Ragus sought to distract himself from his misery. He began looking at the paved road as the course of a videogame and the piles of manure as reward tokens. He tried to avoid thinking about how far he had to go. That would only depress him. He simply forced himself from one pile of shit to the next, making a *ding* sound between panting breaths as he ran past each. The game worked for a while but he eventually reached a point where he was too tired, too sore, and too depleted to continue running. He slowed to a walk.

He was feeling demoralized when he spotted a solitary apple tree in a field beside the road. Even this late in the season there were a few apples stuck to the branches. He could only imagine how wonderful they would taste. Making sure there was no one around to bother him, Ragus climbed up the shoulder of the road and ducked through a barbed wire fence.

With a little climbing and branch shaking, Ragus brought down several apples. They were not perfect and he had to trim away a few wormy sections but they tasted delicious. The sugar spread through his body like a magic potion, revitalizing him. He ate two and put the rest in his pack. With his craving temporarily abated, he wanted nothing more than to lie down at the base of the tree and close his eyes, knowing he would drop right off to sleep.

He held his hand up and saw the sun was four fingers off the horizon. He had about an hour of daylight and should keep moving. If he could keep walking he could cover a few more miles before dark. Though a nap was tempting, there was nothing he wanted more than to find Barb and keep her safe until Conor caught up with them. If the opportunity presented itself, he would rescue her himself, but he would not put her in danger by acting stupidly. He would never be able to face Conor if his actions led to Barb getting hurt.

Ragus got back on the road and returned to playing mind games to distract himself from the pain. He told himself that he was not trying to walk five miles but instead only trying to walk to that funny shaped tree a hundred feet away. Then from the funny shaped tree he was only walking to the crooked fence post that jutted erratically from the otherwise orderly row. From the crooked fence post he was only walking as far as the narrow bridge.

Distracted by such games, he walked for another hour and then on the wafting evening breeze he caught a smell that made his stomach knot like a clenched fist. It was the spicy aroma of roasting meat. He prayed his drooling did not deplete what few fluids remained in his dehydrated body.

BOOGER HOLE CREEK wound like a blacksnake through the khaki-colored pastures of western Tazewell County. Near where it crossed under Highway 460 there stood a roadside barbecue restaurant that had been in business for around forty years. The building had once been a barn. Bright paint and flamboyant graffiti covered the fences and exterior walls. With the smell spreading through the air, Ragus was almost convinced they had remained opened despite the collapse, but the herd of horses gathered in the parking lot told him another story. This had to be the people he was following. He had caught up to the kidnappers.

Relief came with the awareness that he'd successfully tracked them this far. There had been multiple instances over the course of the day where Ragus wondered if he was on the right trail or not. He experienced moments of doubt where he thought he would never find Barb or his body would give out before he did. Even at those moments, he could not go back and face Conor as a failure. He could not go back empty-handed. It was not even a possibility.

With his relief came equal concern from the sheer number of men before him. The group had grown since he'd last seen them. There must've been other scouting parties, perhaps doing the same thing, and they had rejoined each other for the trip home. He didn't know how many of the horses were stolen on this raid or how many they brought with them to haul back women and gear, but he thought he could be looking at sixty or seventy horses. How many men went with these horses? Certainly more than he could deal with by himself.

He was having difficulty processing the information his eyes were feeding him. In fact, he had difficulty thinking at all. Thoughts came and went, trailing off without resolution. Any attempt at deciding a course of action got derailed by things as simple as the sensation of sweat running down his spine. It dawned on him that his inability to think coherently was likely a side effect of the dehydration. He needed to get water before he did anything else.

He skirted to the left and found an isolated section of stream not far from the encampment with a good flow of water. Conor told him that it was always better to draw from moving water if you had a choice. He added one of the salt packets and three of the sugar packets to his water bottle then filled it using the Sawyer mini filter. It tasted exactly like what it was, an unflavored sports drink. It was sweet and a little salty. Not entirely appetizing, but he could feel it working its magic inside his body from the first drink, restoring his chemistry and bringing him back to life.

Looking around to reassure himself that he was alone, he slipped off his shoes and socks. He took a seat on a rock jutting from the bank and eased his feet into the cold water. Resting them on the smooth stones of the creek bottom he was overcome by how good it felt. His poor feet had been tortured by the run. He pulled one out and examined it, finding a few hot spots that would probably be blisters by morning. As good as it felt, he wished he had the time to sink his entire body into the creek and let the water pour over him. He had no doubt he'd emerge a new man, ready to take on the world, but he did not have that kind of time.

Perhaps now that he had found Barb's kidnappers, he would not have to push himself so hard. If they were just walking their horses now that they were out of town, he could walk fast enough to keep up with them. It would be so much easier on his body than running the entire time. He fished around in his pack and found a bandana. He soaked it in the water, raised it over the top of his head, and squeezed it, allowing the cool water to run over him. He could imagine the cloud of steam rising from his overheated skull.

He soaked the bandana again, wiping down his face, his neck, and his chest. It both cooled and soothed him, restoring some of his confidence. Whether it was the drink or the effect of the cool water on his body, his mind was beginning to function better. As it did, he began to turn over scenarios. He glanced at his Henry rifle propped against a tree and knew there was no way he could march into this group of men, wipe them out, and rescue Barb.

He wished he had the ability to do that. He wished he was

capable both in terms of skill and firepower to do such a thing. He fantasized about it, storming in like a wraith, like an avenging angel, and killing all of them. He was just a kid though. Any such action would only get him killed and leave Barb still in the hands of her kidnappers with no one to leave a trail for Conor.

Ragus was distracted by the movement of a fish near his foot. He had a hand line, hooks, and sinkers in a tin of survival gear in his pocket. He could find enough insects here to catch fish with little difficulty but he was afraid to build a fire for cooking them. If he played the wind right it would carry the scent of his fire away from the group at the restaurant. It was also unlikely those people would smell anything over top of their own cooking fires but he was scared to take the chance. While it was hard to pass up food, he had to be disciplined. He had to be tough. Hunger was just pain and he could handle pain.

The sun dropped over the horizon while Ragus sat there cooling his feet. The play of light in the changing leaves was beautiful around him, a peaceful oasis in the chaos of his world and his life. He was almost too tired to drink anymore but he forced himself to finish that bottle, then he made another and drank it also. When he finished both bottles, he made another to take with him, and refilled the empty hydration bladder. The full three-liter bladder added a lot of weight to his pack when he was running today but it would be more tolerable if tomorrow's pace was slower.

Ragus reluctantly pulled his feet from the soothing water and wiped them down with the bandana. They were sore to the touch and would be worse tomorrow. He used his mostly dry t-shirt to finish drying them off. His water bottle had several wraps of duct tape around it and he tore off some small squares to adhere over the blisters forming on his feet. As much as he hated to, he pulled his clammy, sweat-soaked socks back onto his feet and shoved them into his reeking boots.

When he stood, he felt significantly better than when he had arrived at the creek. He put his t-shirt on and walked back to the road. He needed to find a good vantage point from which to surveil the camp. The light would fade quickly now and he needed to learn all he could about the men who had taken Barb. He ate the peanuts and two of the beef sticks as he walked. If he was going expend this level of energy, he couldn't ration food. His body would not have the endurance to push all day long and he would bonk and collapse. He decided that when he found a spot to hide he would open a can of tuna and eat that too. He had never really liked tuna but he liked hunger even less.

11

Conor followed the trail by the same prominent features Ragus did, focusing on the distinctive marks made by the homemade rebar horseshoes. That was not his only assurance he was on the right path. He couldn't miss the branches bent at intervals along the edge of the road. Someone was snapping the end of tree branches as they went, a clear means of trail marking, and Conor was certain it was Ragus because he'd taught him the technique. Not only did those bent branches reassure him he was going the correct way, it told him the boy was safe.

Plodding along at the fastest pace an old shop-rat could manage, Conor had a lot of time to think. When there was nothing to do but put one foot behind the other, what else could you do? The mind wandered in attempt to distract from the physical discomfort. Sometimes he thought about what he was going to do to the men when he caught them. Sometimes he thought about what he might have to do to prevent something like this from happening again.

He was starting to wonder if perhaps his entire approach to keeping himself and Barb safe was flawed. He'd hoped they could maintain a low profile and avoid contact but they had violated the basic tenets of such a strategy. They had both been wandering around outside of the compound.

They had no guards on the perimeter of their geographic boundaries. Their community had no system of alerting each other to danger, no defensive perimeter. Conor had not wanted to do any of those things. He had not wanted to assume responsibility for so many people. He had not wanted to take charge. But that strategy–avoidance—had allowed strangers to come into their territory. It had allowed his daughter to be kidnapped.

If he wanted to keep his ridge safe, his entire community safe, he had to become the sheepdog and drive the wolves away. The only thing wolves understood was violence, and a good sheepdog was willing to rise to a level of violence above that of the wolf. You had to be as willing to kill as the wolf was and the wolf had to be aware of this, had to be afraid.

Conor had no problem with that. He'd been coached on violence his entire life. As a child in Ireland, the unwitting apprentice of two generations of bomb makers, he'd absorbed a lot. Not only about making bombs, but about killing and the motivation for killing. It didn't stop there, though. Conor's relationship with violence and his understanding of the role it played in the world was a long, complicated story.

When young Conor and his mother Moira came to the United States, they settled in the Boston area. There were a lot of Irish folks there and they were able to take advantage of connections with people who were either friends or family of people they knew back home. That helped his mother find an apartment and a job. Still, meeting people with connections to the old country was not entirely comforting. She met people who not only knew who she was but who her husband and father-in-law were. There were people in Ireland who would pay money for that information. People who lost family members to the bombs. They would see her and Conor as fair game. She realized she and her son were not safe in Boston.

Moira worked as a waitress in a restaurant. She told her boss, a well-known local businessman named Bertie, she was interested in moving to a small town somewhere. She wanted a place where she wouldn't be known and where Conor would not be in danger from people seeking retaliation against things he had no part of.

"I might be able to help you with that," Bertie offered.

Ever the suspicious type, Moira had cocked an eyebrow at Bertie, assuming that all help came at a cost. Being a woman with no husband, she was pretty sure she knew what the cost would be but she was wrong. Bertie put matters of money before concerns of the flesh. He was a greedy bastard and, as the Irish put it, he'd sell you the eye out of your own head.

"You ever thought about the mountains of North Carolina?" Bertie asked. "It's a beautiful part of the country and damn near identical to home. Many of the families there are Scots or Irish by blood."

Moira shrugged. "I don't know this country well. I haven't taken my plan to the point of picking a place to move. Moving requires money and I figured I'd have to save for a while before I could make the move."

"North Carolina is far enough that news from Boston doesn't make it down there," he pointed out. "That's part of why I may be able help you out."

"I'm cut to the onions with all this talk. Tell me what you're hinting at, Bertie Mooney." Moira had no tolerance for beating around the bush.

Bertie had to laugh at this woman who showed no deference for who or what he was in the community. Maybe she didn't know. Maybe she didn't care. Perhaps she'd spent so much time around men of violence that they were not a novelty to her.

"I have men, employees and associates, who catch a little local heat sometimes. I've found the best solution is to get them out of town for a couple of months until things blow over. When it happens, I have to make arrangements and find someplace to send them. It's happening often enough that I've been thinking about a place of my own to send them. You could provide that place. I'd pay you a little money every month for room and board of these men. It will never be more than one or two at a time. Sometimes there won't be any there at all but you'll get the money every month. For that money, I expect there to be a bed and a hot meal available if I send somebody."

"Are these rumbly blokes? How do I know these men will be safe for my son to be around?" It was notable that Moira made no reference to her own safety. She was not scared of men.

"Regardless of what crimes these men may or may not have committed, I swear I will only send you men who are good family men. Men you don't have to worry about. Men who will not present a risk to you or your son."

Moira processed that. "You say it's just for a short period?"

Bertie shrugged and held up his hands. "A few days, a few weeks, a few months. Just until things blow over and they can come back home."

"How much would I get for this?"

Bertie considered. "I'll give you three hundred dollars a month. That includes room and board for whoever I might send. I think that's more than fair. You can probably even find a house in North Carolina you can rent for less than that."

She studied Bertie and found no signs of guile or deception. She had a good sense of men and felt this one was being honest with her. She'd known him to be a good man. He'd been helpful to her and kind to her son when the lad came by the restaurant to eat.

She extended a hand and they shook on it. "You have yourself a deal."

Bertie smiled, reaching into his shirt pocket to fish out a wad of bills. He licked his thumb and plucked three hundred dollar bills from the stack. He extended them to her. "First payment. You call me when you get set up down there. Send me a mailing address and a phone number. I need directions to the house and the name of the nearest airport."

By that chance conversation with her boss, Conor's mother began an informal rooming house for Irish mobsters on the run from the law. A couple of times a year they would host a grandfatherly assassin, a handsome thief, or some other high-profile criminal that needed to escape the Boston underworld for a few months. True to his word, Bertie only sent men who seemed like decent family men. Conor, missing his dad and grandfather, was anxious for male influences in his life and most of these men eagerly took on that role to break up the boredom of country life.

They told Conor stories and took him fishing. They washed dishes and helped Moira in the garden. Whether born in the United States or the old country, these were decent Irish blokes and Moira found them to be an honest and trustworthy lot. She had no idea, though, that her inquisitive son persisted in badgering each man with questions until he eventually figured out the score. He had enough street knowledge to figure out who and what these men were. By the time he was eleven years old, Conor knew the inside scoop on pretty much every major crime the Irish mob committed. The boy knew who the bosses were, who pulled off all the major heists, and most entertaining of all, who had whacked who.

Moira understood Conor's need for male influences in his life but she'd have been extremely upset if she understood that these men continued Conor's education in crime, murder, and mayhem. It wasn't their fault. Once Conor figured out why these men kept showing up, he badgered them for stories about their way of life. Once that gate was open, it was like they picked up exactly as his father and grandfather left off.

One of the lessons that stuck with him was the significance of vengeance. You didn't let people get away with acting against you or they would continue to do so. You hit them back and you hit twice as hard as they hit you. It was like the sheepdog and the wolf. You let the wolf keep picking off sheep and it was going to keep coming back. The only way the wolf learned a lesson was if you killed one of them and hung it at the boundary so all the other wolves knew the score.

Conor remembered one story in particular, about an old Irish gentleman named Patrick who liked to take his great niece swimming at the neighborhood pool. There he picked up talk about a loser who spent a lot of time at the pool and always looked at the little girls a little too long, in a way that was not paternal but predatory.

When Patrick heard the pervert had offered his great niece a candy bar, he couldn't let it sit. After all, who knew how many children this slimeball had probably molested? Patrick didn't want his niece to be next.

One day while the pervert was at the pool creeping on the little kiddies, Patrick broke into the perv's car. In his pocket, he had a baggie of crystal drain cleaner that he ground with a hammerhead until it was as fine as baby powder. Using a funnel and a teaspoon, Patrick filled the air condition vents in the guy's car with the powdered drain cleaner. He aimed all the vents at the driver's seat and turned the fan switch to the HIGH position. He wiped down everything he touched with a handkerchief, locked the car door, and retreated to a distant corner of the parking lot to wait for the slimeball.

Patrick was sitting on a bench smoking a cigarette when the creep got into his El Dorado and started the engine. The next thing he knew, the guy was rolling around in the parking lot, screaming and rubbing his eyes. The guy ended up going losing his sight but he saw the writing on the wall. He got the hell out of the neighborhood and never came back.

With that and similar revenge stories playing through his head, Conor pushed himself onward with thoughts of what he was going to do to Barb's kidnappers when he found them. There would be no restraint or mercy. It would be a sheepdog gone mad, tearing men limb from limb. It would be a display of excess and violence that would become the stuff of legend. It would make any future troublemakers think twice before crossing into the land of The Mad Mick.

12

Barb did not sleep. She was wide awake, sitting on the floor and reclined against the cold block wall when the door was shoved open the next morning. Harsh morning light flooded the interior of the sparse building, singeing retinas and forcing those who were awake to cover their eyes. Barb had tried to sleep at some point in the night, stretching out on the floor, but was unable to get comfortable. Where she'd been hit by the blunt arrow caused a dull pain if she moved the wrong way. Unfortunately, lying down was one of the "wrong ways" she couldn't move.

When her eyes adjusted to the stabbing pain of the light, Barb could see the women who'd managed to find sleep stirring beneath the white tablecloths they'd used as blankets. Barb knew she'd pay a price for her lack of sleep. She'd struggle to stay awake in the saddle and wouldn't be at her maximum ability.

"Rise and shine, ladies," sang an all too cheery man sent to wake them up. He brought in a fresh bucket of drinking water.

They'd finished yesterday's bucket last night and had not been offered a refill. Another man came in behind the first bearing a tray of meat scraps straight from the smoker. Last night, from the interior of the building, they'd heard the men outside feasting on steaks and ribs while they got off-cuts and scraps. Still, Barb was glad they were given anything at all. Maintaining their strength would be critical if they ever hoped to fight back or escape.

She stood and walked to the tray of meat left sitting atop the empty water bucket. She grabbed a handful and went back to the wall where she sat down, tearing chunks of the meat free with her teeth. There was no knife to trim the fat away so she concentrated on taking in the calories, trying not to gag on the thick chunks of fat.

Another five gallon bucket and a stack of napkins had served as their toilet overnight. The reek from that bucket made it difficult to eat but JoAnn forced herself. When she found she could not force *all* of the food down in such an unappetizing environment, she secreted away the rest in her bra, hoping she would find an opportunity to finish it later. She didn't know where the next meal was coming from.

The women rose, talking quietly, eating, drinking, and using the makeshift toilet, which had been an easier proposition in the pitch black last night. A person could at least imagine they were in a more private setting instead of sharing their bathroom with an army of other women. Barb needed to go but could not force herself to go under these degrading circumstances. She would hold it, though she might pay a price later for her stubbornness. There was no guarantee they'd stop and offer a better opportunity.

A different man appeared in the doorway, the blinding light leaving him in silhouette and obscuring his features. "Okay ladies, here's how we're going to do things today. Everybody has to be zip tied again with your hands in front of you so you can hold onto the pommel of your saddle. We're also going to zip tie an ankle to one of your stirrups so don't be getting any ideas that you're going to leap from your horse and make a break for it. We'll try this with the hoods off today but if any one of you breaks the rules, it's hoods for everyone." He gave that a moment to sink in.

"Should we bring these tablecloths we used for blankets?" Barb asked.

The man reacted as if it were the dumbest question he'd ever heard. "I reckon you should if you don't want to be cold tonight. Your comfort is not my concern."

Barb wanted to stalk across the floor and knock him on his ass but she showed some restraint. The time for that would come, and she hoped she personally would have the opportunity to deliver the blow.

"Where are you taking us?" cried one of the women. She was holding a younger girl, a teenager, against her.

"Why, I'm taking you home," he said cruelly. "Oh, but before you get too excited, I mean to your *new* home, of course. Not your old home."

"I want to go home," the teenage girl moaned.

"Your lives started over yesterday. The sooner you realize that, the better off you'll be. They call me Top Cat and I'm your new boss. When we get to your new home, I'll introduce you to my boss. His name is Bryan. You'll be fine as long as you obey Bryan's rules. If you break the rules or get to be a pain in the ass, your stay will become very unpleasant."

When there were no comments, Top Cat backed out of the building. "We'll talk more later," he called from the doorway.

Barb looked at JoAnn and saw nothing but fear. Were it in her nature to be more nurturing, she would try to comfort the other woman, but that was not how she did things. She would encourage fighting back, killing, and plotting vengeance. She would not encourage indulging in emotions.

13

Ragus managed to sleep but he was certain it was only the result of sheer exhaustion. Since meeting Conor, he always carried sleeping gear in his pack just in case he was forced to spend the night in the woods. He had a 10' x 10' backpacking tarp constructed of silver nylon that weighed next to nothing. He could use it as a ground cloth, a shelter, or even pull it over his head as a poncho if he was caught in a downpour. With no indication of rain, he laid it out on the ground and slept under a fleece blanket.

When he awoke, he crawled to a position where he could observe Barb's kidnappers again. People were packing horses so he assumed they were preparing to take their leave. He glanced around his own position, halfway hoping he would find Conor approaching so they could end this right here, right now. He did not have the ability to take on this group of men by himself. He wouldn't even know where to start. He was confident Conor could come up with a plan though. The man was good at this kind of thing.

Ragus quickly bored with watching the kidnappers go about their routine, although he couldn't let his attention completely lapse because it was critical he pick up any information he could about the group. Some men were seated at the outdoor dining area, breakfasting on water and warm beef fresh out of the smoker. Ragus took the opportunity to slip back to the creek and refill his water bottle and hydration bladder.

Returning to his watch position, he used his bandana to wipe down the Henry rifle, which was looking pretty grimy after yesterday's sweaty slog. His watch, also a gift from Conor, indicated it was 9 AM. He wondered why these men weren't on the road already. They were wasting good daylight. The more he observed them, he came to the conclusion that it was not a strategic decision but more attributable to apathy and disorganization.

Tendrils of wood smoke seeped from the rusty black smoker behind the restaurant. The breeze carried the scent directly to Ragus, taunting him, and it nearly drove the boy mad with hunger. He pulled a bent stick of jerky from his pack, peeled it open, and chewed, but it was no substitute for fresh smoked beef. He ate and watched, noticing one man was now moving from one cluster of folks to the next, his demeanor that of a person giving orders. Sometimes he shouted out but Ragus could not hear the words. The tone and gestures were familiar to him. It was not unlike a coach calling out instructions to his team.

Apparently those instructions were marching orders, as the loose assembly of men began breaking down their gear, repacking it, and lashing it to pack horses. Ragus raised his rifle and viewed the activity through his low-power rifle scope. The magnification was not great but it did give him a slightly better picture of what was going on.

A couple of men stood at the entrance to a squat cinderblock building that looked like an old garage with its rusty tin roof and mismatched paint. A man shouted inside and a woman haltingly emerged out of the door. She extended her hands in front of her and they were zip tied together. Another man led her to a horse and helped her mount, then zip tied her hands to the pommel of the saddle, then zip tied one leg to a stirrup. When Ragus returned his eyes to the building a second woman was being led off, her hands tied, another woman replacing her at the door.

Better understanding what was going on now, Ragus focused on that door with laser intensity. He only cared to see one girl coming out. Then there she was, the seventh to emerge. Even before his eyes and brain recognized her, his heart already sensed it was Barb. While she stood still for her hands to be zip tied, he got a better look and was certain. It was her. She was alive and unharmed but her body language was telling. She was not happy about her circumstances. Knowing this girl, Ragus could only imagine her thoughts over the past day. She was a strong-willed and vicious thing. Were she unleashed in her current state, she might wreak more death and destruction on this group than even her own father was capable of.

Ragus followed her with the scoped rifle as she was escorted off and led to a horse. She didn't resist but she could have. Ragus had seen her spar with her father before. She was skilled in martial arts he couldn't even pronounce. Once, while watching her train at her dad's compound, he'd apparently worn an expression that was a little too close to a smirk for her liking. He mentioned he'd been a wrestler. When she challenged him to a match, he'd declined, saying he didn't want to hurt her.

That was the wrong thing to say.

The words were no sooner out of his mouth than she had him wrapped up in a submission hold on the ground. He was so stunned he barely had the wherewithal to tap out before he lost consciousness. Conor thought the whole thing was a hoot.

With her hands tied, Barb required the help of two men to mount her horse. One helpful gentleman placed both his hands on her backside and leered as he helped lift her into the saddle. This provoked her sharp tongue. Though Ragus didn't hear the words, the man stiffened in anger. He drew back an open hand, ready to strike Barb, but the other man would not allow it. When prevented from beating the tied woman, the groper sought his consolation by using all his strength to zip tie her leg to the stirrup. Barb would not give him the satisfaction of flinching as the binding dug into her flesh. The man spun and walked away, calling out something to Barb as he left. Ragus assumed it was a comment to the effect that their little conflict wasn't over yet.

Aware that Barb had no circulation with the tight zip tie cutting off the blood flow, the other man whipped out a knife and sliced the tie free, replacing it with another, looser one. Ragus watched Barb as this took place, all of his attention focused on what she might do. He did not see her acknowledge this action, the way this man had protected her and loosened her bonds. She would not thank an attacker. She would not accept kindness from someone who had kidnapped her against her will and was taking her away from her home. She would kill this man as easily as the other.

It took a little time before every woman was on a horse and tied in place. Most of the men mounted once this task was done. They took up the reins of the pack horses and the long leads of the horses carrying the women. When they began moving out, two men remained by the smoker. Noticing that these men were cutting up meat and wrapping it in foil from the restaurant, Ragus assumed they must have been left behind to deal with the meat, which was not quite ready for travel. Having smoked meat they could easily reheat over a fire at night would be helpful as they travelled. He could understand them not wanting to leave it behind, even if it meant splitting up the group for a couple of hours.

In the distance, the caravan of riders and pack horses disappeared into the broad blanket of morning fog hanging over the vast green fields. When Ragus was satisfied the group was not returning, he reached into his pack and removed a canvas drawstring bag Conor had given him. He released the cord lock and opened the mouth of the bag, tipping it into his hand. A metal tube about ten inches long slid into his palm. It was one of Conor's custom rifle suppressors and it was threaded to fit the .22 caliber Henry rifle.

When Conor gave him the suppressor he reminded the boy it would not silence the weapon. It would, however, alter the sound in a way that would make it harder for people to use the sound of his shots to locate him. "It'll make you a little harder to track down when you're hunting, lad. Give you a little piece of mind."

He'd used the suppressor for hunting numerous times and he would use it again now. Taking up his Henry, he removed the steel thread protector from the tip of the barrel. The little cap kept him from banging up and distorting the threads during daily use of the rifle. He dropped the cap into the drawstring bag and pulled the cord tight, sliding the cord lock in place. He put the bag back into his pack and carefully threaded the suppressor onto the rifle barrel. The suppressor affected the balance and weight of the rifle but it had proved its worth to him. His intention this morning was not to silence his shots, but that the suppressor might keep the men who had already left camp from returning to check on their men.

Ragus packed away his remaining gear and slipped his pack on his back. With fewer people remaining in camp, he wanted to ease up on them and see what he could hear. Perhaps the men, distracted by their work, would let slip some bit of information that would help him know where they were headed, providing some insight as to the men's intention with their captives. Or maybe, tapping into his rising anger at seeing how Barb was treated, this would become more than an eavesdropping operation. He fully accepted he might have to pull the trigger on someone.

Ragus dropped down out of sight and used low-lying bottoms and draws to hide his approach. At intervals, he would poke his head up like a gopher and make sure the men had not changed position. Soon, he found himself at the edge of the gravel parking lot. He was not a soldier or a cop, with their training in tactics and assault positions. He had no complicated plan of approach. He treated this as if he were stalking two deer and not two men. He scanned the surrounding area. When he was certain there was no one to see him, he climbed from the weeds and moved across the parking lot to the rolling barn door that served as an entrance. He was nervous and wanted to run flat out, to get this exposed section over with, but was afraid the sound of his feet on gravel would attract the men's attention.

Flattened against the front wall of the bright red barn, Ragus listened intently for any indication he had been seen or heard. He kept himself tight against the wall, easing around the corner from the front of the building to the side. He was now against the long wall leading back toward the smoker. The restaurant had an outdoor seating area and Ragus carefully wound his way between the scattered tables and chairs.

These people are fucking pigs, he thought. The place was trashed. Discarded bones, silverware, napkins, and paper plates littered the floor. Had there been beer bottles or red plastic cups scattered in with the rest of the debris it would have looked like the remnants of one hell of a party.

Approaching the rear corner of the building, Ragus flattened himself against the wall again and steadied his breathing. He heard the men talking, laughing. This was a regular day for them. Just doing another job for whoever they worked for. A regular day for men who ran around kidnapping women from their families.

Ragus raised the Henry in front of him and pushed down on the lever. When he saw the dull glint of brass he closed the action. The rifle was ready to go. He thumbed back the hammer, shouldered the rifle, and raised it into a shooting position. All he had to do was step around the corner and open fire.

If these men were still doing what they'd been doing when he saw them last, they were packing meat and had no weapons at hand other than holstered side arms. Ragus took a deep breath and let it out slowly. Then he took another, trying to get his nerve up. He reminded himself of what these men were doing here and what they had done. He wanted to harden himself so there would be no hesitation if he needed to pull the trigger.

He forced himself to move around the corner and face the men. The first to notice him looked up in surprise, as if Ragus were one of his own group and had returned for some reason. When it dawned on him that Ragus was an unfamiliar face, he dropped a hand to his holster. Ragus was ready. He already had his crosshairs centered on the man's face. He pulled the trigger. The rifle cracked and the man's hand flew to his face like he'd been stung by a wasp. He staggered and was holding his face when he dropped over backward, hopefully out of the fight. Ragus worked the action and chambered another round.

The second man held a slab of greasy ribs in his hand was caught in a void of shock and indecision. Ragus could see the thoughts going through his head. Should he drop the meat? Draw his gun? Run for his life? Ragus understood that confusion because it was much like what was going on inside his own head, mixed with a heavy dose of terror.

Ragus was already aiming his rifle at the second man's head. He decided to make his decision for him. "Set the meat down and raise your hands."

The man didn't move. He was trying to decide if he had a play available to him or if he needed to comply. Ragus and the man stood about twenty yards apart. From this distance, Ragus dropped squirrels with headshots on a regular basis. This man's melon was a hell of a lot larger. He dropped the crosshairs to the man's thigh and squeezed off a shot.

The man flinched, dropping the ribs back onto the table. His greasy hands clasped his thigh. He stared in wonder at his own blood before looking up at Ragus with murder and outrage in his eyes. "What the fuck, dude? What the fuck!"

Ragus had already chambered another round and had the crosshairs of his scope on the bridge of his nose. "Straighten up, mister. That leg will keep. And I ain't asking again about the hands. Put them up!"

Wearing an expression of pain on his face, he tested his leg, putting a little weight on it, and flinched. He extended his hands above his head. "You didn't have to do that. You didn't have to shoot me." His tone was childish and accusing, as if there were rules to this game and Ragus had violated them by using a real gun and real bullets.

"Yeah I did have to shoot you. Now lower your left hand and unfasten your gun belt."

The man displayed the same hesitation, like he was replaying his options again. He was obviously a thick-headed son-of-a-bitch.

"I'll shoot you again. It's nothing to me. Ain't my leg, ain't my blood leaking in the dirt." Ragus' matter-of-fact tone hid his pounding heart and nervousness.

His threat carried some impact, though, and the man complied. He fumbled to unlatch his belt with a single hand as requested. When he was done, he dropped the brown leather belt with his holster and sheath knife to the ground. He raised his hand back up above his head and glared at Ragus. "What you want, boy?"

"I need to know where you're taking those girls and why."

The man hesitated again, challenging. Ragus was tired of being disrespected and not taken seriously. It pissed him off. Each second he wasted, they were getting farther away. That thought dialed up his panic even further.

He dropped the crosshairs to the man's kneecap and pulled the trigger before the man even had time to react. This time he fell over backwards, writhing on the ground, and screaming in pain. Ragus kept his rifle leveled on the man but moved over and kicked the gun belt out of the way. While he was there by the smoker, he confirmed the man he shot in the chest hadn't moved. Unsure if he was dead, Ragus kicked him twice in the head and the man didn't flinch. The sensation of kicking the head left him a little queasy. He'd been unprepared for both the sound and the sensation but it told him what he wanted to know. If the man was still alive he was either a tough bastard or a good actor.

"You son of a bitch!" the injured man screamed, cradling his knee. "I'm going to fucking kill you."

The threats meant nothing to Ragus. He wasn't even listening to them. He had work to do and he was behind already. Without taking his eyes off the man, he eased out of his pack and let it slide to the ground. In an outer pocket he had about a dozen sturdy zip ties Conor had given him. Ragus had never zip tied anyone before but he pulled one out and tossed it to the wounded man. "Tie yourself up."

The man didn't react, rolling around in the dusty gravel, cursing and crying. Ragus patiently waited him out, then reminded him of the request. "If I have to ask again, I'm putting another hole in you."

The man growled and gritted his teeth. "It takes two," he hissed. "Two zip ties."

Ragus shook his head at the man's persistent lack of cooperation but tossed him another. "Always some excuse with you. You're just one of those people, aren't you?"

The man pushed himself to a sitting position, wincing at the pain. He reached for the zip ties.

"Make it good now. Don't try to bullshit me. You have plenty of places left I can shoot."

With some awkwardness the man zip tied one wrist, then slipped a zip tie through it and tied the second wrist to the first.

"Hold them up. Show them to me."

The man did as he was told, scowling at Ragus with a murderous glare. Convinced he was a little less of a threat now, Ragus approached the man, still holding the rifle on him. He checked the man's extended wrists, then grabbed the loose end of each zip-tie and yanked it tight.

The man jerked and cried out. He looked at his hands with frustration, then back up at Ragus. "They don't have to be that tight. It'll cut the circulation off."

Ragus shrugged. "Another couple hours and it won't matter. You'll be dead anyway."

The man appeared stunned by that revelation, perhaps imagining Ragus would let him go and he could hobble off for help. It wasn't going to happen that way. There was no forgiveness in the scared boy's heart. He dragged the man over to a steel pole which supported an upper deck eating area. He used more zip ties to secure the man's hands to the post. Slightly concerned that the man's blood loss might kill him before Conor could catch up with them, Ragus put a zip tie around each of the man's thighs as a tourniquet.

"I'll lose my legs if you do that."

"We done chewed that fat," Ragus said. "Ain't chewing it again."

Not convinced the zip ties alone were sufficient to hold the man to the pole, Ragus went to one of the pack horses and found a coil of rope. He used it to lash the man to the pole. Finally comfortable the prisoner wasn't going anywhere, Ragus used his own knife to trim off a piece of smoked beef. The flavor spreading in his mouth was nearly an ecstatic experience. He couldn't recall ever tasting anything so good in his entire life.

He didn't want to waste time but he could also not pass up this opportunity. He needed the meat, both for now and for the coming journey. Having the provisions he needed on the trail would mean fewer stops to forage for supplies. He also needed to see if he could get anything out of the prisoner.

"What's your name?" Ragus asked.

The bound man moaned, a futile wailing like mating cats. "I ain't gonna tell you nothing," he said. "You might as well let me go."

Ragus shrugged nonchalantly, as if they were going back over old territory. "It ain't no nevermind to me. If you don't tell me, you'll damn sure tell the man following me. I don't have a doubt in the world."

That shut the man up. He retreated back to his suffering.

Ragus continued eating patiently, sipping from his water and watching. Then he turned his attention to the horses. There were two saddled and two pack horses. One of the pack horses was already burdened with gear and other had empty saddlebags which Ragus assumed was for the meat the men had been packing when he came upon them. Ragus wasn't a horseman. In fact, he'd never been on one in his life, but he was getting ready to learn. No way was he passing up transportation to keep traveling on foot.

He sliced off a dozen hunks of the meat, then made himself a healthy package of meat for the trip. He put all the unsliced meat back in the smoker and closed the door. Conor should be coming along soon. If so, some meat and a horse should rejuvenate him in the way it had Ragus.

He conducted a hasty search of the dead man and collected what gear he could find. He took a decent knife off the dead man. The men were using the same type of pistol and Ragus didn't see any point in carrying both of them so he took one with all the spare magazines and the box of ammunition each man carried. They had military-style rifles like Conor had. Ragus didn't know a damn thing about them except they were called AR-15s. He decided to take one and some spare magazines for it. It might be useful if he could figure out how to work it. He also found a really nice rain poncho that beat the hell out of anything he had.

"You ain't going to leave me here like this, are you?" the bound man begged.

Ragus regarded him and nodded. He finished packing his gear onto one of the horses. In his pocket, he had a plastic baggie with sliced meat in it. He took out a piece and shoved it in his mouth, chewing it slowly while he pondered the one last thing he had left to do. He pulled out his own knife, the one Conor had given him, then fell upon the protesting man.

~

FOLLOWING the kidnapper's trail was much easier on a horse. While not an experienced horseman, Ragus was figuring it out. Occasionally he had to dismount and check signs from the ground but the kidnappers were mostly sticking to paved roads. That made Ragus think they were from out of the area and using maps to navigate, rather than being locals who might be inclined to take common shortcuts. Their crude horseshoes and the trail of manure continued to make it easy to discern their direction of travel. Ragus faithfully moved off the road at regular intervals, snapping branches to mark the trail since he hoped Conor would catch up with him soon. He imagined him finding the bound man and the extra horses. Ragus would like to see the look on his face when he did.

Ragus had considered bringing a pack horse with him but opted against it in the end. He was afraid it would be twice as much trouble for a fellow just learning to ride a horse for the first time. He'd learned a lot from riding with his gear today and would have a better idea how to pack things tomorrow. He'd probably have to lose the five-gallon bucket that hung from the saddle horn. It was convenient storage for him but the horse didn't care for it rubbing and bumping against him with the rhythm of its stride.

The markings on the plastic bucket had stopped Ragus in his tracks when he found it while searching the restaurant. Even as he'd regained his emotional footing and rode off on the horse, he found his mind returning of its own accord to that stupid bucket. It was a white food-grade bucket from a grocery store and the label told him it once held white cake icing. Ragus had seen a lot of those buckets in his life.

For most of his childhood, his mother worked in the bakery section of a local grocery store. To a kid it sounded like a dream job. He assumed that all day she was able to pluck up donuts, cookies, cupcakes, and rolls from the display case and shove them in her mouth whenever the urge struck her. She laughed at him and said she wasn't allowed to do that, though she did bring home the day old bread and other baked goods that had to be discarded. Even if it wasn't of the magnitude he imagined, it was still a perk.

Each year she baked a special cake for his birthday. She made them at work and brought them home already decorated with his name on them. Since they didn't have a lot of money, the cakes were a luxury. That illusion, that each cake was made special for him was shattered on his thirteenth birthday. She must have had a busy day at work because she was working on his cake when he got home from school. Through the window he saw her using a butter knife to scrape another child's name off an unclaimed cake from work.

He was angry and upset, but not with his mother. He was angry at the world for making him poor and forcing his mother, a sweet and kind woman, to have to do such a thing to make her child feel special on his birthday. He could barely stand to eat the cake that evening, so sick with the revelation of their place in the world. The cake sat in his stomach like a ball of indigestible stone.

His anger only grew when the world saw fit to so cruelly kill his mother and take her from him. When you only had one thing and it was taken from you, what did you become in this world? For whom did you remain good, moral, and decent? Had Conor not stepped in and taken the time to help him channel his anger, Ragus would probably have become a criminal, robbing and killing folks for their food.

Although Ragus' experiences had not distilled into an acid that completely eroded the goodness from him, they continued to shape him each day. While he did not fully understand the evolution of his development —his growth—he understood that the world was completely what you made of it each and every day. There were no promises or guarantees. There were no shortcuts, no avenues that allowed you to bypass the worst of what the world had to offer.

His mother was a good person, raised him to be a good boy, and died a miserable, excruciating death. There was no justice, no *rightness*, in this world except for what each man brought to the table. Perhaps there was a higher power up there somewhere. His mother seemed to think so. If there was, he'd lost track of Ragus and his mother in all the bad things that had happened. Maybe their small mobile home, wedged as it was in a forested cleft in dense and inhospitable mountains, was just too minute in the scheme of things.

The somber procession of his thoughts screeched to a halt when Ragus came across something new on the road. It was horse urine, puddled and running in a rivulet with the pitch of the road. It could not be more than minutes old or it would have soaked into the sun-warmed pavement. As a single rider with no prisoners and no pack horses, he made better time than the group he was chasing. A short distance ahead, Ragus dismounted at a pile of horse manure and tentatively touched the fragrant balls of horse shit. They were warm.

He reigned his horse to the right and pulled off the trail. Comfortable now that he was close, he needed a better vantage point. He nudged the horse with his heels and steered it up a treeless knoll to the right of the road. Grazing cattle had denuded it of all but a stubble of pale green grass. The hill was steeper than Ragus had thought and he had to lean forward and clutch the saddle horn to stay atop the horse as it lunged with each step.

At the top, Ragus shouldered the Henry rifle and found the group of kidnappers through the scope. It was a slow-moving cluster of disjointed riders. There was a pronounced front to the group which made him think the leader, the man he saw shouting orders back at the restaurant, must enjoy riding lead. Behind him were the bound and kidnapped women. Lines of riders surrounded them on both sides, making it difficult to reach the women if they were attacked. It also made it difficult to shoot at the kidnappers for fear you might accidentally hit one of the women.

Ragus had no idea how he would get Barb back, but he was tempted to come up with a plan each time he caught up with the group. He decided it was best to stick to the plan and let Conor figure it out. His job was to track and mark a trail. Should he see any indication she was in immediate danger, he would have to think on his feet and react accordingly. It might mean throwing his plan out the window, but not just yet.

On the knoll, Ragus made the decision that it might be best to flank the group and ride alongside of them. It would be easier to see what they were doing. Perhaps he would even find himself in a position to overhear something. He didn't want to get too close but he was probably a mile behind them now, and that seemed too far. He could do better.

14

Breaking off his pursuit for the night nearly crushed Conor's soul. He couldn't be certain the kidnappers were pausing, and if they kept moving through the night his daughter was getting farther and farther away. His instinct was to stay in pursuit. He had night vision and a headlamp, but what if he missed some critical trail sign because of limited visibility? That was easy to do when working at night. You tended to only focus on what was immediately within the circle of illumination. If he ended up a couple of miles in the wrong direction he may never find the trail again. He could lose days backtracking, trying to pick up where he'd left the correct trail.

Resigned to calling off his search for the night, Conor didn't make any effort to look for lush accommodations. He wandered off the main road at the first dense cluster of woods he found and threw up a hammock for the night. At this time of year, a hammock and light sleeping bag could hold him through most conditions. He had a tarp he could stretch over the hammock if it was raining.

He was on the trail early the next morning, as soon as there was sufficient light. He stopped at a creek to filter water and refill his bottles, but other than that, he slowed for nothing. Although he had no appetite, he tore the top off a sports gel and squeezed the pudding-like substance into his mouth. It was a concentrated source of carbohydrates and caffeine that cyclists and runners were fond of. Even with no appetite, it provided fuel for the body. He drank on the move and pissed in the middle of the road when the need struck him.

All morning, he continued to see the broken twig markers. He had to assume Ragus was leaving those for him. He was not a religious man but he prayed it was Ragus. Conor knew the boy carried a flame for his daughter. Barb had done her best to try and extinguish it but the boy was not to be deterred. Conor didn't know if the boy was pursuing his kidnapped daughter out of devotion to her or to Conor. Either way, he was grateful.

A few miles from where he began his day, Conor topped a rise and saw the barbecue restaurant. The first thing that hit him was his hunger. He'd eaten at that place more than once in different times and it was damn good. His mind could not help replaying those meals in slow motion...smoked prime rib, barbecue ribs, pulled pork, homemade French fries...

"Lord, I'd kill somebody for a bag of barbecue," Conor muttered, pulling himself back together.

The second thing that hit him was the faint, acrid smell of wood smoke. Conor eased to the shoulder of the road. The grass there was overgrown and brush was encroaching on the road. There was more opportunity for camouflage and even for actual cover if he had to dive into the ditch. He press-checked his rifle and went on heightened alert while he closed in on the restaurant. He could see nothing amiss and could see no people from his position. There was no rising smoke but the smell could simply be coming from a smoldering fire remaining from the previous night. Moving cautiously, he reached the point where the driveway connected to the highway. The gravel entrance was pocked with the hoof prints of a small army of horses.

Conor harbored no hope he would find his daughter here. The prints were going both ways, showing people had come and gone already, but perhaps there was a clue to where they were going. He also picked up the smell of cooling grease, like that of a barbecue grill after a large cookout. Perhaps the kidnappers had found a way to fire up the restaurant. They appeared to have a lot of folks to feed. He certainly hoped they were feeding his daughter. The thought of them not treating her properly stoked his rage. There was no doubt her kidnappers were going to die, but they would die slower, more painful deaths if they'd treated her poorly.

When all the signs told him the kidnappers had left already, Conor was tempted to just keep moving on up the highway. Every moment he wasted on this little side-jaunt was a moment his daughter was getting farther away. He stood from examining the tracks and tried to make himself walk off, but something kept pulling at him. He was considering his options when he heard the sound of a neighing horse and everything changed.

Conor scrambled for the weeds. He crouched down and re-examined the scene but couldn't see a horse anywhere. He reminded himself that the presence of a horse didn't necessarily mean there was a rider but it *did* mean he couldn't move on now without checking the scene out.

Listen to your instincts, he silently reminded himself. *They were trying to tell you to check this place out. Quit listening to your gut and you'll get yourself killed.*

He thought the sound came from around back but he chose to sweep the perimeter. Fortunately, the restaurant didn't have a lot of windows, but that didn't mean there wasn't a rifle already sighting in on him. At the right side of the restaurant, a crude board fence rose above his head, painted in garish red and covered in graffiti put there by the owners. Conor raised the latch and swung open a creaking gate just wide enough for one person to walk through. He had his rifle at high ready, scanning for threats.

This was the place where the cooks smoked their barbecue when the restaurant was operational. It was apparently the site of a brief encampment, also. There was trash scattered everywhere. Cups, plates, plastic ware, paper towels, and even tablecloths. Now that he was closer, Conor could indeed see a fire smoldering nearby with the finest wisps of smoke rising above it. Beside a blackened steel smoker lay a pile of hooves, scraps of hide, and the large leg bones of a steer.

An irresistible aroma latched onto Conor, clawing at his belly. Several horses were tied to a fence, obviously the origin of the sound Conor heard from the road.

He went to the smoker and held a hand near it. It was still warm. He unfastened the latch and swung open the heavy grease-encrusted door, cringing as it squealed nearly as loud as a car alarm. Inside he found several large cuts of meat. He touched a charred cut with a finger and found a little give to it. The meat was fresh. In fact, it was perfect.

"Mary, mother of God," he muttered, reaching inside for a chunk of blackened meat. His brain quickly overruled his stomach, warning him he needed to clear the area before he started feeding his face. Still, what could it hurt to tear off a tiny morsel to chew while he searched the place?

"Is someone over there? Help me!" cried a faint voice.

Conor spun away from the smoker feeling like an idiot. He could already be a dead man. *Should* be a dead man. He threw his rifle back up and scanned the area.

"Hello?" the voice repeated. "Who's out there?"

Conor pinpointed the voice as coming from an outdoor dining area, surrounded by a waist-high wall of red-painted cinderblock. He knew it could be a trap but he couldn't leave without investigating. He approached slowly, the gravel crunching beneath his feet with each tentative step. He paused when he got close to the wall.

"Come out with your hands up!" he bellowed.

"I can't," came a desperate voice. "Some bastard kid shot me and tied me up. I need help. I need a doctor."

Conor's mind raced at that bit of information. *Some kid?* He had to be talking about Ragus.

On high alert, Conor peeked over the wall, ready to rain fire on anything that wasn't right. He found an injured man tied to a steel support post. Conor hopped over the wall and made certain the area around him was clear before focusing on the tied man.

"Are you alone?" Conor hissed.

The man nodded. He was a mess, with bloody wounds on both

legs. Clotted blood clung to the fabric of his pants. Zip ties had been applied as tourniquets around both legs but they weren't tight enough and fresh blood seeped over the clotted masses like lava oozing from a volcano. The man's shirt had been cut away from him and lay in a pile beside his body. A message had been scribbled on his chest with permanent marker.

It read: *He's one of them but he wouldn't talk.*

Conor's jaw clenched to the point he thought his teeth might shatter. That message could only mean one thing. Ragus was telling him this man was one of the kidnappers. Conor moved his gun to the man's forehead, the black maw of the barrel just inches away.

"Where's my fucking daughter?"

Conor could see the shift in the man's expression as he realized Conor was not a savior but instead his executioner. The boy had mentioned something about a man who might be following behind him. A more dangerous man. He hadn't believed him, thinking it was just talk. But here the man was, in the flesh.

"Go ahead, shoot me. I'd rather be dead than left here to bleed out."

The man had mustered some defiance but Conor knew how to break that down. He moved the tip of a stained boot to the man's bloody knee. He let it hover there a moment, studying the man's expression. There was a flicker of fear. Conor knew he would talk then.

"The boy shoot you in the knee?" Conor asked.

The man nodded frantically.

"Hurts like a bitch, doesn't it?"

The man nodded again. Conor smiled at the man and he smiled back. Then Conor stomped on the knee. Once. Twice. Three times.

While waiting for the screaming to stop, he went back to the smoker and sliced off a piece of the smoked beef. This might take a minute. He might as well make the best of it. Chewing and ruminating, he eyed the horses. They were his now. He'd pick one when he left and the pace of his pursuit would change. On foot, his quest had felt doomed. The odds were now much improved. He wasn't a horseman but if he could stay atop the damned thing it would give him a fighting chance. Things were looking up.

When the injured man's scream trailed off to whimpering, Conor finished his scrap of meat and dusted off his hands. There was work to do before he left. He needed to extract any information the wounded man had before sending him on to his maker.

15

Barb's bladder was near exploding when they finally stopped for lunch. A man with a large Bowie knife came around and sliced the zip ties that bound each woman to a stirrup.

"I need to pee," Barb told him.

"Then pee," the man replied, looking at her dumbly, as if the solution should have been obvious.

"These clothes are all I've got. I'd rather not have to ride in my own piss for the rest of the day."

The man blew out a breath of frustration and called to the man in charge, "Top Cat, this one is wanting a bathroom break!"

Barb wondered if that was the man's name or title. She spoke to him as he rode up, ignoring the man who had relayed her message. "I need to pee. Now."

"Then go," he growled. "Don't let us stop you."

The man who had cut her free smiled. "See? I told you. Great minds think alike."

Barb frowned at him, then focused her attention back to Top Cat. "I need my hands free to balance myself and I would prefer a little privacy."

"And I would prefer to be travelling in the comfort of an air-conditioned motor coach but it would appear neither of us is getting what we want," Top Cat shot back.

"That's the best you can do?" Barb insisted.

Top Cat rode off without responding. A different smirking man, this one following the one with the Bowie knife, appeared by her side and extended a hand to her. He helped her down with no groping or wandering hands. Maybe he was a decent one.

"Do you mind to stay handy so I can pee?" Barb asked him. "Between you and the horse, you can at least shield me from the other men."

The man considered the request. "Who are you with?"

Barb looked confused.

"You were picked up with another woman," the man said. "Who?"

"JoAnn." Barb pointed. "Right there."

The man gently helped JoAnn from her horse. When she was on the ground, the man spun her violently, drew his knife, and placed it at JoAnn's throat. He beckoned at Barb with a finger. "Your hands."

Barb approached apprehensively, extended her zip tied hands. The man delicately cut her bonds, then replaced the knife at JoAnn's neck. "You try anything stupid, you try to run, and she dies an ugly fucking death. We clear?"

Barb nodded, stunned. The man had seemed so harmless only a moment ago. It was just reaffirmation that no one could be trusted in the current state of the world. Nothing was as it appeared, and perhaps no one was harmless anymore.

Barb hurried about her business and was back standing in front of the man in a moment. "You can tie me back up now. Just don't hurt my friend."

The man looked at JoAnn. "Do you need to go?"

JoAnn nodded hesitantly. The man released her, lashing out a hand to grab Barb by the hair and pull her to him. He put the knife to her throat and instructed JoAnn to hurry.

It took all Barb had not to kill the man. She'd studied Krav Maga and Jujitsu nearly all her life, her father insistent that she never be a defenseless sheep. This man, obviously inexperienced with the blade he wielded, had left her several openings. Before he was even aware what was happening, she could spin out from beneath his blade, twist his wrist, and shove it into his neck. But how long would she live beyond that moment? How long would it be before she, and perhaps JoAnn, were shot down by the rest of the men?

She choked down her rage and let it pass. For now. But she would remember this man and she would kill him if her father didn't get to him first. She would enjoy the looks on their faces. She would enjoy seeing the awareness of how they'd misjudged her. They would wish they'd never seen the likes of her.

With their most pressing needs taken care of, Barb and JoAnn were ushered to join the group of other women. While there were no fences, the women were basically corralled in the center of the men and horses. They were forced to the ground and several water bottles were distributed. Barb wasn't pleased with drinking water of unknown purity that had been passed between several unfamiliar mouths but she saw no choice. She gritted her teeth and took several swallows, reminding herself this was about surviving, about keeping herself strong to fight when the time was right.

Predictably, the group lunched on smoked beef.

"Where do you think those other son of a bitches are?" asked the man who was slicing and distributing chunks of beef.

A different man, compact and muscular, probably someone who worked with his hands in his previous life, shook his head. Barb had heard him addressed as Lester. "Who the hell knows? They had a little work ahead of them and they were probably in no big hurry to catch up with us. I'm sure it's a lot more peaceful riding along without a care in the world. I don't know if I'd expect them before dinnertime."

A different man, taller and with unkempt hair, walked over with a canteen and stood beside Lester. It was the one called Top Cat, which she thought to be a pretty stupid name.

"At the next intersection there's a huge distribution warehouse for one of those superstore chains. It's fucking enormous. Probably the biggest building in this part of the state."

"You want us to check it out?" Lester asked.

Top Cat shook his head. "Not you. I'm making you responsible for these women. Put two men on it and two pack horses. I'm sure the place is looted and torn all to hell but there's probably stuff we can use back at the farm."

"Most of the horses got loads on them now," Lester replied. "Those asshats we left cutting up that steer kept the only empty pack horses we had."

Top Cat spoke as if he was getting frustrated, as if he were tired of having to explain every little detail to people who weren't bright enough to tie their own shoes. "Before we set out again, shift the loads to free up two horses. Most of the food is probably gone from the warehouse but if they come out with a couple of sacks of toothpaste, toothbrushes, tampons, and soap I'll be happy. We got guns and food under control but we need more of the basic shit we can't make right now."

"Sure wish we had a couple of trucks," Lester complained.

"Yeah, you and every other sore-assed son of a bitch on this ride."

Barb listened intently. Barb hoped her father had caught up with the two men who were left behind at the restaurant. She hoped the real reason for their delay was that he'd killed them and left them for the buzzards. Nothing would give her more pleasure than knowing her father was somewhere back there, killing everyone who lagged behind.

The ladies were prompted to make sure they had all personal business taken care of before they mounted their horses again. "Ain't going to be no more stops until we camp for the night," Top Cat announced.

The kidnappers repeated the process of placing each woman back onto a horse and tying a leg to a stirrup. Each time they did this it fueled Barb's fire. She wasn't one to suffer indignities without returning the pain tenfold and she was stockpiling her anger for the moment she had an opportunity. She remembered the face of every cruel man who had strapped her to the saddle. She remembered the face of every slobbering perv who groped her under the guise of helping her remount. They would all pay.

The entourage headed north and Barb imagined from a distance they must look like a group of settlers from the old days. That image dissolved when she took into account their setting, which included modern buildings, abandoned vehicles, and paved highways. Another less obvious difference would be those earlier folks were accustomed to the saddle and this slow mode of travel. For modern folk, travel on horseback was archaic and cruelly slow.

Barb, in particular, was a woman used to being on the go. She worked hard physically each day and worked out diligently. She trained in her martial arts, lifted weights, and did a variety of functional fitness activities to keep her sharp. Accustomed to that level of activity, she found it tortuous to be strapped to the back of a horse and had to find mental diversions to keep from going insane. It was a tool taught to her by her father, specifically for passing time during tough endeavors.

One of those first games was creating names for each of her kidnappers. To that, she added a fictional backstory she knew would anger and embarrass them were they privy to it. There was the man she referred to as Potato Man, named for his tanned skin and shapeless form. She imagined him to be the product of the union between two slow-witted and shapeless people who were too closely related.

Another she referred to as Dinosaur Arms, because he reminded her of the T-Rex with its short and useless forearms. She imagined him to be secretly saving money in an old coffee can to have the longer arms of a corpse grafted onto his own, hoping he might one day be able to zip up his own pants without awkward contortions.

There was Hair Bear, whom she imagined to be the offspring of an extremely hairy and unattractive woman. Barb decided she could only have produced such an unattractive child by engaging in a bestial relationship with a mangy bear. There was Bugs Bunny, named for his buck teeth and incessant chatter, and MacGyver, named for an old TV show character because he always seemed to have whatever anyone needed in his bottomless pockets.

Barb's childlike distraction served its purpose and she'd nearly gone through all the men when she noticed something taking place within the group. A man from further back in the group rode ahead and spoke to Top Cat. After a brief exchange, he peeled away and another rider, leading two pack horses, fell in behind him. These must be the two men heading to check out the distribution warehouse.

The warehouse was right beside the road. Barb assumed a nearby exit would probably lead them to the front entrance. Horses didn't need roads and they didn't need exits. The men rode over the shoulder of the road and cut their way through a fence with bolt cutters. They slipped through the opening and were gone into tall, golden weeds. She hoped this was an indication the ride for the day was nearly over but that was not the case. One of the men asked Top Cat when they were stopping and he said they'd ride until sunset, which was a ways off.

Not far past where the men cut through the fence, Top Cat pulled a similar move. He guided his horse down over a gentle embankment, rode through some tall weeds, and joined a secondary road running parallel to the highway. For the first time, Barb felt a rush of panic. If her father was indeed back there, he might easily miss the signs of their turn and continue travelling on the highway. If he did that, there was no telling how far he might go before realizing his mistake. He may never rediscover their trail.

Her mind raced, trying to find something she could drop, something he might recognize as belonging to her. She had a few useless things in her pocket and she tried reaching for them but could not shove her zip tied hands inside them. She had a belt her dad might recognize but she didn't know if she could pull it off without drawing attention. She only had seconds to figure something out. The herd of horses was moving closer to the shoulder and, once there, anything she dropped would be lost in the tall weeds.

Then she remembered her necklace.

It was her mother's and it was one of the few things Barb had that belonged to her. Her father had only given it to her when he decided she'd gotten old enough to take care of it. The idea of tossing it to the ground clawed at her soul, yet her father would understand. He would want her to take this chance. If he were here, he would tell her the necklace held no value if she was not alive to wear it.

She feigned a swipe at her neck, as if she'd been bitten by an insect. It was not so dramatic as to draw everyone's attention, but would appear legitimate to anyone looking at her. While her hand was on her neck, she clutched the gold chain around her neck and casually broke it loose from her neck. She had one second to glance down and take a last look at the gold shamrock charm with its inlaid diamond. She committed it to memory in case she never saw it again.

She dropped her hand and let the chain slip through her fingers, watching from the corner of her eye to see it hit the ground and did not snag on anything. It hurt her to let it go but she had to look at it like a resource. It was like a gun, a bullet, a lighter, or any other tool.

Barb hoped her father caught up with them soon. She craved nothing more than the moment he cut her loose and she was unleashed on her kidnappers. She thirsted for the moment she saw fear in their eyes, for the moment just before the blackness of death fell over them like a shadow. Growing up without a mother had made her different and she knew it by this point in her life. Despite the things her father had done in his life, despite the violent acts he had committed, she sometimes felt he was too soft and encumbered by a morality she didn't feel. She would not hesitate to kill all of these men when the time came. She would spill rivers of blood and she would be fine with it.

16

From an isolated stand of deep green hemlocks, Ragus saw the pair of riders with their pack horses split from the main group of kidnappers. The horse he had randomly chosen back at the restaurant was a quiet, well-disciplined mount who made no unnecessary noise and sat patiently when Ragus stilled him. It was the one blessing he'd been given on this journey, that he, through no exercise of knowledge or understanding of horses, had chosen one that did not work against him, making an already difficult mission even harder.

Choosing to follow the two men instead of the larger group was an easy decision. While Barb remained with the larger group, Ragus had no hope of wresting her from their grip. There were too many men, too many guns. He hoped Conor would join him at some point and take over this mission. He was certainly better suited for it. Yet what if he didn't show up? What if Barb's rescue depended entirely on his own efforts?

In either regard, Ragus needed to whittle down the numbers some, a much easier feat when he took them on in small groups. He had successfully taken down two men already and felt certain that with a similar approach he could take down two more. Over time, should they continue to allow men to wander off in smaller groups, perhaps he could kill enough of him that he could swoop into the larger group like a Sioux brave and drop the remainder of them.

He wasn't too concerned about allowing the larger group to proceed without him. He didn't expect they would go much farther. They'd already demonstrated they liked to travel during daylight. He expected another hour or two was all they had left before they'd stop for the night. He could easily close that distance in half the time should he push his horse to a decent trot.

He followed the two riders and their pack horses once the coast was clear. There was no doubt where they were going with the distribution warehouse clearly in sight of the road. There wasn't anything else anywhere nearby. When he found a secluded spot, Ragus tied his horse to the branches of a low willow oak and proceeded on foot. He carried his go bag and the suppressed Henry rifle. Conor had impressed upon him the necessity of always having the bag with him just in case his plans went to shit and he had to run for it.

At the edge of the parking lot, he laid in a weedy ditch and watched the riders circle the warehouse. At first he thought they were looking for a door, then eventually realized they were trying to make sure no one lived there, which might be a reasonable assumption. If a group could defend it, this warehouse full of domestic goodies would definitely be a nice play for weathering this storm until the power came back on and the gas began flowing again.

Finally satisfied the warehouse appeared to be unoccupied, the riders completed their circumnavigation and returned to Ragus' view just as he was steeling himself to go looking for them. They tied their horses off to a yellow traffic bollard and conferred, making the decision one man would go in alone initially while the other watched the horses.

Ragus confirmed the Henry rifle was topped off with rounds and eased the action back to double check there was a round in the chamber. He gave the suppressor a quick twist to make sure it had not loosened during the travels of the day. Returning his gaze to the warehouse, he realized approaching the entrance was not going to be an easy proposition. Distances in open spaces like parking lots could be misleading. They could take longer to traverse than you thought, leaving you exposed and vulnerable.

The distribution center was a warehouse for shipping goods to superstore locations and was not a retail location itself. Instead of being set up with landscaped parking lots and grassy islands, the building was surrounded by vast stretches of pavement where semi-trucks could easily access the dozens of loading docks lining the side walls of the building.

Ragus worked his way around to the side of the building so he was blocked from the sentry's view. There were a few scattered cars in the parking lot, perhaps belonging to employees who had run out of fuel or travelers who had become stranded and thought this might be a safe place to leave a car. Those cars offered the only concealment in the otherwise barren lot. Scared of being discovered, the hundred yards between Ragus and the store looked more like a hundred miles.

Careful to keep his steps silent, he moved from car to car, always trying to keep one between him and the building. He ran out of cars when he got closer to the building and had to bolt for it, flattening himself against the side of the structure. He slipped around the corner to move along the front, using a line of overgrown hedges as concealment. He moved hedge to hedge, not hurrying. He focused on smooth movements and quiet steps. Stealth over speed. He gradually closed the distance between himself and the front door, turning one hundred and fifty feet into eighty, then to sixty, closer and closer.

Ragus checked the sentry's location from each position and monitored his activity. For a while, the man clutched his rifle and vigilantly scanned his surroundings. But as the riders' presence went unchallenged, the sentry relaxed. He rolled a cigarette from a pouch of Drum tobacco and smoked it with his rifle dangling casually from his shoulder. He'd quickly gone from alert to bored.

The presence of the other man, somewhere in the immense warehouse, concerned Ragus. He wanted to take out the sentry in front of him but he didn't want to be heard. There was a closed door between the outside man and the inside man. It would muffle some of the sound. The inside man could also be hundreds of feet away, wandering the rows of shelves, unable to see or hear anything that took place out front but Ragus didn't know that. Conor had impressed upon him the importance of trying to think situations out like he did in wrestling. If you make a particular move, what will the other guy do? Conor said it was like playing chess, but Ragus didn't know shit about chess. Wrestling he understood.

There were several floor-to-ceiling windows beside the sentry that looked into the lobby and reception area of the warehouse. There were perhaps even a couple of more closed doors between the sentry and the man wandering the interior of the warehouse. He just didn't know. Ragus had a pack of subsonic .22 ammunition in his pack and he wished he'd taken the time to reload with it. While the suppressor was helpful, it worked much more efficiently with the subsonic rounds.

He weighed the options, wondering if he could un-chamber what he had in the rifle now and switch it to a subsonic, but there was too much movement involved. That movement, the mechanical sounds of unloading the weapon, digging the ammo from his pack, all might draw attention. It was just too big a risk to take. He needed to go for it before he was spotted. He needed to take the kill. The sentry was distracted by his smoke break but when that was over, there was no telling what he would decide to do. Ragus might lose his shot.

Not breaking the contour of the bush that concealed him, Ragus slowly extended the rifle through the dense branches. He drew the hammer back and got on the scope. The man was facing away from him now, lost in his thoughts and the enjoyment of his tobacco. Ragus lay the crosshairs on a cervical vertebra. He talked himself up. He could make the shot because of squirrel hunting. He knew his capabilities, and what the rifle could do.

There was still something inside him that made him hesitate to pull the trigger on a person. Sure, he'd done it already, but it wasn't easy. Maybe it should never be easy. He reminded himself of the thing that made this killing acceptable. That made it necessary.

This man kidnapped one of the only people left who cares about you and shows you any kindness. You know you'll never forgive yourself if she's injured or killed. You know there's no choice. This has to be done.

Part of his brain was ready to offer more encouragement. Part of his brain was waiting for that encouragement. Another part had already heard everything it needed to hear. That part took the lead, squeezed the trigger, and the rifle cracked. The projectile poked a hole exactly where it was intended to. The man stiffened and arched, his arms flying upward in a gesture of supplication while his rifle clattered to the ground. Then he toppled over, arching and gesticulating. Trying to shout. Trying to put words to his wonder at what happened to him. Trying to understand he was dying.

Ragus realized he was holding his breath and he gasped, starving for air. His heart pounded and his synapses fired. He was in the fight now. Part of him wanted to bolt upright and enter the building, stalking and killing the other man. Another part of him, trained by Conor, knew better than to put himself at risk like that. He forced himself to sit there and breathe, not taking any action until he calmed down since that option was available to him.

He imagined the interior of the warehouse. Darkness with light coming from high skylights, row after row of shelves at tall as some buildings, and the other man wandering through there looking for salvageable goods among the trashed wreckage. There would be miles of shelving and the boy couldn't imagine trying to hunt someone in that vastness. It was too risky. He needed to get the man back outside where he had an advantage.

Breaking cover, the boy carefully approached the body and made sure he was no longer a threat. He tapped the man with the toe of a boot and got not reaction. He couldn't tell if the man was dead or not but he was definitely out of the fight. His eyes bulged from his head in a gruesome manner. His mouth gaped open and his tongue lolled out. Ragus didn't want to see the fruit of his violence—what normal person would?—yet he forced himself to look at it. Seeing the consequences was part of what helped you retain your humanity when you were forced to commit acts of violence. It was something Conor told him and it was beginning to make more sense now that he was racking up a body count.

He chanced a quick glance at the building and saw no one visible through the glass front. He stooped and picked up the man's rifle, slinging it over his back. He crouched again, grabbing the man by the leg. The position of Ragus' body caused the rifle to come unslung and clatter to the sidewalk. He flinched, then picked it up in his free hand and tugged the body out of sight behind a nearby car.

He pointed the rifle into the air, released the safety, and fired off a couple of quick rounds before returning to the concealment of a bush. He waited, hearing an inner door bang shut before the other man burst through the front door, weapon raised.

"Carlos!" he called. "Where are you?"

With no need to minimize noise this time, Ragus squeezed the trigger several times, pumping four or five rounds into the armed man before he spun and dropped in a tangle. Ragus watched the still body for a moment, hoping the man was not playing dead. When he saw a stream of bright blood running from beneath the man, filling the cracks in the sidewalk, he finally felt comfortable rising from his concealed position.

He walked over and examined him with a little less scrutiny than the first. He was obviously dead and the only thing that stuck out to Ragus was the look of utter surprise on the man's face. That look, like something unexpected–*undeserved*–had befallen the man irritated Ragus. The man had brought his fate upon himself.

"Don't fuck with my friends," Ragus said to the motionless body, "and you won't get killed."

While saying something to the body had felt necessary, he really didn't have time to waste. He'd pulled off the main trail to deal with these two men and now he needed to get back to it. He didn't want to open up too much space between him and the remaining kidnappers. He'd like nothing more than to make a pass through the warehouse and see if there were things he could scrounge. He needed another pack, he needed a good sleeping bag for winter, he needed a warm coat, and several other things.

He could stop here on his way back, but for now he needed to get on the road. He felt better sleeping where he could keep an eye on his quarry, harboring the idea that if things got too bad, if Barb was in imminent danger, he could swoop in and try to save her before they killed him. He would gladly give his life for Barb. If not out of his love for her, out of obligation to her father.

He deliberated for a moment, then went to fetch his horse. Rather than take precious time to go through the men's gear there in the parking lot, he decided to strap all of it—their guns, packs, and sleeping gear—onto his own horse. He could go through it at his own camp and keep the items he needed. Besides, the gunshots may have drawn attention from locals. A heavily-laden horse would be an attractive target.

Once he had everything strapped to his horse, he rifled through the pockets of the dead men. It felt weird, ghoulish, but Ragus could not be picky. He found a cigarette lighter and a good pocketknife on one of the men. He had a pistol belt with a handgun and several pouches of gear. Ragus slung it over his saddle horn to dig through later. He took a similar belt off the second man, and found a pack of cigarettes in his pocket and a switchblade knife.

Ragus had seen cheap switchblade knives at convenience stores in West Virginia. This one seemed decent. The blade had no wiggle to it at all and shot out with a solid click when he pushed a switch with this thumb. He carefully shoved it in a pocket. He already had a knife but who the hell ever complained they had too many knives?

He looked back the way he'd come that day and wondered how far behind him Conor was. Surely he had to catch up with him sometime soon. Ragus didn't want to think about the alternative, that Conor was lost, had been injured, or was otherwise unable to follow. He was also concerned about the change in direction the group took before these men split off. Before he continued behind them, Ragus had to find a way to clearly mark the change in route so there was no way Conor could miss it.

He rode his horse back to the highway, back to where the men rode down the embankment and switched to a small state road.

There were no trees close by for cutting a log marker. He could always get a can of spray paint from the store if they had any and paint a direction arrow on the road. But what if Conor thought it was the police marking an accident or a road contractor marking a needed repair?

Ragus felt the pressing need to get back on the trail but couldn't move on without marking this intersection. He stared down at the road as he thought and spotted a reflection in the last of the evening light. He squinted at it, then got off his horse for a closer look. It was a necklace. He also thought he recognized it.

It belonged to Barb.

It was some kind of clover necklace the girl wore, but she laughed when he called it a clover. She said Irish folks had another name for it. She rattled it off in some foreign language he didn't understand at all. She said it was native language of her people.

Holding the necklace dangling from his palm, watching the light reflect from the gold, he wondered if it had been dropped intentionally or ripped from her neck. It reignited his rage and he now knew how he was marking the trail.

17

Following the kidnapper's trail was becoming more difficult. The hard surface made it difficult for Conor to use even the most rudimentary tracking methods to determine how far he was behind the group. In soil, the definition of the print, the compaction of the soil, told him things. In woods or a field, crushed foliage gave him information. He was in an information vacuum now, blindly following the occasional scuff in the asphalt which he presumed to be made by the homemade rebar horse shoes and by the bent branches he presumed to be signs left by Ragus.

Even the bent branches were becoming scarcer. This section of highway was four-lane with guardrails on the sides. West Virginia had eradicated roadside foliage with napalm and there was very little left vegetation left within the public right-of-way, leaving fewer means by which Ragus could leave markers. The boy obviously had guts but he was lacking in experience. It was just sheer luck the boy had managed to follow the kidnappers this far without getting himself killed.

Earlier in the afternoon Conor crossed the state line into West Virginia, a state he'd traveled through but knew little about. He was unfamiliar with the road system and what cities it passed through. As night neared, he faced yet another evening away from his daughter. As much as that pained him, he was afraid to ride in the dark and possibly miss one of the scant trail signs. If this happened a few months back, he could have called in favors and had satellite footage, drone surveillance, and possibly even a strike team at his disposal.

There was a beautiful sunset that further enraged him because it was the kind of thing he would have pointed out to his daughter had they been home together. It enraged him because her absence reminded him of the absence of his wife, a woman he felt he'd barely gotten to know before she was taken from him. It enraged him because it illuminated the void within him created by all of the things he'd lost in his life from his father, to his grandfather, to his country, to his mother, to his wife, and now his daughter. Nothing hardened a man like loss. Nothing reminded you of the passage of time and brevity of life like a sunset. It could stop you in your tracks but disappear if you looked away for even a second. It was a beauty made painful by the inability to perfectly capture it in words, pictures, or in memory.

Conor was just past Princeton, West Virginia when he noticed the billowing black smoke. Considering the state of the world and the general unrest of people, he assumed the smoke to be the result of a bored miscreant or even an accidental fire. At this stage, he saw it as nothing more than something to keep an eye on. Further up the road, he started to smell the smoke.

It had to be burning tires. There was nothing in the world that smelled like it. Surely if this were the kidnappers they were not use burning tires to cook their dinner. Nor could he imagine any group they would intentionally camp around a fire producing such noxious smoke. The fire was close enough now that he was determined to travel past it before he stopped for the night. If the smoke were related to some sort of civil disturbance, he did not want to be within proximity of it and find himself caught in it tomorrow.

He moved past a cluster of businesses located near an exit. There was a Waffle House, a Bob Evans, several adult bookstores, and a few inexpensive hotels. Ahead in the distance, Conor could now see a furious, intense fire in the center of the road with black smoke churning about it. It could have been as much as a mile distant, although it was hard to tell. Concerned it might be a roadblock or a trap, he moved his horse to the shoulder and proceeded cautiously. Stopping at regular intervals, he used a small pair of binoculars to examine his surroundings.

The fire he saw ahead was definitely the source of the burning tire smell but there was something else there. He didn't see any sign of a trap nor a barricade, and felt safe enough to continue moving toward it. Amidst the denuded backdrop of the interstate highway, Conor saw nowhere he could skirt the scene safely and get a look at it. So in the interest of expediency, he rode right down the middle of the road like he was the most dangerous son of a bitch in West Virginia and he dared anyone to mess with him.

The sun was gone by the time he reached the tires, taking the light and the color of the world with it. Near a minor intersection, a half-dozen tires were ablaze. In some cases, the smaller size marked them as spare tires likely purloined from the trunks of stranded vehicles. The fire scorched the pavement and oily rivulets ran in all directions carrying flames with them. The flickering orange light from the fire was not unlike that of the sun earlier, casting the same tangerine glow to the world. It would have been almost cheery in other circumstances and were it not illuminating a body stretched out in the road.

There was no doubt the corpse was posed, laying on its back in the road with one arm extended toward a break in the guardrail. A heavy rock sat on the cold, dead hand, pinning it in place to assure it remained pointed in a particular direction. On the bare forearm, an arrow had been drawn with permanent marker to make sure the intention of the outstretched arm was not lost on Conor. The number eighteen was written on the dead man's forehead. Conor had no fucking clue what the number meant.

Of equal significance was the name scribbled just below the number. It read *Ragus*. The boy wanted to make certain Conor knew who'd left the message. It was a small but important confirmation.

Most folks may have found the boy's improvised route marker to be a little over the top, perhaps even a sign of some type of mental derangement. Conor understood, though, that a person didn't go through the kind of things Ragus had gone through and not find himself changed. Conor had gone through similar things and he was changed by them as well. Ragus had watched the only person in his life die and he'd had to deal with that himself. He'd had to carry her body outside by himself, dug a hole, and put her in the ground, then bury her.

How did that not change you? Not damage you somehow?

Conor pulled out his headlamp and followed the directions from the dead guy. At the gap in the guardrail, he found trampled grass and disturbed sod from the feet of dozens of horses. The kidnappers had left the road here. Had it not been for this extreme signpost Ragus left him, would Conor have noticed the change in course? He didn't know.

It was getting too dark to follow the trail now. He would put some distance between him and the fire, then he'd set up a quick camp for the night. Courtesy of the men back at the restaurant, he had a decent supply of smoked beef. That and a little grape Kool-Aid would make for a lovely dinner.

18

When the kidnappers finally stopped, the day was completely gone, the light changed to the monochromatic blue gloaming of late evening. Of the eighteen kidnappers present, three cruel bastards were selected by Lester to manage the prisoners. One by one, and in the same touchy and inappropriate manner, each woman was cut loose and helped from her saddle. Those released from the saddle were clustered together on the ground, seated nearly on top of each other as the men gaily went about their work. They commented without shame on the various physical qualities and attributes of the women they touched. The women bore the indignity with withdrawn stoicism, aware there was no recourse available to them, and that to protest might invite worse upon them.

It amazed Barb that these men could be such jerks even in the midst of their own suffering. They were all covered nearly head to toe with some vile rash. They scratched all the time. Some of them had pockets of infection from constantly digging at their itching arms. It made the men even more disgusting than they already were.

In the absence of any structure in which to lock the women, Lester informed them they would remain bound together for the night. "I'm sorry to you. I know it will be a little uncomfortable. All I can say is it sucks to be you. I'll have a man watching you all night. Any of you try anything stupid, I'll make an example of you. You probably don't want to know what that involves."

Barb's wrists were already raw and aching from the sharp edges of the plastic zip ties, having cut into her hands as the horse jostled her around all day. She wasn't the only one in such discomfort so it would have done no good to complain. While these men were not overt sadists, they *were* bastards. They made it clear the comfort of their *cargo* was secondary on this mission.

The group was served a dinner of smoked beef, canned peas, and canned peaches. As the cold beef was cut and distributed, the last of the smoked beef, the unspoken question on everybody's mind was what had happened to the two men left behind at the restaurant. It was their job to cut up the remaining beef, pack it onto the horses, and then catch up with the remainder of the group. They should have caught up hours ago.

Barb was fairly certain she knew what had happened to them. The fact they had still not shown up made her think her dad may have crossed paths with them. If he had, she could only guess how it ended, but she felt she was safe in assuming the men would not be rejoining their party. The absence of the two men was not openly discussed in front of the women but Barb overheard comments between Top Cat, Lester, and other men. There was debate as to whether a couple of men should be sent back to search for the two who were AWOL.

"You don't throw good money after bad," Lester said. "I'd rather be certain of having the men I've got than to take a chance on losing more. Who the hell knows what happened to them? They could have met some women. They could have found a bottle of liquor stashed in that restaurant somewhere. They could be back there having a barbecue and living it up."

"That better not be the case," Top Cat growled. "I get wind something like that is going on, I'll drag the pair of them behind their horses all the way back to Douthat Farms."

As warned, the women were bound together. A single rope was threaded through each woman's arms, which they could not escape because of their hands being zip tied together. Any woman attempting to escape would have to drag all the others along with her unless she had a means to cut the rope.

As darkness settled over them and a gibbous moon rose slowly in the southern sky, the men built a campfire. Women began drifting off to sleep, practically elbow to elbow beneath the tablecloths that served as their blankets against the chilly night. The accommodations were not comfortable but the women were exhausted and sheer tiredness raked them into sleep.

Barb was awake, listening to JoAnn's breathing slow and grow deeper. The kidnappers settled in for the night too, laying their sleeping bags out on crinkly blue tarps or off to the side, directly on the ground. Barb listened intently, hoping she could learn the watch plan for the night. Instead, she found Lester and Top Cat discussing the new glaring absence among the group.

"Those two clowns we left at the warehouse should be back by now too," Lester said.

Top Cat sighed loud enough that Barb heard him over the crackling of the fire and the snores of the sleeping. "Yeah, I don't know what to think about that."

"I guess they could've found some alcohol to get into. They know you won't let them bring it into camp so they might have stayed behind to live it up for the night."

"Same deal as with the other men," Top Cat said. "They show up late reeking of booze and I'll make an example out of them."

"I hear a lot of talk about you making examples out of folks but I see few *examples* of you making examples out of folks. You get what I'm saying?"

"If you don't like my management style you're free to go," Top Cat said.

Lester bit his tongue. He didn't want to go. He wanted Top Cat to go.

There was a lull in the conversation and Barb listened to the crackling of the fire, the chirping of the cicadas. In the distance coyotes started their song, yapping and howling.

"If it ain't drinking or women, what do you think it is?" Lester asked. "That's four men. The odds of four men not coming back are slim, wouldn't you think?"

"Spit it out. What are you thinking?" Top Cat asked. "Get it out of your system."

Lester looked at his boss with the same reluctance and grave seriousness one might use when bringing up the sighting of a ghost. "You think somebody might be following us?"

Top Cat made some sort of dismissive grunt. "I fucking doubt it. There's twenty-two of us. Who's going to set out after twenty-two men?"

"There *were* twenty-two men. There aren't anymore. You're counting men who haven't come back and might not ever come back."

"I'm going to sleep," Top Cat said, signaling an end to the conversation. "You should do the same."

"I'm taking watch," Lester replied.

"You're a boss. You can make someone else do it."

"I'm good. I'm not ready to call it a night yet."

Lester voluntarily taking a watch concerned Top Cat a little. Although he suspected the man might be up to something, he wasn't ready to lose sleep over it. The man didn't like him but he didn't think he'd do anything about it. Yet.

∼

IT TOOK a while but Barb allowed herself to fall asleep, knowing she'd need her rest for what lay ahead of her. Later, she awoke with a start as if something inside her mind had elbowed her awake. The forest was silent except for the deep breathing and snores of the people sleeping around her. It was the deepest part of night. It was time. Her odds were the best they would likely be.

She shifted, acting as if she were simply stretching in her sleep.

She positioned her head to where she should have been able to see the guard but she didn't see anyone. Men were strewn about the camp like discarded toys in a playroom. Some lay collapsed awkwardly as if their batteries had run down and they toppled over. It was impossible to tell which of them was supposed to be the man on duty.

From her father's background in covert operations, Barb had learned the importance of having basic survival gear on your person at all times. Conor always carried enough kit with him that, should he be separated from his gear, he'd be able to make it to safety, whether safety meant an embassy, a hotel room, a foreign border, or a forward operating base. He'd impressed the importance of everyday preparedness on his daughter as well.

Conor started off carrying a money belt that contained some basic survival gear. Eventually he found a better belt. He and Barb each wore one now as part of their everyday carry. Unlike money belts, this one didn't require removing the belt and unzipping it to access the hidden compartment. It was constructed of two layers of webbing sewn together at the bottom and sealed with Velcro at the top. With a little effort, you could work a finger between the layers and access the hidden compartments while wearing the belt.

Each item was affixed in place so you always knew where it would be located on the belt. A single stitch of thread held a handcuff key where it could be accessed in an emergency and pulled free. A single drop of hot glue held a packet of fishing line and hooks in a fixed position. A short ferro rod for starting fires was in a sleeve beside a sealed plastic bag of Vaseline-soaked cotton balls. Most importantly at this moment, a spot of hot glue held a single edged razor blade inside the belt, protected by a cardboard sleeve.

Barb had to move painfully slow to avoid tugging the rope and waking the other prisoners but she finally worked a finger into the belt. The belt was cinched fairly tight, which worked against her. She'd lost weight like most folks as a result of the change in diet and the increased level of physical activity. That meant a tighter belt to keep the jeans from falling off. Despite that restriction, she was eventually able to get through the Velcro and between the layers of webbing exactly at the point where the razor blade should be.

With some deft manipulation of her finger she found the protected back edge of the blade. She twisted her fingers to widen the opening in the belt as much as she could, then pinched the razor blade. Holding tightly, she pulled it from the spot where it was glued. Once she had it in front of her, she used her other hand to slip the protective sleeve from the blade. She formed a small loop of rope in front of her, holding it tightly so she could apply cutting pressure without creating any unnecessary movement. The brand new razor blade cut quickly and in a few careful strokes she'd severed the rope and unthreaded it from between her arms.

JoAnn and Barb had been sitting side-by-side on the ground when they were roped together. The overall length of the rope restricted how far the women could move apart, so to some extent they slept like a pile of puppies in a basket. As the tablecloths they used for blankets provided little warmth, the contact of the other bodies was also a welcome source of heat. This meant Barb needed to move slowly and carefully to avoid jostling a neighbor. That was difficult for her. With her hands free, it was like someone had stepped on the gas pedal and flooded her with adrenaline. Barb wanted nothing more than to bolt upright and run like hell.

She slipped her hand over JoAnn's mouth to muffle any cries of surprise and placed her mouth next to the woman's ear. "Wake up, JoAnn. It's Barb. We have to go. Don't make any noise."

Barb could only see the faintest outline of JoAnn's face but knew her first expression would be panic. It must have been the hands on her that stirred this fear reaction but it quickly subsided as Barb's words registered. JoAnn nodded. She understood and was ready. Barb gave a gentle tug of the rope and pulled it through JoAnn's zip ties. With a flick of the razor blade, she severed those plastic bonds. With no safe way to store the razor blade for travel, Barb reluctantly dropped it to the ground. The two women were free.

She sat up slowly, like a child awakened and confused about where she was. If anyone was awake, her movement would not immediately raise an alarm. She scanned all the sleeping forms, not finding a guard. She felt comfortable there was no one awake. She eased up onto her feet, careful not to wake the other women. She slipped a hand under JoAnn's bicep and helped her up. Barb knew every second they were in camp increased their chances of getting caught. It was not safe to waste time looking for a weapon, a pack, or even a bottle of water lest that hesitation result in them being caught.

The women's eyes were fairly well-adjusted. Coupled with a clear night and gibbous moon they had a fighting chance against the darkness. Barb also paid close attention to how they had arrived at the campsite earlier in the evening. She wanted to have a basic knowledge of an escape route just in case the opportunity presented itself. Barb was in the lead, pulling JoAnn's hand. She took small steps that would make it easier to recover from any obstacles she might trip over. JoAnn started to speak a couple of times but Barb shushed her, not wanting to break the silence until they had a good distance between them and camp.

Barb was fairly certain she knew what JoAnn was going to say anyway. She was going to ask about the other women. Barb had already thought about that. Part of her wanted to help every woman escape but she could not imagine wrangling that many women out of camp without waking their captors. Add to that the fact there were women among the group who appeared to relish the idea of being provided for, even if it meant living as a slave. They showed no indication of wanting to escape and going back to a life of providing for themselves.

Completely abandoning the women was not the plan. Once she got free of the camp and met up with her father, they would return, free the women, and kill all these kidnapping bastards so they could never do this to another woman again. While that may have sounded cold, Barb had no intention of allowing them to continue roaming the land, marauding and stealing women as they pleased. Like her father, Barb was undergoing a change of heart on how to best weather this societal collapse. It was no longer about self-preservation and staying out of other peoples' fights. This had become about being the sheepdog and killing any wolf who strayed too close.

The two women stumbled through tall grass and overgrown roadside weeds, closing the distance to the road until they felt pavement beneath their feet. The blacktop still held some warmth from the day's sun. With her feet firmly planted on pavement, Barb paused for a second to get her bearings and determine the direction of escape. She wanted to make certain she was going away from camp and toward home. When daylight caught up with them, they would move from the road to travel concealed in the deep woods, hidden from eyes and from anyone who might be trying to track them.

No more than a few seconds passed before JoAnn squeezed her hand tightly and hissed, "Listen!"

Barb did as instructed, fully prepared to hear an army of men bearing down on them, but this was a different sound. It was a rhythmic grunting that could have been a black bear or feral pig heading right for them. While the women were trying to interpret the sound a light clicked on mere feet in front of them. The woman named Bonnie, one of those so eager to be taken captive, was standing in front of Lester, pulling her pants back up.

Barb's reaction was instant. She beat feet and sprinted away from the man, making sure she took off in the right direction, knowing there would be little time to put any distance between them. It hit her that she was by herself though. JoAnn did not have the reaction time and was gathering the impetus to move when Lester's strong arms latched around her neck. Barb heard her cry out and paused. She had put thirty feet between her and the kidnapper by now. She could get away. There was no way he would catch her. Then JoAnn cried out again.

There was the pop of a fist pounding into flesh and Barb knew Lester had punched her. Wrestling with her obligation to this woman she barely knew, Barb stood in the road anguishing over the decision, torn between freedom and obligation. The man had control now. His light was clutched in his fist, glaring upward into his face and illuminating JoAnn's, which was clenched in a brutal headlock. The effect of the strong under-lighting only accentuated the ghastly nature of his face and the suffering on JoAnn's.

Seeing now that he had Barb's attention, that she had paused in her flight, Lester drew back a fist and punched JoAnn in the face again. She cried out, and he did it again. His eyes were not watching his actions nor JoAnn's reactions, but were instead glued to Barb. He was enjoying this. He was enjoying seeing her torn between freedom and responsibility. He was making her suffer by remote control and he liked it.

Lester had no idea who he was messing with. He lowered his eyes to JoAnn's tortured expression, relishing it. He drew back his fist to pummel her again but Bonnie cried out. Lester barely raised his eyes in time to see Barb cartwheel in front him, her legs falling on either side of his head. Barb's momentum unsettled him and he fell over backwards.

Before he even hit the ground, those legs were tightening around his neck like a vise. They crashed to the ground but she did not let go. If anything, her grip only tightened. She gritted her teeth, grunted, and put all her effort into choking him out. He tried beating on her legs, tried gouging his fingers into the soft tissue of her legs, tried *everything* but he could not get her to let go.

His head was getting foggy and he knew time was running out. He only had a short amount of time to fix this or he was a dead man. He remembered a knife on his belt and reached for it, but as quickly as he did, Barb grabbed one of his fingers, tugging it from the knife. His first reaction was almost amusement. She thought with her weak girl's grip that she could do any damage to him?

He felt pressure against the tip of his finger then blinding pain as she snapped the bone at an acute right angle. He screamed but it sounded far away, lost in the pounding of the blood trying to get to his brain. He was starting to lose consciousness but her grip weakened, her legs loosened, and he rolled away. He couldn't even function enough to raise his head from the pavement.

Through his blurry vision he saw Bonnie with the flashlight in her hand. She drew it back to hit Barb across the head a second time.

"No!" he groaned. As much as he enjoyed seeing that bitch get what she deserved, these women were his responsibility. He couldn't let her be killed or disabled. He was already going to be in enough trouble over this.

He collapsed to the pavement, gravel pressing painfully into the back of his head. He could hear the other woman, the one he'd punched, crying.

"The other men are coming," Bonnie said. "You better get up."

Lester tried standing but the world was spinning. He staggered sideways a couple of steps before falling back down. He surrendered to it, lying back on the pavement and watching the stars spin over his head. The next thing he saw was Top Cat's face over his own, illuminated in the ambient light of several flashlights. Even through his foggy brain he could tell his boss was not happy.

19

No one at the camp got much sleep after the escape attempt. Top Cat obviously blamed the whole thing on Lester. If Lester hadn't decided to sneak off with that woman there would have been a guard there to catch the troublemaker before she even got out of camp. If Lester had done his job, the same troublemaker wouldn't have a nasty wound to the head.

"If she dies, you're explaining this to Bryan," Top Cat raged, spittle flying from his mouth and hitting Lester in the face. "We can't afford to lose any of these women. I want you taking care of her yourself. I want you to babysit her for the rest of this trip. If she dies, I'm not responsible for what happens to you."

Lester grumbled but took his medicine. He hadn't really intended on fraternizing with the prisoners but that chick Bonnie made it clear she was available. She was his if he wanted her. Now he could barely move his neck from that ninja bitch trying to take his head off.

In a shitty mood that only got worse, Top Cat made them pull out at first light. He ordered all the women saddled and tied with no breakfast. His own men got nothing to eat either, and had to pack all their gear by flashlight. Top Cat told them they could eat from the saddle while they rode but people grumbled. Top Cat wasn't a tough guy but he was serious about discipline. He probably wouldn't hesitate to kill one of the crew if they risked screwing up the mission. There were plenty of men living around Douthat Farms who would gladly take their place for the promise of regular hot meals

As if Top Cat's mood weren't bad enough, Lester had to point out the obvious, bringing up the fact they had missing men. "The men we left at the warehouse still aren't back."

Top Cat glared at Lester as if deciding whether he should go ahead and kill him right then. Lester was bound to only cause him more headaches. Should he just cut his losses and pop the guy right in front the whole crew? It would send a message.

"Thanks for pointing out the fucking obvious. You're a very astute individual. Shame you didn't get to finish your education. I'm sure you were destined for great things."

Lester ignored the commentary. "I think we should send somebody back for them. If something happened to the guys we left at the warehouse, then the guys we left at the restaurant might not find the turnoff. Those guys could just be back there wandering around lost. This could turn into a goat rope."

"It's already turned into a goat rope," Top Cat grumbled, impatiently shoving gear into his saddle bags. He was ready to be back at Douthat Farms where life was a little more predictable. "What are you proposing?"

"Let me pull off two guys. Riding at a good pace, they could be at the warehouse in about forty-five minutes. It shouldn't take them more than a half-hour to poke around and figure out what happened. I'll tell them not to worry about any salvage. Just see if they can figure out what happened, then haul ass back here. If they make a good pace they should be able catch up with us by 10 or 11 AM. That might also help us answer the other question we talked about last night."

Top Cat slapped the flap on his saddle bag shut and buckled it. "What question?"

Lester lowered his voice. "Whether we're being followed or not."

Top Cat shook his head in disgust. "You haven't given up on that dumb-assed idea?"

Lester shook his head. "I have a weird feeling. I feel like I'm being watched."

The remark went ignored. "It's light enough to ride now. Let's get out of here."

Perhaps Top Cat should not have been so quick to dismiss Lester's hunch, because the group was indeed being watched. Ragus had slept through the previous night's escape attempt and the ensuing fight, and he was up early. He wanted to take advantage of the opportunity to collect some intelligence on the kidnappers. They were camped on the playground of an old school. While the grounds were relatively flat and open, they were surrounded by a chain-link fence approximately four feet tall. The fence was overgrown with ivy and weeds, creating a nearly impenetrable wall behind which Ragus was hidden and listening to their conversation.

He had a small pair of binoculars he had stolen from one of the men he'd killed. He pressed them against the fence, trying to catch a view through the dense greenery. Among the bound women, he spotted Barb and was shocked by her condition. She had a bruised cheek and her face was stained with dried blood. He hadn't been able to get a good look at her since catching up with the kidnappers but even at a distance he felt he would have noticed her condition. This had to be recent. It made him want to rush into the camp and kill all of the men. If he'd had even a glimmer of hope that he could accomplish this, he would have done it. He had several rifles and a couple of handguns now. His level of firepower had increased. The problem was that his level of manpower had not, and that was what he needed more of. Something to improve his odds of success.

From his concealed position, Ragus listened to the plan to send men back to the warehouse. He saw this as another opportunity to level the playing field. If he couldn't add more men to his fighting force, he could continue to reduce the size of their force. Gnawing away at their numbers would slowly improve his odds. He needed to catch those men at a safe distance from camp and ambush them, then get back on the trail of the main group of kidnappers.

When the men started putting the women on the horses, Ragus saw for the first time how each captive was tied to a stirrup so they could not even dismount without assistance. Their hands, bound in front of them, were zip tied to the saddle horn. He needed to remember that little bit of information. Whatever rescue he put in place, he should not have the expectation that Barb could just leap from her horse and take off running.

He withdrew quietly and returned to the horse he'd tied a good distance away. He backtracked a little, finding a good position along the route the men returning to the warehouse would have to take. There was a good straight stretch where it was open and there was nowhere to hide. Just the right spot.

He dismounted and tied his horse in the bushes where it would be hidden from the road and hopefully safe from any flying bullets. He tied it loosely with the hopes that if he were killed the horse would be able to pull itself loose and escape. Tied to the back of his saddle, he had two of the shorter military-style rifles Conor had taught him to shoot. Conor referred to them as M4s.

The boy had no illusions he'd be able to keep all the weapons he liberated but he wanted to keep some of them. These two M4s seemed to be pretty standard among the kidnappers. With each man he killed, he was able to collect more ammunition for them. He'd also taken a handgun, a Glock, and carried it in a holster on his waist. Despite his growing arsenal, he felt that the right weapon for this job was the Henry. The .22 caliber was small but the suppressor would help minimize the noise. He only hoped there would be enough distance between him and the larger group that no one would hear what happened. That also meant making sure the men didn't have the opportunity to shoot back at him. A shot from their unsuppressed weapons might bring the entire group riding back to lend aid. If that happened, he would probably die.

Ragus had manned his outpost in the bushes for perhaps twenty minutes before he heard the clatter of shod hooves on the paved county road. He already had his rifle raised and the barrel resting in the crotch of a maple sapling. He let the men get close enough that he would have a clear headshot on the first and should be able to get several more off at the second man before he found cover. Ragus rested the crosshairs at the very top of the man's head and squeezed the trigger.

The rifle cracked and a hole appeared in the tanned expanse of the man's forehead. His expression didn't even really change. He merely stiffened then toppled out of the saddle. The other rider must have heard the muffled crack but did not immediately associate it with a rifle shot. He was more distracted by his concern at his friend falling off his horse. By the time he put two and two together and determined there might be a threat, Ragus had already squeezed the trigger again.

The shot placement had not been so easy on the second man because he was moving and his horse was spooked. The shot caught him in the cheek below his eye socket and ripped away a chunk of flesh the size of a quarter. The man flinched as if he'd been stung by a bee. He gritted his teeth and his hand flew up to his face.

Watching through the riflescope, it wasn't immediately clear to Ragus if the man even associated the rush of pain with a gunshot wound. Before he could take any further action, Ragus levered the action, positioned the crosshairs, and squeezed the trigger again. The solid-point projectile punched a pencil-sized hole in the man's cranium and penetrated his brain. He tumbled off his horse, which panicked and bolted for the woods. Ragus was not certain the men were dead but he did not want to have to apply the coup de grace from point-blank range. He wasn't sure he was ready for that kind of personal killing. From his cover, he aimed carefully and put another shot in each man's head. They weren't getting up from that.

Ragus had no interest in gloating over his victory. This was not a particularly proud moment. This had not been a fight, it had been an ambush. It was not *his* skill overcoming his *opponent's* skill, but simply the bad luck of two men to have been in the wrong place at the wrong time. Add to that the fact that, as a group, the kidnappers had crossed the wrong kind of people. People who didn't quit.

Without looking too closely at them, Ragus posed the men in the road, pointing their arms in the appropriate direction. He made a cursory check of their gear and food for anything he needed. One man's saddlebags had a handful of Snickers bars and Ragus nearly cheered out loud. He was suddenly starving and planned on eating all of them.

20

When the dark of night began moving toward a predawn gray, Conor stirred in his hastily strung hammock. He had always been sensitive to light. Unless he was flat out exhausted he found it difficult to sleep outside during the daylight or in a lit room. His work ethic was so engrained he felt if he could see, he should be working. By that same measure, if it was light enough for him to see the ground and not miss a sign, it was light enough to be on the move.

He was certain he knew which way to go now. There was no mistaking the objective of the morbid directional markers Ragus had left him beside the burning tires. This other road was a secondary road with a lot more turns and intersections than the highway, and he would have to remain alert for places where the kidnapping bastards may change direction. The distinctive scuffs left by the rebar horseshoes were becoming more difficult to spot. Conor assumed they were becoming worn down by all the walking on hard surfaces. The distinctive scoring that made the prints so easy to follow were slowly being ground off by the asphalt. This secondary road was made up of older pavement, already scuffed and harder to read.

Conor was a fit man despite all the ribbing from his daughter but had to admit he felt a little old for this type of pursuit. His back hurt from being jostled in the saddle all day yesterday. He was not used to being on a horse. He was not complaining about that, though. He'd gladly take the horse over the pace and exertion of trying to keep up with the kidnappers on foot.

When he did find his first set of prints on the new road he hopped off his horse, crouched down, and examined them closely. He wanted to make a mental note of any changes in their appearance so they would be easy to look out for. He was also pleased to note that this road passed through more forested terrain. With more roadside vegetation, Ragus had taken to breaking the tips from branches again as a trail marker. It was an easy indicator that didn't require Conor to hop off the horse and lose time deciphering prints. It was also easier for Ragus than having to pose a dead body at every intersection.

While the dense vegetation made it easier for Ragus to mark the trail, traveling in the forest made Conor much warier. The brilliantly colored changing leaves formed a canopy, looming over and embracing the road. There were a lot of places to hide. There could be men anywhere. This road also passed through communities and there would be houses along it. There could be traps or ambushes anywhere and he might not see them until they were sprung. Days in this terrain, under these conditions, were tense and exhausting. It was a far cry from the peaceful country drive one would have experienced traveling this road a year ago.

Conor was perhaps an hour and a half down the secondary road when he came up on a straight section with some sort of obstruction in the distance. His first thought was it might be a trap. He raised a pair of binoculars to his eyes and squinted for any sign of something fishy. Instead, a smile curled the edges of his mouth.

"I like your style, kid."

The *style* to which Conor was referring ended up being a new pair of directional markers. There was no intersection here that required clarification so Conor had to assume these dead men were targets of opportunity. Ragus may have no choice but to kill them or he'd killed them to reduce the number of enemies they'd face down the road.

When he reached the bodies, Conor found there were two of them laid out neatly in the road. Each man's hands, outstretched above his head, was weighted down with rocks to assure they remained pointed in the correct direction.

"Hey buddy, can you give me some directions?" Conor asked one of them.

The wounds on the face told Conor the story. The kid had taken them out with head shots. They appeared to be .22 caliber. An M4 in 5.56 would have the same size bullet but there would be more trauma. He suspected Ragus was using the Henry rifle he'd given him with the suppressor. Conor was pleased he'd made the decision to give the boy that rifle now. He was also pleased that Ragus seemed to understand the judicious use of firepower. Better to use the stealth approach of a well-aimed, suppressed shot than to blast mag after mag of higher caliber ammo at the target.

If Conor formed a team when he got home, this kid certainly had a place on it. It crossed his mind he might even make a fine son-in-law but Barb wasn't having that. To her, the small age difference, or perhaps maturity difference, was an insurmountable chasm. From Conor's perspective, with the benefit of more life under his belt, the difference in ages would be completely immaterial. There was also no arguing with the fact that Barb badgered and made fun of Ragus every time she saw him. Despite that, it didn't deter the lad. Maybe he sensed the bark was worse than the bite. There was no arguing with the fact the boy was risking his life, and taking others, to try and save Barb, though. If that didn't buy him some points with Barb, Conor was going to have a serious talk with the girl.

One man's forehead was damaged by gunfire, making it a poor substitute for a notepad. The other man's bore a number written in permanent marker, just like the dead man he'd found yesterday. The number was sixteen and the purpose of the numbers was clear now. The previous man read eighteen, minus these two dead men, left sixteen men remaining with the party of kidnappers. The kid was not only leaving him directions but intel as well. He now knew what size force he was dealing with.

"Good move, son."

Conor had been impressed with the boy's style earlier but this was definitely a good way to pass intel onto the folks following you. The purpose of the numbers would not be clear to folks just randomly coming upon this body but would be evident to someone following in your footsteps. The state of the bodies told Conor that Ragus had gone over them hastily, taking only the things he needed. He hadn't taken all the weapons which told Conor he'd already armed himself. That was good. The Henry rifle was clearly doing the trick but additional firepower was always nice. If this turned into a battle, the lever action would not be as efficient as a semi-auto.

The men's horses had been collected and tied off to a nearby tree. Conor removed the gear, saddles, and the bridles. He released each horse with a pat on the rear. No use leaving them here tied up. They could forage until someone new claimed them.

He went back to the bodies and rolled one of the men over, raising his shirt. He examined for post-mortem lividity. The beginning stages of purple blotching told him the bodies had probably been there for at least two hours but not overnight. He lifted an arm and flexed it, checking for rigor mortis. He found no indications of stiffness there so he moved to the eyelids and neck. Changes he found there helped give him an approximation of how long the bodies had laid there. He was guessing two to four hours.

Conor had no formal instruction in forensic sciences but he had more experience than he'd admit looking at dead bodies. He also read a lot of medical information because it helped him design better weapons. Occasionally it struck him that it was probably a little fucked up to read medical books for the complete opposite purpose in which they were intended, but that was the nature of the job. He was the Mad Mick, not Doctor Mick. He was the Master of Mayhem, not the Master of Medicine. He was a killer and not a healer.

He climbed back on his horse and nudged it in motion. A few miles further down the road he came upon signs of a group encampment. A wide trail of beaten-down grass led to a schoolyard where it looked like the group had spent the night. Conor remained on his horse but made a quick pass around the site. He wasted little time there. He only wanted to confirm there were no bodies there, either of captives or of kidnappers. When he found nothing, he steered his horse back onto the road and took off.

He was close. This could happen today.

21

After an hour of riding, Barb began throwing up. She rode with her eyes closed, wavering in the saddle like she could topple over any moment. She was not really sick, she was intentionally trying to appear ill to slow them down, but it was a fine line to walk. A dangerous line. If she appeared too ill, too injured, she suspected they'd just shoot her and leave her behind.

Top Cat wore a strained expression on his face and cut his eyes at Lester. "This is your fault. She's probably got a head injury. Concussion or something. I think that's supposed to make you throw up."

There was a lot Lester wanted to say in his defense but kept his mouth shut. Yeah, he'd screwed up, but everyone had screwed up before. It was not a big deal and he was tired of Top Cat making out like it was the end of the world. If he had to, he could go out anytime with a smaller group of men and bring back more women. He didn't get this whole thing of making out like they were precious cargo. They weren't. They were cattle, and there were plenty more cattle out there.

When she came up with this plan, Barb was concerned she wouldn't be able to make herself throw up because her hands were bound to the pommel of the saddle. She couldn't move her hands far enough to get a finger into her throat. Fortunately, she'd once had a nauseating experience that unfailingly made her stomach churn. She hated to draw upon that experience to fuel her nausea but she had no choice. She recalled an incident from a few months back when she was helping her father track down an apparent roof leak in the compound.

Since a lot of the finished space in the various buildings had once been offices, there were suspended acoustical ceilings throughout much of the facility. A damp ceiling tile had caught Conor's attention. He was meticulous, and if there was a roof leak he wanted to stop it before it did any significant damage. While Conor climbed on the roof to investigate the leak from the top, Barb remained inside staring at the ceiling tile.

Not one for inaction, she got a ladder and decided to explore from the bottom. She pushed the tile up to see if she could find anything but the ceiling tile was snagged on something and didn't want to go up at all. Try as she might, Barb could not get the tile to move. The adjacent rectangles in the ceiling grid held numerous useless things that prevented her from just moving to an adjacent tile and raising it. Two held florescent lights, one held a heating duct, one a cold air return, and another an exit sign.

Barb decided since the tile was ruined anyway she could use her finger to push a hole up through the soft tile. Perhaps she could feel something and if any water was trapped there it would then be released by the weep hole her finger created. She got a mop bucket and placed it beneath where she thought the water might run, then put her finger in the center of the damp area on the ceiling tile. She twisted it back and forth, drilling her finger into the soggy tile.

Her finger hit what she thought was wet insulation, which would have been consistent with what they'd found in other parts of the building. She removed her finger from the hole, squinting and peering upward, shining a flashlight toward the hole. Just then, a gooey stream of maggots poured forth from the hole and ran into her face, her hair, and her open mouth. Barb was neither weak, nor was she squeamish, but the stream of maggots was carried by a liquid that looked like thin red gelatin but smelled and tasted like rot and death.

Her reaction was instantaneous and involuntary. Springing backwards out of the stream, she half jumped, half fell down the three steps of the ladder. Carried by her momentum and off-balance, she staggered backwards several feet and hit the wall. She brushed furiously at her face, trying to clear the maggots from her face and mouth. She kept spitting but could feel them moving inside her mouth, between her lips and teeth.

The vomiting came of its own accord.

She didn't know if it was the taste, the palette of sensations, or the putrid smell like a rotten fish smoothie. She was on her hands and knees throwing up into the mop bucket when Conor came in.

"I can't find a damn thing," he said before spotting Barb collapsed against the wall, a look of panic on her face, which triggered his own panic. He was uncertain as to what had happened to her. His eyes went to the overturned ladder. He crouched at her side and put a hand on her back. "What's wrong, my girl? What happened?"

Before she could respond the soggy ceiling tile gave way, crumpling and falling to the floor just feet away from them. As the chunks of disintegrating tile hit the ground, the decomposing body of a fat raccoon landed atop it, hitting the floor with the sound of a soaked bath towel dropped onto a tile floor. Odiferous coon fluids splashed around the entire room, hitting both Conor and Barb.

Conor, who had certainly seen more ghastly sights in his life than his daughter had, simply wiped the spray from his face and curled his nose in disgust. "Well, ain't that a sight."

He took his daughter by the arm and led her to an outside solar-heated shower, helping her into the stall. She was ready to cry and might have had nausea not overruled every other sensation.

When Barb got out, her dad handed her a glass of clear liquid. "Vodka."

"I don't drink," Barb said. "I'll just throw up again."

"Don't drink it. Just swish and spit. It will cut the taste of coon juice."

Barb's stomach heaved but she heeded her dad's advice. It did indeed cut the taste of coon juice but she hoped that was a folk remedy she never needed to resort to again.

～

"Do we need to cut her loose?" Lester asked. "Just leave her behind? Or take her off to the side and kill her?"

Lester had never killed anybody like that in his life, shooting them in cold blood at point-blank range, but he thought he could do it. Certainly portraying the image that he could perform such an act would strengthen his position among the group. In this type of social order, almost like the correctional system, the willingness to kill so easily and so personally gained you respect. While he wouldn't admit it to anyone in the group, if Top Cat had given him permission to kill her, he'd probably have just left her behind with a warning, firing a couple of shots into the ground to make people think he really killed her.

"No, you're not fucking shooting her," Top Cat grumbled. "I've told you, we can't spare any of them."

Barb experienced a little relief in overhearing that, concerned she had overplayed her hand and puked herself into being euthanized.

"How about we leave somebody here with her to see if she gets any better?"

"We're already down enough men," Top Cat replied. "And what if she didn't get better? What are we supposed to do with her then?"

"With this sized group and these pack horses, we're moving pretty slow," Lester replied. "We can let her stop and rest for an hour or two, then double-time it to catch up with us."

Top Cat looked indecisive, shaking his head doubtfully. "I don't like this thing of us being strung out all over the place. Our strength came from the size of the group, and this group is getting smaller by the day. It gets too small, we lose our intimidation factor and we might get challenged by locals."

Lester was fully aware the group was shrinking and he had his own opinions about why that was taking place. Top Cat was just not listening when he offered them. Lester persisted, and Top Cat finally gave in, giving him permission to leave the injured woman behind in hopes a little rest would improve her condition.

"You better hope she snaps out of this and there's no permanent damage. I'm not lying to Bryan about this. I'll tell him your fuckup cost us a woman. I expect when he hears that you'll be carrying her load for a while. You'll be doing laundry and working crops, all that shit."

That was exactly what their boss back at Douthat Farms had assured them would happen if they injured any of the women. He'd told them whoever was responsible would have to carry the workload originally intended for the injured prisoner. Lester thought that was a crock of shit. In fact, he thought Top Cat being in charge of him was also a crock of shit. Lester was practical and realistic in his awareness of his own limitations. He did not have the broad range of knowledge required to operate Douthat Farms like their boss Bryan did. Lester could never take over that operation and run it with the same efficiency. He could never manage all the people and personalities. He knew nothing of agriculture, solar power, or construction.

Top Cat, on the other hand, was no better in those departments than Lester was. He wasn't a better leader, any smarter, or any more skilled than Lester was. As far as Lester was concerned he could just as easily do that job. He was tired of taking orders from Top Cat. If the man persisted in being a dick, the injured girl might not be the only person left behind. With all the people who had already disappeared from this expedition, one more might not make any difference. He could slip a knife in Top Cat's back and roll him off into a ditch somewhere, no one the wiser.

"I want to leave Howell with the girl," Lester said.

Top Cat looked over at him curiously. "Howell? Really? I thought you didn't like him. You're always complaining he's useless."

Lester shrugged. "Well, if he's totally fucking useless then I guess we won't miss him being left behind with her, now will we?"

"I guess not," Top Cat agreed.

The riders left Barb and Howell at a shady spot by the road. It was little more than a wide place to pull off by a scenic creek. It looked like a spot where people stopped to fish or picnic. Howell protested being left behind, presenting a variety of reasons why he thought it was a bad idea, but he wasn't fooling anyone. They were all pretty sure it was because he was scared. He'd shown signs of it before but he was a decent follower and you had to have people like that.

Lester complained about the guy all the time. He was always shirking the hard physical labor at the camp. That would be okay if he compensated for it by carrying more of the guard duties, but he didn't like those either. He complained about snakes, bears, and the bugs. If it was Lester's call, he'd simply cut the guy loose and boot him out of camp but he didn't get to make those decisions.

Lester left Howell with a water filter and a couple of empty bottles. He also gave them a half-dozen cans of pears from one of the pack horses.

"You don't got peaches?" Howell asked. "I like peaches better."

"I don't give a shit what you like. It's the pears or nothing," Lester replied.

Howell pouted. "Be that way then." He took the pears and wandered off to take a seat on a rotted log.

Barb laid on a vinyl tablecloth in the thick grass. She was alert and listening to everything but she put on a good show of whimpering and acting semi-conscious.

When the larger group rode out of sight Howell began to express his frustration with Barb. As far as he could tell, she couldn't hear him. She was practically delirious. As long as he didn't hurt her, or at least leave any marks on her, he figured he could do what he wanted. Certainly berating her was within the scope of what he could get away with.

"Stupid bitch! You're the reason I got stuck here babysitting. A grown-ass man and I got to look after you."

Barb was concerned about the man hovering over her and mumbling. She expected at any moment for him to lash out with a foot or punch her in some soft spot that wouldn't leave a mark. She needed to do something to put a little space between them. She needed a deterrent. All it took on her part was recalling the revolting mouthful of fermented raccoon juice and the smell of it on her face, a mix of rotted fish and corpse. She gagged deeply, turned her head, and threw up a puddle of bilious liquid at his feet.

"Jesus Christ!" Howell muttered, stepping backward. He grew even more disgusted at her and stalked off to look over the creek bank. There were boulders along the edge the size of wheelbarrows. A man could stand on them while fishing.

Howell wandered back to her a few minutes later. "I'm going to fill these water bottles. If you move an inch, you'll live to regret it. There won't be any marks but you'll hurt just the same."

Giving no reaction at all, Barb continued to give the impression she was barely coherent. Bored with her, Howell walked off to fill the water bottles. Relieved he'd gone about his business, Barb lay there on the ground fully aware that, while she wasn't as bad off as she acted, she really didn't feel very well. Her ribs and sternum ached from the blunt arrow she'd taken to the chest on the day she was kidnapped. Lying on the hard ground only caused that pain to resurface, and she was not entirely certain she didn't have a mild concussion from the flashlight blow she'd taken to the head last night.

Concerned that Howell might be a loose cannon despite the warnings not to hurt her, Barb decided while he was over the bank filling water jugs she would pretend to pass out. Her fitful tossing and moaning only agitated him, reminding him of her presence, and of the unwanted babysitting duty he'd been unfortunate enough to draw.

She needed to think. She had a decision to make. She felt an obligation to JoAnn and didn't want to abandon her. If she killed Howell and took his weapon, could she then get JoAnn back by herself? Perhaps she would run into her dad along the trail and enlist his help, but she wasn't even a hundred percent certain he was out there. All she had was a feeling and the knowledge that he would follow her with everything he had. That still didn't mean he was close enough to help with a rescue.

Unfortunately, the easiest way to keep JoAnn safe was from the inside, as a captive. Even in her injured state, she was aware she could not stop thinking like a sheepdog. It was about obligation and protection. It was about taking care of folks who couldn't take care of themselves. She should just try to relax and take a nap. When she woke up she would pretend to feel significantly better, then she and Howell could rejoin the main group.

She heard the loathsome man returning from the creek, the heavy steps of his boots in the overgrown weeds, then scuffing against the gritty dirt. He rinsed his mouth out with a drink of cold water and spat it on the ground then shuffled over toward her. She could sense him standing above her, an ominous, menacing presence. She could feel the gears grinding in his head and hear his dark thoughts. The side of him of him that followed orders was losing out to the other side. Why was he just standing there above her? Why didn't he sit down somewhere else and keep himself occupied while she rested?

The water bottle lid was unscrewed again and she heard him drinking. There was a spitting sound and a warm spray of water hit her in the face. He'd rinsed his mouth again but this time he chose to spit the water on her instead of on the ground. She was so startled she broke her act, opening her eyes and looking up at him. She was greeted by the grinning visage of a man who had come to a decision, and it was not a decision she would like. He resolutely put the lid back on the water bottle and tossed it casually in the direction of his pack, then returned his gaze to her. There was a smile on his lips. A glazed expression in his eyes.

Barb would have given anything at that moment to have her hands free. With her martial arts background she was confident she could grapple with this guy and kill him with her bare hands. He'd have no idea what hit him. With her injuries, and with her hands bound, she was less certain of her abilities. If he chose to carry out whatever disturbed plan he was concocting, she may be powerless to stop it.

She watched his eyes and saw he'd progressed. He'd passed the point of deciding to act on his thoughts. He was now struggling with how to initiate it. He was trying to get his nerve up. His indecision showed her he was not a career criminal. He was probably not someone who'd even committed a violent crime before in his life. He was just dumb and she was a target of opportunity. He was a weak man and could not resist the impulses of a sick, immature mind.

Then he pounced, dropping heavily onto her body and straddling her. He sat on her stomach with a leg on each side. The impact stunned her, the pain in her ribs taking her breath and making her eyes water.

"You don't have to do this," she said through gritted teeth, finally recovering enough to speak. Her voice was low but firm. Commanding.

He grinned at her, his sense of reason, morality, totally gone. There would be no changing his mind. He was sure where he wanted to go and he would not be deterred. Howell placed one hand on her throat and with his other began unbuttoning her flannel shirt. He could only undo two without shifting his body lower.

"You don't have to do this," she repeated firmly.

Again, he did not answer. He was beyond answering. Not wanting to hear anything else from her, Howell raised his hand from her neck to her mouth and pressed down hard, mashing her lips painfully against her teeth. Howell leaned over and began kissing her neck. Still uncertain how to resolve this, Barb considered forcing herself to become sick again, to throw up on his head. It would not be difficult. His mouth on her neck provoked the same nauseous reaction that memories of the raccoon had.

But how would he react if she became sick? Would it stop him or simply anger him? Would he then beat her, further injuring or debilitating her? Would he kill her?

She studied his balance and his body position. The hand pressing so heavily on her mouth was his support hand. It was the pivot point from which all else was balanced. She jerked her mouth open as wide as it would go. With his weight on that hand, he could not yank it away immediately. Part of his hand slid into her mouth and she latched onto him with her teeth.

She bit him hard, attempting to bite through the flesh of his hand, but she did not hang on. Yanking his hand away from her mouth was purely a reaction and it caused him to lose his balance. Losing the support hand was like snapping the leg off a tripod. He dropped awkwardly across her chest, right on top of her arms and bound hands, pinning them against her.

In order to kiss her neck seconds earlier, he'd scooted his legs down her body and was laying directly on top her. She flung her legs apart now, wrapping them around his waist. When she did that, clutching him in her powerful grip, he reacted by putting both hands on the ground to either side of her body and trying to raise himself off her.

That freed her bound arms from where they'd been trapped between them. She clasped her hands together, yanking them upward and to the left. By sweeping them to the side of her body she knocked one of his hands out from under him. Losing his balance yet again, his body tilted and he fell heavily on her chest. He was not a grappler and had no defense against her moves. Before he could recover, Barb rained devastating elbows down on his head.

He tried desperately to push himself away, getting a hand beneath Barb's chin and pushing. That further dialed up the excruciating pain she was experiencing from her ribs. She did her best to block it out, using her adrenaline to mask it. She focused only on driving elbows down onto his head. Her blows were stunning but not entirely debilitating. Then one split his forehead open and blood began to run between them.

Howell shoved angrily at Barb's face but could not push himself back far enough to line up a punch. Another elbow shattered the bridge of his nose. Howell realized he had to get away from the elbows. He had to put distance between them because the blows were taking a toll. He tried turning his body away from her and she allowed him do it. In fact, she was relieved at his action.

It was a crucial mistake and the one Barb had been waiting for. By rolling over and presenting his back to her, he'd set himself up for the choke. She looped her bound arms over Howell's head and drew her zip tied wrists hard against his throat. Too late, Howell realized his mistake and began clawing at her hands. He pried at her fingers, tried rocking to each side, anything to roll away from her, but her legs trapped him, kept him close against her body.

Using his superior weight advantage he did manage to roll onto his side and then his stomach. That accomplished nothing. Barb rolled with him and, despite getting a face full of dirt, she was now in an even more superior fighting position. Her legs were pressed against the ground, trapped between his body and the earth, which locked them into position. Howell was weakening, his arms pushing feebly against the ground, unable to do anything to counter her attack. Anxious to end this, she painfully arched and extended her back, pulling her cramping biceps as tight as she could, trying with all her might to rip his head from his body.

The act was incredibly painful and she cried out, screaming with the effort, screaming to block the pain messages firing in her body. "Die, you fucker!" Tears welled in her eyes, both from the pain and the satisfaction. She could feel him struggling beneath her but less now. He was dying. He could not escape.

From nowhere, hands were on her back and she knew there was now someone else in the fight. Taking Howell out required everything she had. She had nothing left for another attacker. If they wanted to kill her there was nothing she could do to stop them. She was not a quitter, but she'd given this fight her all. If the man at her back wanted to stick a knife in her, she was uncertain as to whether she could even raise an arm in her own defense.

She could hear a voice but her heart was pounding so loudly it drowned out everything else. It was a freight train roaring through her mind. Through her murderous fury, it then hit her that the hands on her back had not pulled her away from Howell, nor was the voice imploring her to release him. It was just repeating her name, patiently.

Barb whipped her head to the side and saw a face. It was familiar, but in her frenzy, in her rage, it took her a moment to put a name to it. Then she realized it was the boy. Ragus. She looked at him in confusion. Had it been him all along that had been following them, and not her father? Was it him nipping away at the men they left behind? Her arms finally failed her, so flooded with lactic acid she could no longer control them. She sagged onto Howell's body.

"What are you doing here, kid?" she breathed.

He helped her disentangle herself from Howell's body and she flopped painfully over on her back, sucking in a breath. Ragus rolled Howell over, saw the ligature marks from where the zip ties had contacted his throat. There was swelling and deformation there, as if she had crushed his windpipe. His eyes were open, red and bulging. He was dead.

Ragus crouched over Barb. He whipped out a knife and sliced her bonds. "It's okay, Barb. You're safe now."

She stared at Ragus. He was different now. Or seemed different. He had risked his life for her. Had that changed him? Or had it just changed how she saw him?

"It was you all along? Behind us?"

Ragus nodded. He continued to gaze at her in a way she'd never seen from him before. Or never noticed. It was not a boy's look. It was a man's look.

"My dad?"

"I think he's somewhere behind us. Probably not far."

She let out a gush of breath and almost smiled. That was good news. "What the hell kind of name is Ragus, anyway? Where'd you pick that up?"

He smiled at her. "It's my real name. If I told you what it meant, I'd have to kill you."

She did smile at that. "I'd have to let you. I got no fight left."

"Oh yeah," Ragus said, remembering something. He dug a finger into his pocket and pulled out a gold chain, dangling it in front of her. "This yours?"

"You found it," she whispered, touching it lightly with a trembling finger.

Ragus nodded, pleased with himself. Then there was a thud and Ragus' head shook from an impact. His eyes glazed over and he fell forward across Barb's body. At first she had no idea what happened to him, then she saw Lester's grinning visage over the raised buttstock of a rifle.

"I knew there was some son-of-a-bitch following us. I just couldn't get ole Top Cat to believe it. But here he is, in the flesh. He'll have to believe me now. I can't wait to see the look on his face when I haul this asshole into camp."

Barb would not give Lester the satisfaction of seeing her cry. The only other reaction she could muster was to glare at him with pure hatred. She would kill this man one day, perhaps even as personally as she'd just done with Howell, squeezing the life from him with her bare hands.

Lester nudged the dead body beside her with the toe of a dusty work boot. "Shame about Howell," he said, his voice lyrical with mock sincerity. "He was such as an asset to the organization."

Returning his eyes to Barb, he dug a handful of thick zip ties from his pocket and dangled them in front of her face. "Time to hit the road, sweetie."

In this world, or more precisely, in the previous world, there were several things Barb hated with resolute passion. She hated bullies, she hated Brussels sprouts, and she hated being called sweetie. She extended her arms, trembling from the exertion of choking Howell, wishing desperately she had the strength to show this smug bastard just how much she hated that name.

22

The kidnappers stopped at an abandoned convenience store for a late lunch. Every window was shattered and the interior of the store was carpeted with damp-smelling trash. Birds flew in and out of the windows, carrying material for nests. Rats still found edibles where the people couldn't. The area was overrun with them, much to the disgust of the travelers. The flat metal awnings over the pump provided some relief from the sun, though, which was strong even in the midday of fall. They cooked up a couple of boxes of spaghetti in a big pot and squirted a bottle of off-brand ketchup in it for sauce. It was a depressing and sobering meal, a statement of the times.

All eyes turned to the road and the *clopping* sound of approaching horses. Guns were put back down when everyone recognized the returning Lester and the captive Barb. They were confused by the horse Lester led on a tether. A man lay on his belly across the saddle, his hands bound to his feet beneath the belly of the horse. People assumed it to be Howell's body, an indication he'd met some unfortunate fate.

Lester dismounted and cut the rope holding the body in place.

Ragus oozed from the horse like a clump of mud separating itself from the wheel well of a truck and slid to the ground. He rolled to his back and moaned, raising his zip tied hands to rub at the back of his head which had met abruptly with the hard ground.

"I may have hit him a little too hard," Lester said.

"Who the hell is he?" Top Cat demanded, squaring off with Lester.

Lester glared at his boss, not intimidated by the man's stance in the least. "I told you we were being followed. You should have listened."

Top Cat didn't respond, unable to argue with the presence of the man on the ground in front of him. Top didn't take it all at face value, though. He wouldn't put it past a man like Lester to lie right to his face or to orchestrate this whole scenario just to make him look bad. The man had never liked him, had never liked his position within the organization. There had always been jealousy and resentment.

"Where's Howell?"

"Dead. They killed him."

"*They* killed him?" Top Cat confirmed. "As in the boy and the woman?"

Lester nodded.

"Are you sure of that?" It was an open accusation. No subtlety, no inference.

"You think I killed him? How would that benefit me at all?"

Top Cat ignored the question. There would have only been one benefit and that was to make Top Cat look bad, which would have been reason enough. "Where's his body?"

"I'm assuming it's where I left it. Right there beside the road."

"That the best you could do? You couldn't bury him or bring him back for the rest of us to bury?"

Lester shrugged. "He weren't no kin of mine."

"How did he die?" Top Cat asked, sounding like a cop interrogating a suspect. He was certain if he asked enough questions he'd get some telling detail Lester was leaving out.

"They choked him to death."

"You didn't try to stop it?"

"By the time I got there, he was already dead. His eyes and tongue was bulging out like a squashed frog." Lester stuck a hand in his shirt, his face scrunching in pain as he scratched at raw, irritated skin. When he was done, he returned to the same stoicism.

"You knew we were being followed and you used Howell for bait," Top Cat concluded, shaking his head with disgust. "It makes sense now why you wanted someone you didn't like to stay back with her."

Lester bristled at the accusation. "His death is on you," he growled, pointing a finger at his boss. "I warned you and you didn't listen."

"So you hauled this asshole back here to rub it in my face?" Top Cat said, gesturing at Ragus, still floundering around on the ground.

"Yeah, pretty much. And to show these other men who has their backs." Lester acknowledged this loudly, wanting all the assembled men to hear what he had to say.

Top Cat looked hard at Lester, seething. "I know where you're headed with this. You sure you want to go there? You're just determined to keep pushing, aren't you?"

Lester wasn't scared of Top Cat. They were roughly the same size, but Lester was pretty sure he'd been in a lot more scuffles than Top had. Top had been an employee at the college where their boss, Bryan, worked. In the physical plant, some kind of fancy maintenance man or something. Lester had been a pipeliner. His days had been brute physical work. Sometimes there were men you didn't get along with on those jobs and the men settled them with fists. What happened out on those jobsites in the middle of nowhere usually stayed there, even if it resulted in black eyes and bloody noses. Lester was certain if it got physical that he was coming out on top.

He shrugged noncommittally. "I'm not taking it anywhere, Top. This is just where the road leads. I have a feeling we'll end up in the same place, regardless of what we do today."

Top Cat knew Lester was probably right. This had been brewing for a while but had stayed under wraps because neither man wanted to lose his cushy position at Douthat Farms and all the benefits that brought. Their boss would not tolerate infighting and would usually banish both men rather than take sides. But here on the trail, without supervision, this was coming to a head. Top Cat was beginning to wonder if they would both make it back to camp alive. Maybe it was just going to be one of them. The question was just whose body got left in the dirt.

"My advice to you, Lester, is to put this behind you. We got shit to do and you're just wasting time and energy."

The tension was thick. Every man and every captive was mesmerized by the drama playing out in front of them. It was like high noon on the streets of an Old West town. They were like the townspeople watching from windows or board sidewalks, waiting to see if this conversation ended with gunfire.

"So now that you've rubbed it in my face, what are you going to do with that one?" Top Cat nodded at Ragus. "Kill him and leave him for the worms? Hang him from a tree?"

Lester shook his head. "I don't think so. The boy is stout. We could put him to work back on the farm. He might take some of the load off the rest of us."

"If he's that stout he might fight back. He might be more trouble than he's worth."

"Maybe we can cut him in a way that will make him less trouble but still allow him to work. Cut out his tongue and one eyeball or something."

"That's your problem," Top Cat said. "He shits the carpet, you clean it up."

"Understood."

Turning his attention to Barb, Top Cat approached her horse and assessed the woman. "This one doing any better?"

"Good enough. She rode here with no complaint. I reckon she's good for the rest the day, anyway."

"Saddle up!" Top Cat yelled.

"I could use some lunch," Lester protested. "At least some rest. It's been a long damn morning."

Top Cat gave the man a cold look. "You'd have got rest if you hadn't been off on your own mission. Your choice. Now get everyone saddled back up and let's get on the road. We're burning daylight."

23

Riding down the road, Conor had nothing but time on his hands. He was making a good pace and his horse was comfortable with it. Vigilance was so natural to him at this point in his life that his mind wandered, even as his eyes and the limbic region of his brain watched for danger. He could feel in his bones that he was gaining on the kidnappers. Any moment he expected to come around a corner and find Ragus in the road ahead of him, riding along with the Henry rifle slung over his back.

He hoped the boy was doing okay with the killing. He hadn't grown up with violence the way Conor had. It was surely a new thing to him and he'd probably had a hard time pulling the trigger on a man for the first time. It was never easy. Despite training, despite bravado, and despite knowing it was the best course of action, it forever changed you.

Conor had to assume Ragus did it the same way he himself did, by reaching into that inner rage and using it to his advantage. Losing someone who was a vital part of you changed a person. Conor had lost his wife; Ragus had lost his mother. Those experiences left both of them with a vast well of frustration and a sense of injustice. If

Ragus learned to tap those emotions as Conor expected, it would help him manage this cruel and unpredictable world.

There had been a lot of death around Conor when he was growing up. From his earliest childhood, he remembered *the troubles*, or what the rest of the world called the Northern Ireland Conflict. Conor knew it as a war, a guerilla war that was fought in the streets and homes of his town. It affected where he could play as a child and who he could play with. It affected who his mother could talk to in the grocery store and who she avoided. It affected where his father Pat and grandfather Sean could work. Hell, it even affected which pubs the men of the family could drink at. They were Irish Republican Army, or IRA. Conor's father usually referred to those men, their comrades, as *the lads*.

Conor knew the men of his family and *the lads* met frequently, both at the pub and in private homes. When he was younger, he had no idea what they were meeting about. In his child's mind, he just assumed perhaps all adults went to as many meetings as the men of his family did.

He was around seven years old when he was let in on the secret. He popped into the basement one day to see what his father and grandfather were up to down there. Wherever they were, he wanted to be. They were full of stories and played with him. He was also at an age where he was pulling loose from the apron strings, seeking the company of the men in his life more than his mother and grandmother. Conor found them in the back room of the basement that his father used as a workshop. The walls were lined with tools and a beat-up kitchen table set in the center of the floor served as a workbench. His father and grandfather were sitting at that table in old chairs. Pat was using a popsicle stick to take pink goo from a can and smear it around a section of thick water pipe.

"That smells bad," Conor said of the goo.

The men looked up in surprise. Pat looked guilty, like he was about to send Conor back upstairs, but Sean opened an arm to Conor and waved the boy over.

"There's things you need to know if you want to be part of this family, lad," he said. "There's people that feck about without a care in the world and there's people who feel a sense of duty to do what's right. We're a family with a sense of duty to do what's right for us and what's right for our people."

Conor didn't understand much of what was being said at that moment. He had no frame of reference for words like *duty* and he wasn't sure what his grandfather meant about *our people*, unless he was referring to the members of their own family.

Sean told him about *the troubles* and why there was war going on in their country. Although Conor didn't understand the details, his grandfather made a basic concept very clear to him: There's *them*, there's *us*, and you're one of *us*.

Sean and Pat allowed him to watch them assemble a bomb for the first time. When the pink goo, which his dad called *body filler*, completely covered one side, Sean dumped a worn paper sack of steel nuts and ball bearings into a bowl. Conor reached to pick one up but his grandfather grabbed his hand.

"Only with gloves, Conor. You don't want your fingerprints on them."

Conor knew a little about fingerprints from television. The bomb itself was a rather abstract thing to him, though. His grandfather explained that it was like a gun that killed a lot of people at one time.

It was a gray afternoon in his ninth year when Conor saw a man die for the first time. A couple of squaddies, British soldiers, were raiding a house in Conor's neighborhood. They didn't find the man they were looking for, only managing to break a few things around the household and make his young wife cry.

"Those fuckers," Conor's dad cursed. He stood fuming in the front window, ranting about the way they rolled in like an occupying army and disrupted the lives of decent people. Then he disappeared for about five minutes, running next door to Conor's grandfather's house. When he came back, he was sweating and panting. Conor asked what he'd been up to but his father didn't answer.

His grandfather showed up and the three of them watched the street through a gap in the pulled curtains. Conor didn't know what he was watching for, only that his grandfather had waved him over and told him to watch.

"They're leaving," his dad whispered.

"Shhhh!" his grandfather hissed.

The soldiers climbed back in their vehicle. When the driver climbed in, there was a loud pop, then a deeper rumble that shook the entire house. Sean nodded with satisfaction. Conor would later understand, as he dissected the bombing from a professional's perspective, that his dad had used a quick and dirty method to take out the vehicle. He'd taped a pipe bomb to the fuel tank and tied it into the brake light circuit. When the driver pressed the brake pedal, it applied voltage to the triggering device and detonated the bomb.

"Close the curtain now, lad," Sean said.

Hoping to see more action, Conor ran up to his room and looked out from his window. The military vehicle the squaddies had driven into the neighborhood was aflame, all of the windows blown out by the explosion. A soldier, his clothes burned and his face soot-blackened, was crawling up the sidewalk, trying to put distance between himself and the burning vehicle. He left a trail of blood behind him. There were bones exposed from both legs and an arm hung awkwardly from a joint that didn't exist previously.

When the soldier got as far as he could go, he rolled onto his back and began screaming for help. He continued to scream for several minutes and no one came to help him. Conor wondered why. He went down to the kitchen where his dad was sharing a toast with his father.

"There's a man hurt in the road," Conor said. "Should we go help him?"

Pat and Sean looked at each other, the smiles fading to seriousness. Sean took Conor up in his arms.

"We don't help squaddies, Conor," his grandfather said. "We're at war and they're the enemy we're at war with. When we make bombs, this is why we make them. We take the bastards out one at a time until they decide to get out of Northern Ireland and leave us the fuck alone."

It wasn't until that very moment that Conor understood the purpose of the bombs he watched Sean and Pat make. It was not a fun activity he and the family did, like working on an old motor bike or repairing a car. It was not a craft project. The bombs were tools of murder or justice depending on your viewpoint, and bombs were the family business. It all came together at that point.

"Aye, that bloody screaming," Pat said, slamming his glass on the counter. He walked to the front door and stared out.

"We should probably disappear for a while," Sean said. "There'll be more of them here soon and this was right on our doorstep. They'll go house to house."

"I'll be damned," Pat muttered, his attention captured by something outside.

"What?"

"Mrs. O'Kane."

"What about her?" Sean asked, wandering up to the door, Conor still in his arms.

"She's out there in the street trying to help the bastard," Pat said incredulously. "What does she not fucking understand?"

Conor could see now that was exactly what she was doing. The old widow next door, Mrs. O'Kane, was crouched in the street comforting the British soldier. Sirens could be heard in the distance. Help would be there soon but the poor bastard would probably die anyway. She was just trying to ease his suffering, to prevent him from having to die alone.

"Fucking slag," Sean hissed, setting Conor down at his feet and pushing by his son.

Conor and his father watched from the doorway as Sean strode boldly across the yard, crashed through their sagging, peeling gate, and stomped into the street. Mrs. O'Kane watched him curiously. In front of God and the entire neighborhood, Sean whipped a revolver from his waistband and shot the squaddie in the forehead. The soldier's screaming stopped abruptly, only to be replaced by Mrs. O'Kane's.

Sean spun on her and aimed the gun at her head, his face screwed into a mask of rage. "I suggest you get back to your house, bitch, and you keep your damned mouth shut."

The way the words slithered from his mouth, oozing with venom, made it clear that he was not to be argued with. Mrs. O'Kane stood and backed away from Sean, finally turning and running to her home. She slammed the door behind her.

It was a complicated moment for Conor. One moment his grandfather was carrying him in his arms, hugging him and talking to him with nothing but affection. Less than a minute later, he murdered a man in the street and was threatening an old lady who gave Conor macaroon bars and Galaxy Truffles. He wasn't certain how to process that experience at the time but it was a pivotal point in his life. He was certain that he probably presented such an enigma to his own daughter when she learned who he truly was. He was a loving and jovial man who killed for a living.

The men of Conor's family disappeared for a few weeks after that bombing but were never formally accused. No squaddies raided the house and terrorized his mother. No one ratted out his grandfather for topping the man in the street. Conor expected that to be the end of the story but that was not the case.

While Pat and Sean were laying low and visiting relatives in Cork, a group of *the lads* paid Mrs. O'Kane a visit. They took her for a ride and everyone in the neighborhood watched her go willingly but she was never seen again. Rendering aid to the mortally wounded enemy of the people was a betrayal *the lads* could not overlook, even from a kindly old widow.

∼

CONOR RODE AT A BRISK CANTER, secure in the knowledge he was on the right path because he was still finding the broken branches Ragus left for him. The boy was smart enough to not bother with them during the uneventful sections of road where no direction was needed, but he was meticulous in his route-marking anywhere clarification was needed. Despite the rapid pace, Conor scanned for threats with a practiced eye, weapons handy, and ready to steer his horse into the brush at the first sign of trouble.

Then the corpse caught his attention.

Conor remained in the road at first, sitting on his horse and taking in the scene where Howell's body lay. He watched and listened. His horse became skittish, perhaps sensing death, but Conor forced it closer to the body. He examined it from horseback initially and, even at that distance, cause of death was clear. This poor bastard had been strangled.

It raised a lot of questions. Had Ragus killed the man? Everyone he'd killed so far had been shot with the Henry, a .22 caliber round or two ending their life. Why was this one different? Why had he gotten special treatment? If this had been Ragus, there could only be one reason for breaking his mode of operation. Something had gone wrong.

Conor slid from the saddle, rifle in his hand. While most of the area was overgrown with weeds, this spot where people used to park was sandy dirt and was enough the grass was slow to grow back. There was a fire circle of blackened stones. A couple of crushed beer cans with some of the paint burned off lay among stubs of partially burned firewood.

Starting at the body and walking in widening circles, Conor examined the ground thoroughly. Near the body, the silty soil was compressed and footprints were obscured. It was as if someone might have laid there or rolled around on the ground. Closer to the road there were indications that a lot of horses had stopped here. A lot of grass had been pulled up, as if the horses had a moment to grab a bite while their riders stood still. Their shod hooves pawed at the ground while they stood there but it didn't appear they all dismounted. Most of the horses never left the shoulder of the road.

Conor returned to the body and examined it closer. He rolled it to its side and pulled up the shirt as he had with the previous body to look for signs of livor mortis. Beneath the body a glint of gold caught his eye and he frowned. He brushed at the dirt, removed a tactical glove, and plucked a delicate chain from the soil, a charm dangling from it. It was the shamrock pendant he'd given his daughter on her sixteenth birthday. It had been a reminder to hang onto her Irish heritage. She'd been wearing it all the time lately, figuring she needed all the luck she could get.

There was the sound of movement in the brush and Conor reacted before he even took the time to process what it might be. He could figure that out from the safety of cover. He rolled away from the body and scrambled behind a tree, throwing his rifle up, ready to fire. The sound continued and Conor tried to interpret it. It sounded like a man moving through thick brush.

He waited several moments, safety off, but the noise didn't get closer. He wondered if it was a bear or deer. Conor slipped from behind the tree, his rifle at high ready, and moved steadily across the clearing, barely even breathing. He took cover at another tree and listened. The noise was still there, but moving no closer.

The rustling continued coming from the same direction. It was close but the position didn't vary. Conor stalked through the underbrush, moving silently toward the noise while praying he didn't run up on a snake. The bastards were thick along rivers and he wasn't sure he could contain a childish scream if he were to step on one. Even a big, bad, bomb builder had his weaknesses.

There was a snort and a whinny, telling Conor there was a horse and it had picked up his scent. It still didn't tell him if there was a rider on it, or worse, a rider who was now on foot and watching him at that very moment, waiting for a clear shot. When he finally saw branches moving, Conor could see that a leather rein was tied to a branch at chest level, where a rider might naturally tie it as he dismounted. The branch was high enough off the ground that when the horse plucked at the sparse grass it tugged on the branch.

While that solved the puzzle of the noise, it didn't solve the issue of the missing rider. On high alert, Conor watched the woods for any movement, knowing the rider might he camouflaged. Hell, he could be wearing a ghillie suit for all Conor knew. His eyes returned to the horse, which had lowered its head again, trying to reach the next tuft of grass.

With its head lowered, Conor got a better view of the saddle. He didn't recognize it but he certainly recognized the gear tied to it. There was the pack he'd given to Ragus as a go bag. A half-full water bottle hung from a strap looped over the saddle horn. He recognized that too. Conor approached the horse, stroking its flanks to reassure it. He was tempted to call out the boy's name but he couldn't make himself do it. He didn't want to call attention to himself in case there were other people around.

He removed the boy's gear, stashing it in the bushes and covering it with a garbage bag from a side pocket of the go bag. He knew it was there because he'd put it there when he packed the bag for the boy the first time. He covered the gear with the saddle, the saddle blanket, and then released the horse. There would be more of them. The only thing that worried him was the possibility that the boy might be wandering around here somewhere and that Conor was stranding him by releasing the horse, but it just didn't seem likely. He had to assume that, after all this distance, the boy was either on Barb's trail or dead. He'd also not found the Henry rifle. He had to assume it was with the boy. At least he hoped so.

The condition of the body told him it was only a few hours old. Perhaps less than two. Maybe today was the day this all ended.

Before mounting his horse again, Conor rechecked his gear. He confirmed mags for his primary and secondary weapons, confirmed the presence of his fixed blade knife and his tactical folder, checked for his tourniquet and blowout kit. He unfastened the flap on each pouch on his plate carrier and confirmed that smoke, flash-bang, and fragmentation grenades were where he expected them to be. That was shit he'd never have if not for his previous line of work. He accepted lots of forms of payment. Sometimes people had an off-the-books job and the form of payment they had at hand was munitions. Conor loved munitions.

When he was certain his kit was in order, he dug into his pack and removed a long canvas bag with a drawstring at the top. He unfastened it and drew out a tactical tomahawk. It clipped onto the back of his plate carrier with the handle accessible above his shoulder. It could be awkward to wear in stealthy situations, the handle snagging on branches and other gear, so he only used it for special occasions. It reminded him of Celtic warriors and the hand-to-hand combat that was his heritage. He expected this to go hand-to-hand. He expected to wield that tomahawk before the day was over. Getting his daughter back and inflicting justice upon the men who took her would be one of those special occasions.

∼

Riding at a brisk pace, the spare horse following on a long rope, Conor studied the GPS strapped to his forearm. Knowing his daughter was close by, he wanted to be as familiar as possible with the terrain. He wanted to know what lay ahead of him in terms of advantages and disadvantages. They were approaching a more mountainous area carved by a river gorge. The nearly vertical hills were lined with hemlocks, poplars, and oaks. With this steep terrain, most residents lived in the bottom of the valley, near the road. The chances of encountering random strangers and locals was getting higher. That was the last thing he wanted. He hoped the very sight of him, a heavily-armed and hopefully terrifying rider of the apocalypse, discouraged conversation.

He'd gone perhaps seven miles PDM—Post Dead Man—when he found horse manure on the road that looked significantly fresher than anything he'd seen up to that point. Without a thought, he climbed off his horse and nudged it with his toe. Whatever information that gave him prompted him to drop to his knees and sink a finger into the fragrant horse apple.

It was still warm.

No expert on the rate of heat loss in equine droppings, Conor nevertheless interpreted this as a sign he was closing in. He sprang back onto his horse and took off. Every time he got to a rise in the road he'd raise his binoculars and scan the path ahead of him. Most of the time he saw nothing. Still expecting nothing, his heart skipped a beat when he saw there was indeed something filling the glass of his binoculars. It was a large group of riders and pack horses. He'd found them.

"Got you, fuckers."

He studied them as best he could through the binoculars, trying to glean any useful piece of information he could, but he was too far back. He studied his GPS. The riders were several miles ahead of him. They'd be crossing a bridge over a decent-sized river before the day was out. The bridge looked like it might make an excellent spot to ambush them. The lines on the topo map of his GPS indicated extremely steep ridges on either side of the road. It was a perfect chokepoint.

This would take some thought. He couldn't set some kind of trap that might put the captured folks at risk. He would have to get more intel. He needed to see how the group traveled, how the kidnappers rode in relation to their cargo of women.

Part of him thought the best way to run this operation was at a distance. Figure out who the leaders were and remove them with precise shots from cover. He was comfortable shooting this particular rifle to four hundred yards. He could probably drop several of the men before they figured out what was going on if they were close enough to each other. That would be cold and surgical. It would be *too* removed from the fight.

But it wasn't just about that. Sniper shots would give them warning and they would hole up. This could become a long, drawn out affair, a battle of tenacity. Worse yet, it could become a hostage situation where they started killing captives to force him to give himself up. He couldn't fight that way.

There were no rules of engagement, no mission parameters. He would wade into this fight. He would let the men see there was one killer and one executioner. He would free his daughter and, if he was alive, free Ragus. They would fight together. As much as he wanted to spare his daughter the violence, he knew a little about how a child of his would process her experience. She needed vengeance to put this to bed. She needed satisfaction and closure. That would come with spilled blood. That would come with knowing that the men who had taken her could never, ever do it again, to her or anyone else.

24

The blow to his head had not significantly injured Ragus. He briefly lost consciousness after he was struck and woke strapped across the horse. Most of his current pain was due to the awkward riding position. He felt like his ribs had been crushed and it had been difficult to breathe while in that position, but knew those were not permanent injuries. He'd known worse pain. He also intuitively understood it was to his advantage to pretend to be more injured than he really was. Perhaps it was instinct, perhaps it was the influence of movies and television, but as long as he appeared to be somewhat addled he would not be considered a threat and no one would watch him as closely.

When the prisoners mounted up, being tied to their saddles again, Ragus was allowed to ride in the proper position. No one prevented him from riding beside Barb but conversation was prohibited. He learned this the hard way when he asked Barb a question and one of the kidnappers shot him with an airsoft gun. While it was not a life-threatening injury, it stung enough to serve as a deterrent.

Barb and Ragus patiently established a means of communicating with whispers, hand signs, and nods. Ragus found that being there beside Barb made it all worth it. If he had to do it all again, he would.

If he had to die for her today, or another day, he would. He'd never had a girlfriend before and was inexperienced in such matters, but he knew what he felt. Seeing her and looking into her eyes reaffirmed for him that he loved this girl. Now there was only the small matter of convincing her to see things the same way. Then, of course, there was the other matter of getting back home alive.

Through their discreet communications, Ragus managed to tell Barb he had not seen or directly spoken to her father but had left clear route indicators along his path. If he was on their trail there was no way he could miss the signs Ragus had left. Barb asked him how he could be so certain but Ragus didn't want to explain how he'd used dead bodies as pointers. Of course, knowing how tough this girl was, he wondered if she'd even bat an eye at it.

She told him about the kidnappers who had been left behind for various reasons and never caught back up with the group, and thought it must be a sign her father was on her trail. When Ragus didn't respond, she gave him a sideways glance.

Ragus pointed at himself and nodded, admitting he killed those men. An unusual look crossed Barb's face. It was one thing to know a man had risked his life to try and save you, pursuing you for days on foot and horseback. It was quite another to know a man had taken lives for you. The boy had crossed a line for her and it was a line he could not cross back. It was a gesture she could never forget.

It reminded her of something her father said, commenting how Ragus reminded him of himself when he was younger. Barb could see that now. She could see the determination, the willingness to kill when it had to be done, and his unfailing loyalty to family and friends. That was Conor. Apparently it was Ragus too.

Barb offered him information he knew was important when he heard it, despite not having the tactical wherewithal to ask the right questions. She pointed out who was in charge of this group and where she thought they were going. She told him she'd overheard they were to be used for farm labor and should not be injured. Ragus was uncertain as to whether that commitment to not harming prisoners extended to him. It clarified for him that until the moment to strike was at hand, his best odds of survival came from being as little trouble to these men as possible. If he became a pain in the ass, they'd just shoot him and leave his body behind.

That raised the question for him of why he wasn't already dead. "Why didn't that guy kill me when he caught me?" Ragus whispered.

Without looking toward him, Barb whispered back, "The two lead guys have a beef with each other. I think the number two guy wants to take out the number one guy. He'd been claiming for the last day or two we were being followed but the number one guy, they call him Top Cat, wouldn't send anyone back to check. The second guy, Lester, decided to leave me and that rapey bastard behind as bait. He only brought you back to prove a point to the rest of the men. He wanted to prove he was right and Top Cat was wrong."

Ragus let some time pass, making sure they weren't drawing any attention. "Do you think the disagreement between them is anything we can exploit?"

Barb made a sound of dismissal.

"You don't think we could get in Lester's head?" Ragus hissed.

"I'm going to get in his head alright," Barb replied faintly. "With a rock, a knife, or whatever the fuck else I can find. We've tangled already and I won't go home until I've spilled his blood."

The comment was a reminder to Ragus he shouldn't see Barb as a scared victim here. While she was indeed on the losing side of this situation right now, she was probably taking it more in stride than he was. She seemed braver and more determined. It occurred to him she might not accept victory by escape. She might require victory by conquest. She was, after all, her father's daughter.

They fell into silence. Everyone in the group, captive and captor, was lost in the mire of their own thoughts. Ragus lost track of time until he noticed the sun on the shoulder of the mountain, the light going orange and angular before fading. His watch said 6 PM. The warmth of the day quickly disappeared. They were due for a heavy frost soon. It would be unpleasant if it came tonight.

They came upon a massive suspension bridge spanning a turbulent river. Exploring the possibility of him and Barb escaping by jumping off the bridge, Ragus looked over the edge and quickly thought better of it. It was a very long drop to a boulder-strewn river. It was nearly a certain death. Ragus didn't mind the odds being against him but there were no odds there at all.

The riders at the front of the pack halted on the bridge and Top Cat rode back to face his captives.

"We're staying here tonight," he announced. "I'm putting guards on either end of the bridge. Should you think jumping is an option, think again. You wouldn't survive it. You'll be cut loose from your bonds as soon as someone can get to you. We'll bring food when it's ready. Sleep is wherever you find it."

Ragus didn't have any sleeping gear. He expected he'd stretch out on the hard pavement and try to stay as warm as he could. No way was he asking Barb to cuddle up with him to stay warm. The look she'd give him in response might be colder than anything this fall night had to offer.

Shortly, a gruff man with a hunting knife came around and cut loose the leg that was bound to a stirrup. With a flick of the blade, he severed the zip ties binding each of their wrists. Ragus rubbed his, trying to restore the circulation and ease the cramping. He bent over, stretching his back and then his legs. The riding had been miserable.

"I don't know how much more of this I can take," he mumbled.

Barb shrugged impassively. "You'll take it as long as you have to. Toughen up, buttercup."

He'd meant the remark as more of a conversation starter than anything else, still not entirely comfortable with this bold young woman. Stung yet again by her remarks, he sat down against the guardrail and withdrew into himself.

"You can't be sensitive if you're going to be around me," Barb said, taking a seat beside him. "I've got my own type of people skills. They weed out the squishy bastards."

"I've noticed," Ragus said, not meeting her eye.

There was a lot Barb could have said at that moment. She considered her options. She could have thanked him for coming after her. She could have acknowledged how well he did in tracking her and in dealing with the men he encountered. It wasn't her way, though. She was appreciative but felt this was not the time to let down her guard and have a kumbaya moment with this young man who was clearly so enamored with her. She'd thank him when they were safely riding home.

"I would expect my dad tonight if he hasn't encountered trouble," Barb said. "If the boy you sent to him relayed the message and he got on the road the same day, he probably wasn't far behind."

"I left him horses and directions," Ragus said. "As long as nobody took them from him."

That brought a smile to Barb's face. "No one took them from him, lad. There's no one out there more dangerous than my father."

"That's comforting, in a strange way."

"It is, isn't it?" Barb agreed. "I feel exactly the same way."

The smell of wood smoke reached them. Whoever was on cooking duty was starting a fire. Other men were refilling water bottles, collecting firewood, and setting up a secure perimeter.

"What should we do if your dad shows up?"

"*When*," Barb clarified. "*When* he shows up."

"So what should we do *when* he shows up?"

"Join him."

"We shouldn't take advantage of the distraction and make a break for it?"

Barb shook her head. "He's not coming here to create a distraction so we can run. He's coming for revenge. He won't stop until every kidnapper is dead. So to answer your question, you take up a weapon and join the fight. Just don't get in his way."

Ragus nodded.

"You look scared," Barb observed.

"I am, a little," Ragus admitted.

"No shame in acknowledging that," Barb said. "Best to be honest. Just don't let fear control you. You're braver than you think."

"If fear controlled me, I'd be dead already."

"Good point."

"Stick with me," Barb said. "We'll fight our way out of this together. Just stay on alert. Watch for anything unusual, any indications he's out there and the fight is starting."

Ragus frowned.

"What is it?" she asked.

"I'm not sure I chased you all this way to let you get killed. I'm not anxious to let you get in the middle of a gunfight without a gun."

She raised an eyebrow. "First, it's not up to any man to *let* me do a damn thing. I do as I please. Second, I'll have a gun by the end of the fight."

Ragus looked at the ground and shook his head. She understood what he was thinking. He was letting the heart crowd out the gut. She put a hand on his forearm. Ragus moved his eyes to it but didn't let them meet hers.

"I know what you're thinking. Don't let this get into your head. You relax, you rest, while you can. You fight the fight when it's in front of you. There's nothing to be gained by trying to fight it now inside your head. Take it a minute at a time. That's all you can do."

"I'm still not sure about this."

"It's not up to you to be sure," Barb said. "It's only up to you to fight your best fight. And I recommend staying out of my way."

She smiled at Ragus and he knew she wanted him to smile back but he couldn't do it. His gut was twisted with anticipation, anxiety, and worry.

25

Conor's unique line of work, building specialized weapons and explosive devices, brought him in contact with a wide range of experts and operatives. Being a gregarious Irishman, he liked a good story, but was also interested in tidbits of information he might utilize in a future project. He recalled a story he once heard from an operative, a former member of the U.S. Special Forces who had been involved in an operation in Afghanistan.

The operator, whose name was Rich, was part of a small team being pursued by a group of Taliban riding in *technicals*, which were often a Toyota pickup with a mounted weapon in the back. Rich and his team were on foot, travelling through a narrow gorge with little room for anything but the road both they and the technicals were following. When it was clear they were not going to escape the Taliban forces without an engagement that could end badly for his vastly outnumbered team, Rich called out to his team to deploy a BFR.

His team, all highly experienced field operators and soldiers, looked at him in confusion. When Rich didn't elaborate, just continuing to stare at his team, one of them finally broke the deadlock.

"Dude, we don't have time for this bullshit. What the hell is a BFR?"

Rich broke into a grin. "Big Fucking Rock."

It took them less than five minutes of rushed searching to find the right rock, which was probably the size of two Volkswagen beetles welded bottom to bottom. The rock was big enough to put a serious hurting on any pursuing Toyota but small enough that the team of men, with their legs and backs in it, should be able to dislodge it.

The men waited until the first technical was crawling its way around the corner. They picked this particular section of road because it was steep enough that the rock should roll into the road and then continue rolling back down the road. This removed some of the burden of trying to time the falling rock exactly right in order to crush the technical against the opposite wall. This way, even if they missed, the rock would keep going down the road until it wedged itself against a vehicle, hopefully cutting off all vehicle traffic.

They gave themselves a head start in their effort to dislodge the rock. They didn't know how firmly seated it would be. Rich lined his team up with their backs against the rock and everyone planted their legs wherever they could find a foothold.

"Let's give it a test push first. See if we can budge the fucking thing."

The test push exceeded their expectations. With their adrenaline pumping, each man shoved with all he had and the precariously balanced rock began tumbling down the hill.

"What do you assholes not understand about a *test* push?" Rich growled.

The operators all fell on their backs as the rock shoved out from behind them and started rolling, seriously gaining momentum with each revolution, going from zero to thirty miles to eighty miles per hour in mere seconds. They lay on their stomachs now, staring over the ledge and watching the massive boulder bound toward the approaching technical.

They experienced a moment of panic when the roundish boulder passed across the road and started up the other side of the mountain.

They thought they had overshot their target, the boulder possibly rolling up the opposing incline and becoming lodged there, but it did not. Without losing speed it returned to its channel in the road much like a bowling ball settling into the gutter.

The approaching technicals had seen the boulder now. At least the first vehicle had, because it was trying to back up, but the second vehicle had no clue what was going on. The first backed into the second, causing the driver in the lead vehicle to stick his head out and scream at the second driver. The second driver, unaware of the impending danger, had his own head out the window, both questioning and cursing the lead driver. By the time he noticed the approaching boulder it was too late.

The lead driver had been focused on the man behind them, trying to get him to move, and did not allow himself enough time to escape the oncoming rock. The boulder was moving like a freight train and crushed the technical flat like an alcoholic drywaller crushing his first beer can of the day. Rich thought the first technical may act as a wedge and bring the boulder to a stop but it did not. In fact, the boulder barely slowed at all, ramping over the technical and snapping off the heavy gun mount. The two Taliban in the second vehicle burst from each door as if they were spring-loaded just as the massive boulder crunched into their cab.

The second impact slowed the boulder considerably and it only took a few more tumbles, snapping the gun off the second technical before dropping off the back of the vehicle and coming to a stop dead center in the road. Rich and his team let out a small cheer. Their cry of victory echoed against the stony walls of the canyon and drew the attention of the half-dozen Taliban now gathered around the boulder. Rich caught this in his binoculars.

"They've seen us. Somebody drop those assholes."

They managed to hit most of the six and even place a few rounds in the technicals stopped further back before Rich called for a cease fire. "I don't think they're coming after us. Let's get the hell out of here and call for an evac."

The tale of Rich deploying the BFR became legendary among the special operations community. Over the course of the war, the story spread to where it eventually reached the ears of Conor Maguire. While Conor was not certain a boulder was the right tool for the job, he was certain something similar was in the cards. Disrupt the camp and cause chaos. There was a reason some folks called him the Master of Mayhem.

∼

BY THE TIME Conor reached the bridge, the sun was just dropping over the horizon. The kidnappers had stopped but he couldn't tell how they were dispersed. Wanting a better vantage point, he looked for elevated positions. This being the steep Appalachian Mountains, folks lived and worked on terraced shelves as they did in mountain communities all around the world, whether it was Nepal, Peru, or West Virginia.

On a bulldozed terrace high above the road were the rusty hulks of heavy equipment and box trailers. Conor found a winding road that led up the mountain and forced his horse upward at the fastest pace it could manage. His heart was racing now. The battle was upon him. He had to force himself to be strategic and methodical, to not just wade in shooting and stabbing. It was hard, though. Barb may be a woman now but she was forever a child in his mind. He saw her at four years old, a motherless child being fed by a father who did the best he could to fill all roles while never certain he was doing any of it right. With no other family in America, they were close beyond words. She was not just his daughter, she was his life.

The horse was panting when they reached the gravel parking lot carved into the slope of the mountain. It turned out to be the repair shop for a mining operation. It reminded Conor of his own facility. A yellow pipe gate blocked a road that led further back into the property. Worn out and broken down equipment was crammed everywhere on the site.

He eased to the weedy edge of the bank and stared down on the encampment. Using binoculars, he could tell the prisoners had been forced out onto the bridge, the captors taking advantage of the natural impoundment. A single guard was on the far end. Below Conor, men were building a bonfire and preparing a meal. The horses had been tied off to a single rope at the side of the camp. The saddles had been removed and stacked nearby. Except for the two men guarding either end of the bridge, it looked like everyone was around the campfire with a paper plate in their hands.

A quick count confirmed that the numbers Ragus had provided on the foreheads of the dead men were fairly accurate. Perhaps fifteen kidnappers remained.

Fifteen dead men walking.

A yellow front-end loader, massive and covered in coal dust, stood to Conor's left. He twisted the lever handle on the cab and pried open a reluctant door. He climbed inside, released the parking brake, and the machine started to roll. He stopped it using the foot brake and reset the parking brake. The shop door was open, the lock having been hacked off. Conor entered cautiously, shining his light around. He found a bin of shop rags and a couple of greasy moving blankets. He took them back outside and crammed them into the cab of the loader.

Scouring the lot, he found a half-dozen worn-out heavy equipment tires and manhandled them over to the edge of the embankment looking down on the kidnappers' camp. He stood each tire upright and used a rock wedge to prevent it from rolling off the edge. Inside the shop, he found two five-gallon buckets of a highly flammable liquid used for cleaning parts. Back outside, he splashed the solvent into the absorbent materials packed into the cab of the loader and then onto each of the loader's tires. He took the remaining solvent and poured a puddle into the bottom of each tire. Not satisfied this would give him the flame he wanted, he found a bucket of hydraulic fluid and added that to the mix to thicken things up.

He went back into the shop and looked for a propane torch for lighting his goodies. Most shops had one for heating stubborn bolts. While searching for it, he found a beautiful ball peen hammer. As a machinist, a craftsman, he had an appreciation for a good tool. As a maker of tools of murder and mayhem, he had an appreciation for the destructive abilities of a good hammer. He tucked it into his belt.

When he found the torch, he turned on the gas and hit the red igniter button. A blue flame burst to life. Conor checked that his horse was ready and confirmed his weapons were where he expected them to be. He used the torch to ignite the solvent soaked materials in the cab of the loader and then released the parking brake. The loader eased forward, dropping over the embankment and picking up speed as it freewheeled down the mountain.

Without waiting for it to hit, Conor lit the puddle in each tire, then started them rolling down the mountain. The dispersal of the kidnappers and the captives could not have been more to his advantage. Trapped on the bridge, the captives were protected by the steel guardrails. The kidnappers, on the other hand, were completely exposed to the barrage of missiles bearing down on them.

Conor tossed the torch to the ground and sprang onto the back of his horse. It was time. The hour of these men's deaths was upon them and they had no idea the angel of death was coming. He galloped down the gravel road to the base of the mountain. The gloaming of twilight had crept up on him, the shadows lengthening until they yawed toward night. When the road leveled off, the horse found its rhythm. Conor readied himself. Once the men saw the flaming toys he'd sent their way, they would suspect an attack. They were probably getting ready for him but there was no way they could be ready enough. There was no way they could stop him.

26

Barb and Ragus sat against the guardrail on the bridge picking at soggy paper plates of boiled sausages and canned green beans. It was a nasty meal they ate only for the energy to fight back when the time came. When they heard sounds coming from the mountain above them, they first thought it was a rock slide. Then they saw the flames.

"What the...?" Ragus muttered, spotting the loader barreling down the mountain fully engulfed in flames.

The kidnappers had seen it too, realized it was headed directly for them, and scattered from their positions around the fire. Nearly at the bottom of the mountain, the loader got sideways and a tire dug in. The machine flipped and starting rolling down the hill. Nearly 40,000 pounds of steel bounced and tumbled, shaking the ground. The burning tires spewed molten, flaming rubber in all directions, starting scores of brush fires on the hillside.

"There's more of them!" yelled someone as the first tire came bouncing down the hillside.

Anyone who'd ever rolled a tire knew that they started out rolling, then began bouncing as they covered long distances at high speed. A four foot high truck tire rolled through the fire and into a cluster of kidnappers, forcing them to dive away from the unpredictable missiles. One unfortunate man was hit square in the chest by a bouncing tire and knocked nearly twenty feet. He staggered back to his feet, stunned and injured but alive.

The tires that hit the bridge, trees, or abandoned vehicles eventually rolled onto their sides, sprouting massive pyres that disgorged broad clouds of dense black smoke.

"It's him!" Barb hissed. "Stay down."

She and Ragus flattened themselves against the side of the bridge, taking advantage of the only cover available to them. She called to JoAnn. "It's my dad! Come here."

Word spread among the captives that it was a rescue attempt and people stood, looking for aid.

"Get down, you idiots!" Ragus yelled. "You'll get your ass shot!"

After the loader crashed and all the flaming tires stalled, the sounds of chaos dropped suddenly and ominously. There was the crackle of flames, the rush of water beneath the bridge, and the sound of cicadas chirping on the looming mountainsides. There was the murmur of nervous men and the crying of fearful prisoners. There was the rattle of men readying weapons. Then there was a new sound. An ominous tapping that began like an impatient man rapping a fingernail on a wooden tabletop. It gradually grew louder, turning into the clatter of approaching hooves on the roadway.

Conor burst through a column of smoke like a demon evicted from Hell. The reins of his horse were clenched in his teeth and he held a rifle in one hand, his pistol in the other. Flames from the burning tires reflected off his skin and illuminated the smoke around him. People were too stunned to react but Conor didn't hesitate. He opened fire, his rifle spraying three-round bursts toward the scattering kidnappers. Some fell screaming, rounds sawing their flesh, while others threw themselves toward any available cover.

His horse reared, overwhelmed by everything going on around it— the flames, the bursts of gunfire, the screaming from all sides. Grabbing for the saddle horn, Conor dropped his rifle but the sling caught it. Without breaking stride, he opened up with the handgun. The rail-mounted laser shot a piercing red beam into the night, stabbing through the smoke and finding targets. For several men, the appearance of that glowing red dot on their chest or forehead was the last thing they saw.

"Father!" came a voice through the night.

Barb! He'd found her.

"*Iníon!*" Conor bellowed, the Irish word for daughter. He'd been raised to speak Irish Gaelic and had passed it on to his daughter. He spun his horse in her direction and galloped, still shooting.

Conor did not lose focus that getting his daughter back was not the only objective of this mission anymore. It was also about devastating this group of men who had the audacity to take the only thing of value in his life. It was unacceptable and intolerable. It warranted a death sentence with no mercy and no reprieve.

When the handgun ran empty and the slide locked open, Conor ejected the mag, dropped the slide on an empty chamber, and slapped home a full mag. He looked for his daughter through the smoke, the flickering firelight, and the gray night, spotting her by the bridge railing, waving a hand. He threw the pistol underhanded, letting it clatter to the pavement and slide to her feet. Before he waded back into the fight, he saw her retrieve the pistol and chamber a round.

With Barb armed, Conor spun his horse and sprinted back into it. A hand shot from the smoke and grabbed him by the leg, trying to yank him from the saddle. He raised a heavy boot and stomped the figure square in the face, and the man's nose gave way. Conor thought the man would retreat cradling his broken face but the man had more fight in him. He dropped a hand to his holster and came back with a handgun.

Before he could level the gun on him, Conor yanked the tomahawk off his back and slashed downward in a single motion, cutting across the back of the man's wrist, nearly severing his hand. The useless hand could not hold the pistol and the man screamed, trying to hold his hand on. Blood flowed between his fingers like squeezing wine from a sponge.

Conor wasn't done with him. On his back swing, the hook end of his tactical tomahawk caught the man in the temple, penetrating his skull like a finger jammed through a Styrofoam cup. The man's face froze and he fell over dead.

Conor spun his horse, checking his surroundings, a hoof slamming down on the dead man's face. There was more yelling in the smoke and chaos. Bullets whizzed by him but he wasn't sure if they were aimed or fired blindly into the dense smoke. Conor nudged his horse into a run and sprinted between a pair of burning tires, their smoke forming a solid curtain. Men were in this direction, he could hear them.

Bursting through the wall of smoke, Conor found himself squarely in the sights of an AK clenched in the hands of a terrified young man.

"Oh shit!" Conor tried to raise his leg and slide off the back of the horse, putting it between him and the shooter. No sooner was his leg yanked from the stirrup than the AK opened up in full-auto. Conor's horse flinched and trembled as rounds zipped up its side.

The horse stumbled, then bolted into the night to die, leaving Conor exposed. With the tomahawk already in his hand, Conor desperately heaved it in the direction of the shooter, knowing the whirling blade would force him into evasive action. The man broke off his aim to sidestep the tomahawk. As he did, Conor whipped up his own rifle and pulled off a three-shot burst that plowed up the man's chest and knocked him on his ass.

A standing man was a dead man so Conor stayed moving, sending bursts of gunfire in the direction of any man he saw. He wanted to keep the atmosphere chaotic and terrifying. He did not want to give them time to calm down and think. The biggest flames came from the burning loader and it drew his eye. A trio of men was gathered there and he sent rounds in their direction, forcing them into cover behind the burning machine. He whipped out a fragmentation grenade and tossed it at them, dodging behind a tree as it detonated.

One man staggered out, clutching his ears and disoriented. Conor dropped him with a shot to the side of the head. Two more came after that one, crawling away from the flames on stumps and destroyed legs. Conor launched himself toward them, stopping only long enough to scoop up his tomahawk from where he'd thrown it at the AK shooter.

The crawling men were bleeding profusely. In better times, a tourniquet and advanced medical treatment would have saved their lives, but that was not happening today. These men would be dead soon enough but Conor wanted them to die with his blood-spattered visage forever burned onto their fading retinas.

The tomahawk lashed out, the hook sinking into the side of one man's throat. Conor yanked hard, drawing his powerful bicep taut, and the throat ripped free. Blood and gore showered Conor. The surviving crawler screamed for mercy. He begged, backed away, and offered his surrender. Conor had nothing to say. No witticism, no jab, and certainly no acknowledgment of the request for mercy. He stomped his combat boot onto the man's head and swung the tomahawk into the top of his skull like he was hammering a croquet ball.

Silhouetted now by the blazing loader, Conor began taking fire from several directions. He shoved the tomahawk into his belt. Rounds sang off the thick steel of the loader body. A bullet shattered against a hydraulic cylinder and fragments sprayed the back of his body armor. He couldn't stay there. He bolted to the opposite end of the loader, paused long enough to whip another grenade from a pouch on his plate carrier, and popped smoke. Added to the smoke and hellish flames from the burning tires, this would provide Conor with even more concealment to move within the fragmented group.

Low smoke filled the encampment while he ran forth in a maddened fury. He'd built his career on calculating and precise attention to detail, but tonight was none of those things. Tonight was chaos. It was a blood frenzy. It was a maddened berserker creating centuries of legend in one night. Conor no longer saw or heard, he no longer thought. He only reacted. He was a primal machine set to kill.

A man burst through the smoke, running full blast. He didn't seem to be charging Conor. Maybe he was trying to escape and Conor simply got in the way. Either way, escape was not an option. The man was too close to shoot so Conor slammed the butt of his rifle into the man's face. It was a like a pool cue smashing the cue ball on a break. The blow clotheslined the man and he dropped on his back. Conor pummeled him with more blows from the buttstock of his rifle. Only when a puddle formed in the middle of his face and blood splashed did Conor let up.

He straightened at the sound of more men running through the smoke. He dropped one with a burst of gunfire to the chest. The second was destined for the same treatment but Conor's rifle ran dry. He efficiently ejected the mag, pulled another from the carrier, and slammed it home. He'd done this a million times and could run drills with the best of them but there just wasn't enough time to do it. He didn't get the bolt released and a round chambered before the second man went airborne.

He was a big son-of-a-bitch and wrapped Conor in a bear hug, trapping his arms. Conor released his hands from the rifle but the sling kept it trapped against him. Conor staggered forward, testing the balance and grappling skills of the man latched onto his back. The man had both. He released his grip around Conor's chest and moved an arm up into a chokehold.

While Conor's bulky plate carrier made it difficult for him to maneuver, it also made it hard for the man to get a proper hold on Conor. Despite that, a chokehold could be dangerous even when wielded by an unskilled opponent. The window of time in which he had to react was small. Conor's hand found the ball peen hammer he'd picked up in the shop up the hill. He whipped it from his belt and swung it into the man's shin.

The man screamed, a high-pitched bellow of pain, and dropped to the ground. He rolled around cradling his shattered leg. The man's brain was so overloaded with signals from the damaged nerves that he could not find the words to beg for mercy. It would have been a futile effort anyway. Conor gave no quarter and accepted no surrender. He swung the hammer into the man's temple like Thor shattering stone. Conor drew back to strike again and saw there was no point. The hammer had sunk inches into the man's head, creating a basin of flesh and bone that filled with a vile stew of blood and brain matter.

Conor could hit him ten more times and he would get no deader.

27

Conor's attack on the camp brought a mixture of terror and relief. Ragus was terrified by the chaos but tried to mirror the bravery he saw in Barb. She appeared completely unfazed by everything going on around her. He tried to keep an eye on her to watch that she didn't do something impetuous. When she saw her father and called to him, Ragus experienced a moment of panic, concerned her yell may draw attention in the form of gunfire. When Conor tossed a handgun in their direction, both Ragus and Barb reflexively lashed out a hand to take hold of it.

Ragus looked at Barb with surprise. She looked at him with pure aggravation.

"Seriously?" she asked.

"I need to protect you."

"If you don't take your hand off that weapon, you're going to need protection *from* me."

Ragus let his hand linger there for a moment, gauging the seriousness of her statement. He found no humor in her eyes so he withdrew his hand reluctantly. "I didn't come all this way to watch you die."

JoAnn came crawling over, panic written all over her face. "What's happening?"

"It's my dad," Barb said. "I told you he'd rescue us." She shot a glance to the far end of the bridge, away from all the chaos and fighting. There had been a guard there before but she didn't see him now. He was hiding or had had the good sense to run.

"Get all the prisoners. Move them in that direction. Tell them to stay against the edge of the bridge and crouch down. I don't want anyone catching a stray bullet."

Ragus and JoAnn did as they were told. Starting with the women huddled nearest to them, they got their attention and pointed toward the open end of the bridge.

"Go! Go! Go!"

The first prisoners, spotting Barb running ahead of them with a handgun, fell in behind her without further prompting. JoAnn and Ragus didn't have to do anything else. The movement of those first prisoners was like pulling the plug on a drain, the prisoners flowing in that direction of their own accord and escaping their prison on the bridge.

Barb ran at the head of the column, a two-handed grip on the handgun. When her head moved, the gun moved, always ready to pull off a shot if the need presented itself. There was an abandoned car, which she approached cautiously and cleared. She took off again, waving a hand to urge the other captives forward. Up until the shooting started, the other guard had been walking back and forth in a highly visible position at the end of the bridge. She saw no sign of him.

When she reached the end of the bridge she threw up an arm, halting the prisoners. The pistol had a rail-mounted tactical light to go with the laser and she punched the button. A powerful LED beam cut through the smoke and the fog filling the river valley. She was relieved, concerned the light may have been damaged when Conor threw it to her. She saw no threats and moved the women forward. She took a position at the end of the bridge and directed the prisoners toward an overturned police car.

"Take cover there! Don't come out until I come back for you!"

The women ran unquestioningly. They responded to the fact that Barb had a gun and seemed to know what she was doing. Until Bonnie showed up.

She was the woman who'd been out in the woods with Lester and thwarted Barb's earlier escape attempt. She was the one who'd clubbed Barb over the head and took her out of the fight.

Her expression venomous, Bonnie got up in Barb's face. "If that's one of your people, I hope they kill the bastard," she hissed. "Not all of us have a place to go back to. Being kidnapped probably saved my life and now you're fucking it up."

Barb lashed out with the heel of her palm and struck the woman in the nose. She felt it break under the crushing blow. The blow hurt Barb's palm but she found it very satisfying. Bonnie crumpled backwards, her eyes rolling up into her head as blood erupted from her nose. Barb leveled the gun at her face. "You ever cross me again and I'll kill you. This is the only warning you get. If I see you again tonight, I might throw your ass off this bridge, so I'd recommend you stay clear."

The stunned woman rolled to her knees and started crawling off. Two other captives grabbed her by the arms and steered her toward the rest of the group.

"Did you save her life just so you could kick her ass?" Ragus asked.

Barb spun on him, her eyes flashing. "Did you save me just so I could kick yours?"

"Point taken," Ragus muttered.

The encounter with Bonnie reminded Barb she had unfinished business beyond saving these women. Only two men from this group had struck her and she'd killed the first, Howell. Now it was Lester's turn. She hoped he was still alive so she could have the pleasure of killing him personally.

Since the gunfire erupted, Barb had not seen Top Cat or Lester. They had been at their campfire with the other men eating dinner. When it became clear they were under attack, those two had disappeared in the ensuing chaos. She didn't expect they were gone yet. Whomever this man was back at the farm—the man who had sent him on this mission, and the one they discussed with such deference —held powerful sway over them.

They were concerned about going back empty-handed, about screwing up this mission. She didn't think they would leave without their cargo of captives unless every one of them was dead. She tried to put herself in their heads. Once she did, she immediately knew where to start looking. That pair was a little sharper than most of the men running around getting killed in the smoke and chaos. They would have gone for the stacks of rifles and ammo where the horses were tied up. They probably had horses saddled and waiting in case shit went seriously downhill.

When she confirmed all the captives were off the bridge she turned to Ragus. "I'm going after Lester. That bastard is mine."

"I'm not letting you go alone," Ragus said firmly.

"I'm not taking responsibility for you."

"I didn't ask you to. But I'm going with you, either way. You'll have to shoot me to stop me."

The pair locked eyes and Ragus experienced a moment of concern. Perhaps he'd overplayed his hand. Perhaps she *would* shoot him. He was never certain what she was thinking. He was certain only of one thing, that she was perhaps the most violent, most dangerous woman he'd ever met.

"Come on," she finally said. "Don't slow me down and don't question what I do."

There was a burst of full-auto fire from somewhere within the hellish arena. Barb looked into the smoke, the muted flickering of flames reflecting off her face. Further discussion was a waste of time. She bolted and disappeared into the smoke, Ragus hot on her heels.

He was scared but followed, his only objective to keep up with Barb. She was running at a full out sprint, her arms pumping, the handgun clutched in a single fist. The loud echoes of gunfire and the whine of bullets ricocheting off steel filled the air. There were shouts and screams, roars of fierce combat that Barb knew came from her father doing what he did.

Barb popped out of the densest smoke within sight of the horses and immediately came under fire. A bullet whizzed by her, low and to the left. Two bullets struck the ground in front of her, chewing up divots of earth and spraying her with dirt. Not wanting to give the shooter time to zero in on her, Barb kept running, hoping Ragus would understand what to do. The scene was dark and ominous. The smoke flashed with pockets of firelight, like lightning seen through distant clouds. The sulfurous smoke from the tires choked them with hellish fumes.

With her limited visibility Barb nearly ran into a heavy steel garbage can. It was a bear-resistant can, like you found in parks. If the shooter was using solid point rounds they might penetrate it but this was all she had. Any gunshot, no matter where it hit her, might be fatal. There was no evac, no hospital, and no medics. There was nobody but her dad to fix her if she took a serious bullet wound. Death was a likely consequence of any bad decisions.

More shots came in her general direction though none were close. She caught a muzzle flash that time and saw that whoever was shooting at her was dug in behind the tall pile of saddles. She held her fire, knowing she didn't have many rounds left in the 9mm pistol. It was just as well since the projectiles would not have significant penetration when hitting the thick leather saddles. She needed a certain shot.

There was a lull in the battle and she called to Ragus. "You good?"

"I'm not dead if that's what you're asking," he replied after a brief pause. The attempt at bravado fell flat when tinged with his obvious fear.

There was another exchange of gunfire beyond the curtain of smoke, then another choked scream. Conor was hunting stragglers. Barb heard a sound and squinted in the direction of the saddles. She caught a flicker of movement, a shadow, a body up and sprinting away. She popped off two shots at the fleeing body but couldn't bring herself to waste more ammo than that. It was possible she hit them but she was not confident. She dropped the magazine from the handgun, tipped it to the nearest source of flames, and thought she could make out the glint of at least two more rounds. She slammed it back home.

"So, which asshole are you?" Barb yelled.

The answer came in the form of four quick gunshots, closer than the last burst. There was a high-pitched whine as a round caught the edge of the garbage can. She had to assume he wasn't in the mood for discussion. She looked in Ragus' direction, briefly considering trying to involve him in a plan but he was too far away. Anything she yelled, the man behind the saddles would hear. There wasn't much cover, and she didn't want Ragus to break and try to reach her. He'd just get killed and that would be lousy payback for all the effort he'd put into finding her.

She thought her only option might be to get to the horses. The asshole behind the saddles might not fire into the herd. Not that the guy was an animal lover, but if he had any hope of salvaging this operation he would need those horses. She hopped back to her feet, into a sprinter's position, and launched herself into the darkness, running as hard as she could. Her breath pumped as rapid gunfire erupted in the night. Bullets impacted around her but nowhere close. The man had no concept of leading a running target and she was thankful for that small blessing. Her running startled the horses and they shuffled about, making high-pitched sounds of alarm.

When she reached them, she slipped into their midst. She tried to soothe them in her calmest voice. She stroked their flanks as she eased by, weaving her way through a maze of fur and flesh, trying to keep horses on all sides of her. Her plan was to work her way to his position, hoping that he could not get a shot at her without injuring his horses. It might force a reaction. He might run, but anything was better than a deadlock.

It was very dark where the horses stood. She had less visibility here than she had at her previous position. A wall of decorative trees blocked much of the firelight and though she could catch glimpses of light, it did little to aid her sight.

The horses had grown accustomed to her presence. They were quiet now, no longer shuffling or moving, no longer making sounds of alarm. She pressed her way through them and heard nothing from outside the large herd. Was the man still there? Had he moved? Did he know she was coming?

She heard a noise to her right and jerked in that direction, turning her back to the warm sides of a quarter horse. She realized the noise must've been a ploy, a distraction, when an arm came across the back of the horse and snaked around her neck. Understanding the lethality of a choke, she dropped her gun as she tried to get both hands up under the arm and pry them from her neck. Her attacker had leverage, though, and strength. He was anchored firmly against the horse, giving him a mechanical advantage. By simply tightening his arms he was able to lift her off her feet.

Being unable to use her legs put Barb at a tremendous disadvantage. She was now dangling from his powerful chokehold. His hands were locked together, fixing the hold around her neck. Despite having both hands hooked beneath his arm she could not pry him loose. It was not only his tremendous strength, but the fact that the horse was in between them, preventing her from using any of the typical moves she would use to break a chokehold. She could not throw elbows, attempt to gouge his eyes, bring a heel to his groin, or stomp his foot. She was completely powerless, a feeling she feared more than death itself. She was in no immediate danger of blacking out, but neither could she escape.

She considered yelling for help but what if there was another shooter out there? If both Lester and Top Cat had been hidden behind those saddles, yelling at Ragus would only draw him into the fire. She couldn't do that. She had to solve this problem on her own.

The horse directly in front of her was growing uneasy, worried by the sounds and frantic gestures she was making. He took a step further away from her and it gave her an idea. She raised both her feet and kicked hard against the side of the horse in front of her. The move startled that horse, and also the quarter horse she was pinned against. Uncertain of what was going on, the horses shied away from each other.

The quarter horse behind Barb stepped in the direction of her attacker, throwing him off balance. She could sense his indecision, the knowledge that while he did not want to let go of Barb's neck he could not let himself be trampled. Taking advantage of what she had set in motion, Barb began raining powerful elbows against the side of the quarter horse between them.

It had no idea how to react to such physical aggression. It tried to move away from her, stepping yet again toward her attacker. His grip broke, slipping from her as the horse pushed against his body. It didn't feel like he was giving up. It felt like he was falling or being pulled beneath the horse. Taking a risk, she jerked her body hard and pulled loose from his grip. She dropped to the ground and spun, shooting her arms beneath the horse and finding the man's ankles. She hooked her hands around them and tugged hard, pulling his legs out from under him.

The man grunted as he fell hard, unable to regain his balance with the horse pushing against him and Barb pulling. The instant he hit the ground, Barb wasted no time. She began shooting groin strikes with her powerful right fist. The man cried out and tried to block, to kick at her, but she parried his moves. The horse could take no more and shuffled away from them, stepping on the man's bicep as it slewed away from their combat. The man tried to roll away from Barb's brutal punches, ending up on his stomach. Barb was waiting for this. She nearly smiled as she sprang onto his back and locked him in a rear naked choke.

Barb now knew that the man under her was Lester. She recognized his voice in the grunts and groans as the struggled. He fought valiantly for a moment but he was too beaten down by the groin punches to effectively defend himself any longer. His resistance to the choke was a token gesture. He had nothing left. She felt him give in, submit, and knew then that he would be dead shortly. If she felt anything at all, it was satisfaction.

"Remember calling me *sweetie*?" she hissed. "Sweetie is going to kill you. What do you think of that?"

"Let him go!" a voice demanded from the dark. Then the blinding beam of a flashlight hit her. She blinked but did not release her grip. "I said let him go!"

For a moment she thought it might be her dad. She realized that she hadn't heard gunfire or screaming for the last few minutes. Then she recognized this voice as Top Cat. She released a hand from the limp man, drawing his handgun from the holster on his belt and whipping it up toward the light. "Make me."

The light moved away from her face, snaking slowly across the distance between them before revealing Ragus, his neck locked in the crook of Top Cat's elbow. A .45 automatic was pressed against his temple.

"Surely this boy has to mean something to you. After all, he came all this way to rescue you. Don't tell me you're going to let me blow his brains out right in front of you."

"Ragus," Barb growled. Her cry was a plea of desperation, expressing anger, disappointment, and frustration.

"I'm sorry," he said. "He was on me before I saw him."

"Toss away the gun and get off Lester," Top Cat ordered.

Barb sagged her head in defeat. She tossed Lester's pistol in Top Cat's direction and released her hold on Lester's neck. She sat upright on his back and the man stirred. She got off him and scooted away, then stood, glaring at Top Cat defiantly.

"What did she call you boy?" he asked. "Ragus? What the hell kind of name is that?"

Barb knew this was a sore spot for the boy. He became defiant anytime he was asked. "None of your damn business."

Top Cat shook his head in the harsh glare of the flashlight. "That's no way to talk, boy." There was a flash of movement and Top Cat struck Ragus in the head with the pistol. It was not enough of a blow to knock him out or seriously injure him but the metal base of the grip lacerated his scalp. Blood seeped down over his forehead.

"I asked you a question. I expect a polite answer."

"It's just a name," Barb said. "I asked him before and he doesn't know. It's just some weird fucking hillbilly name his mom came up with. He's a dumb kid. Leave him alone."

Ragus mumbled something unintelligible.

"What the hell did you say?" Top Cat asked, drawing back the pistol, preparing to whack Ragus again if he felt disrespected.

"Ragus is *sugar* spelled backward. My mother named me Ragus because she thought I was going be a sweet baby."

Lester guffawed. "Now that's some stupid bullshit right there," Lester said, staggering to his feet. He retched and gagged, then coughed violently. The moment the coughing spasm stopped, he lashed out with a violent jab that caught Barb off guard. The punch hit her just below her left eye. She staggered and fell backward.

"I thought you were some kind of tough bitch," Lester snarled at the fallen woman. "Get back up! We're not done playing yet."

Top Cat, who usually disapproved of Lester's crude and often violent behavior, appeared to have no problem with it this time. When Barb righted herself, a grin was widening on Top Cat's face in the glow of the flashlight. He was gloating, relishing the moment. He was enjoying the show.

Before her brain could make sense of what she was seeing, a gloved palm wrapped around Top Cat's face and wrenched it violently to the right, followed by a sickening pop. When the gloved hand was removed, the head remained obscenely staring backward, looking Conor directly in the face. Ragus moved away as the hand around his neck released him and the gun dropped to the ground.

Lester was not fully aware of what had taken place but knew that the window of time in which he could get his own revenge was closing. His hand dropped to his left hip, to the fixed blade knife he always carried there, but his hand landed on an empty sheath. He looked down in surprise.

The knife was in Barb's hand, removed when she climbed off Lester's body. She lashed out with the razor sharp blade, slashing the tendons above his right knee. Lester bellowed and the leg folded under him. He collapsed in a heap, unable to control how or where he fell.

With no weapons at his disposal, he opened his mouth to bargain, to beg for mercy, to do anything to see his life spared but he did not get the words out. Barb slid the long blade into the side of his neck. Lester had a moment where some clarity remained, where he pondered the seriousness of his injury, the sensation of the stiff metal object embedded in the soft flesh of his neck. He felt a tug, the blade viciously slashing out the front of his neck, and then he was gone, fading like an old light bulb.

Conor leapt over Top Cat's body and took his daughter up in a desperate embrace. While the overwhelming emotion was relief, there remained an undercurrent of panic, the awareness of how close they'd come to losing each other. The emotional complexity of the embrace between the two blood-spattered and gore-encrusted warriors seemed unfathomable. It was only now that Conor let his emotional armor slip. The tears flowed and he sobbed openly, the tears rinsing ghastly tracks in the blood coagulating on his face.

"I was so scared," Conor said. "I can't tell you what it felt like to know you were out here and I couldn't protect you. I wasn't certain I'd ever find you. I might not have had it not been for the lad."

At the mention of the boy, Conor was hit with the awareness that he and his daughter were not the only pieces to this puzzle any more. Conor raised his damp eyes from his daughter's head and looked at Ragus. The boy stood several feet from them, watching with both hands shoved in his pockets. He looked uncomfortable. Conor knew what he needed. He understood the boy needed closure and de-escalation as badly as they did.

"My boy," Conor said softly, raising an arm and beckoning Ragus with a gory glove.

He didn't move at first, uncertain if he should intrude on what was clearly such an intimate family moment. Then Barb turned to him too, her expression softer than he'd ever seen it, and she opened their embrace to him. They all knew the significance. It was the opening of more than an embrace. It was the opening of a life. Ragus was one of them now.

He walked over tentatively, uncertain as to what to do. Conor lashed out and grabbed him by the sleeve, pulling him hard into them. Father and daughter both hugged him tight and Ragus was overwhelmed with emotion. He knew his place in this world, knew his worth, and knew what he was to these people. He was not alone anymore.

"You're fucking family now, Ragus. You're one of us. When we get home, I'd be honored for you to move in with us. You belong under our roof and at our table. God knows we've got the room."

Ragus had no idea that such a simple statement could have such a profound effect on him. His guard slipped, and the tears flowed. He had not let his emotions see the light of day since he'd shoveled dirt onto his poor dead mother. He understood this was not just a gesture of thanks for going after Barb. He had proven himself to these folks and their appreciation was genuine. As they'd said, he was one of them now. He felt a warmth inside, a peace, that had been absent since the death of his mother. It felt like warm water running back into pipes long left empty. He could never have imagined in the midst of this gore, death, and extreme violence, he would find a family.

No one, neither rescued nor rescuer, wanted to spend the night in the midst of the carnage. The brushfires started by Conor's improvised pyrotechnics had burned their way down to embers, running out of dried grass and brush when they hit rocky sections of the steep mountains. Barb and Ragus kept the former captives on the other side of the bridge until Conor finished dispatching the wounded. He had done such a thorough job of killing that there were few for whom the task was incomplete. There were some who'd caught bullets in non-lethal areas of the body and crawled away. Conor found the suppressed Henry .22 among the saddles, using it to finish the wet work.

When the death detail had finished its rounds, they dug through the kidnappers' gear and found what flashlights and headlamps they could. With those, they saddled the horses and the pack horses then set out. They searched the bodies for weapons, ammo, and gear, leaving the corpses where they fell. Kidnappers and slave-takers were unworthy of the sweat required for a decent burial.

They used some of the weapons and ammunition to arm the former captives who were familiar with operating weapons. Barb would not arm Bonnie, though. She did not trust that woman at her back with anything dangerous. Barb gave the petulant woman the opportunity to take a horse and continue on in an attempt to find a better place for herself.

"What do you care?" Bonnie growled in response to Barb's offer.

"I don't," Barb responded, "but you have to go somewhere."

"I got nothing at home. Nobody at home."

"It's familiar territory. You might do better in a place you know than as a stranger in a place you don't know."

Bonnie chose to go with them, but displayed no gratitude or appreciation. Barb would be surprised if they made it all the way home without her having to kill this woman. While it would probably be wiser to just banish her here and avoid the possibility of the fight, Conor had not raised her that way. She'd try to do the right thing until she couldn't anymore.

They put nearly ten miles between them and the scene of the battle before the adrenaline and the bad memories began to dissipate. Nearly everyone but Conor was nodding off in their saddles. They pulled over and set up camp beneath the canopy of an abandoned convenience store. The women no longer needed the tablecloths, instead finding rest inside the sleeping bags belonging to their former captors.

Conor insisted that he could not sleep and chose to remain on watch for the night. Barb told him she would switch out later if he would wake her up. He promised he would but she knew he was lying. He was her father. He would let his baby sleep, even if that's not what she wanted to do.

28

The ride home with the freed captives was nearly relaxing after the urgency of the days of dogged pursuit. The ability to relax came from knowing that anyone who might pursue them lay rotting in the stark light of a roadside battlefield many miles north of them. It also came from Barb, Conor, and Ragus, now a family of three, being together. They remained vigilant against anyone who might see them as prey, yet had time to talk and get to know each other. There was a lot to learn but things had changed between them by virtue of this experience. They were bonded. They were tempered by fire.

They stopped at the location where Barb had killed Howell and she told her dad how it went down. It was interesting for Conor to hear the details and see how they matched up with his earlier speculations. They retrieved Ragus' gear from the woods and the young man was glad to have his pack on his back again. Conor had reunited him with the Henry rifle after the battle was over. The pack and the rifle had come to feel like part of him. The gear kept him alive on his trek after Barb.

When they passed the dead men Ragus had left as directional

markers, some of the women wondered if they should stop and give them a Christian burial.

"They're undeserving of our sweat and toil," Conor said. "Let them feed the ants. Let people see them and speculate on how they came to end up where they did. They'll become part of the legend and that legend will protect us as it grows."

"What legend?" one of the women asked.

"The only way we prevent this from happening again is we band together," Conor announced. "We work as a group to maintain security and we develop a plan for communicating with each other. The legend to which I was referring is the manner in which we capitalize on this experience. It was unpleasant for all of us and we might as well derive some benefit from it."

Conor withdrew the combat tomahawk from his pack and went to a tree visible from the pair of bodies. He shaved off a circle of bark facing the road at head level. It was nearly a foot in diameter. Using bold strokes of the tomahawk, he formed the letters *MM*.

"What's that mean?" asked the woman.

"The Mad Mick," Ragus replied.

Conor nodded. "As we get closer to home, we leave more of those. It's like the signs for security companies you used to see in fancy neighborhoods. These are protected by ADT or whoever. Except in this case, it means that this area is protected by the Mad Mick."

"And that's you?" the woman asked.

"I may be the face of it," Conor replied, "but it's not only me, it's all of us. It's your husbands and sons. It's you and your daughters. It's all of us working together to keep this from happening again."

"How do we do that? We're not soldiers. We're not fighters like you."

"You do it by spreading the legend of the Mad Mick," Barb replied, seeing where this was going. "You tell the story of what happened on this trip and you make it wilder with each telling. If you're speaking to a stranger, someone from outside our community, you describe the Mad Mick as a dangerous madman who guards our community to keep people safe. He's the sheepdog who drives out the wolves, who protects the sheep."

The woman, in fact all the women, appeared overwhelmed by this but it wasn't just the story. It was everything they'd gone through. The trauma of the experience would be slow passing. There would be nightmares and tears. They would fear strangers for a long time, but perhaps that was the safest response to have. The coming winter would be a hard one with deep snows and long periods of time spent in a single room by a warm fire, just like the pioneers that settled this region. Around those fires, they would tell stories like folks used to. Variations would develop. Stories would be embellished. By spring, the legend of the Mad Mick would reach as far as Asheville, Knoxville, Roanoke, and Charleston.

~

CONOR DID his part to encourage the legend. Every man deterred from bad actions by the legend was one less the sheepdog had to engage. By the time the snows of winter melted, everyone in their greater community carried an ax or hatchet on their forays into the woods. As Conor did that first time on the road home, they shaved the bark from trees and carved crude *MM*s to mark the range of the Mad Mick.

Those markers were on every road and trail in the region. By the following summer they would saturate the area Conor recognized as their community. As people from outside the area learned that the mark was one of protection, they carved them in their communities too. The sign began to have the power of some ancient talisman that warded off evil.

People distant from Conor's community, who knew the meaning of the mark but had never heard the story of its origin, were forced to make up their own Mad Mick stories. Through those, the legend grew epic and feats impossible for any man became attributed to him. Many were pure fabrication, but unfortunately many others were based on truth.

Bad men would continue to come, wolves intent on preying on the good people of his community. Conor was ready for them. Barb and Ragus too. They would take on the fights. They would be the sheepdogs unafraid of violence, unafraid of unleashing a savagery that made people hesitant to meet their eyes. It was the cost of the role. It was the cost of being the shaman that kept the demons at bay.

EPILOGUE

In the midst of December, snow lay heavily on the ground. The full moon made travel easier for the three moving somberly to their dark duty. Ragus was at the lead. This was his trip. His mission. He was the only one who knew where they were going.

The world was silent, muffled by the coating of snow. The road between Jewell Ridge and the town had a few sets of tracks, most made by this very group coming and going with their new horses. They'd ended up with nearly ten. Trading captured weapons they'd brought home on the pack horses had helped them secure feed for the winter. They had a better plan for next year and would store hay and grain, should order not be restored to the nation by that point.

They brought lights but did not use them, choosing instead to preserve their night vision for the advantage it gave them. Nearly two hours later, they rode up a mostly abandoned street in a neighborhood on the fringes of town. Wood smoke hung in the air, an indication that some people were alive and making it. It was the scent of survival in the post-electric world. Fire was life.

Ragus stopped in front of the house. He remembered it vividly. Remembered the beating he took in the back yard. He remembered lying on the ground being kicked, worried about everything but his own wellbeing. He'd hoped they wouldn't hurt him so badly he couldn't make it home to help his mother. He'd worried that his appearance, bloody and bruised, may upset her. He'd been concerned that the longer they beat him, the longer it delayed him from continuing on his mission to find pain medication for his dying mother. He'd sworn then that he'd be back one day. He would take his revenge.

The day was upon them.

Ragus dismounted and handed his reins to Conor. The boy carried a full-auto AK pistol. He chambered a round, slid the awkward safety to the fire position, and walked through an opening in the chain link fence. He recalled there once being a gate there. Shadows in the snow showed a constant stream of visitors. Trash was piled in the yard and deposited against the fence by the winter wind.

There was laughter inside. Obviously the drug-impaired were still able to find their moments of joy despite the despair in the world. There was the glow of flickering light from a lantern or candle. Ragus raised the weapon and pulled the trigger, raking the front of the house. Windows shattered and screams erupted from the darkness. When the mag ran dry, he switched it with a recently-acquired smoothness and lit the house up again. This time he stopped before he dumped the entire mag.

He stood boldly in the front yard, confident that he'd be difficult to spot since the people in the house were accustomed to the light. The occasional *ting* of glass dropping from window frames and breaking against hard surfaces was the only sound. Tattered and bullet-riddled curtains flapped within the damaged window openings.

"Get your ass out here!" Ragus yelled.

There was no response.

He pulled a grenade from his pocket, hefted it in his hand, pulled the pin, and tossed it through the dark chasm where the picture window had once been. The grenade popped and irritating clouds of CS gas spilled into the living room. There was coughing and choking.

"Get out now!" Ragus ordered.

"Don't shoot!" came a male voice from the inside. "We're coming out."

Three men Ragus recognized even in the dark streamed onto the porch. They huddled against the cold, struggling with whether to wrap their arms around themselves in an attempt to stay warm or to keep them raised so Ragus would not shoot them.

"You remember me?" Ragus asked.

There was silence, then one man spoke. "Remember you? I can't even fucking see you."

"I came here to buy pain pills for my mother. She was dying of cancer. I had money. You all beat me and took my money."

There was a moment of silence. The men exchanged glances. Across the distance, in the pale moonlight, Ragus was unable to see their expressions. He hoped there was awareness. Recognition. Fear.

"You shouldn't have come here with such a lame-assed story," the man said. "Do you know how many times we've heard that shit? Hell, most of us have even used it a time or two to try and score."

"I was serious. My mother was dying. I was desperate. I needed help and you all decided beating and robbing a kid was something worth doing. Do you know how that made me feel?"

Silence.

"We're sorry, kid."

"Somehow, I doubt your sincerity," Ragus replied. "But I've thought about you guys. A lot. I thought about you while I watched her die. I thought about you while I dug her grave. I promised myself that this moment would come."

"Listen, kid, you don't need to do anything stupid," the man urged.

There was a scratching sound and a road flare illuminated in Conor's hand. The trio on the porch noticed the other riders for the first time, their ominous expressions harsh in the glare of the flame. Ragus nodded at Conor, who heaved the flare into the house. It hit the curtains and flames rose within seconds.

"What the fuck, dude?" one of the men screamed.

"You have to leave," Ragus announced. "You have to go far away."

"Like where?" the man said, his voice cracking. "It's cold. It's snowing. All our shit is in there. Our coats, our boots, everything."

"You'll find no sympathy in this heart. You can start walking now," Ragus said. "We're going to follow you to make sure you don't bother decent folks. If you stop walking, I'll tie a rope to you and drag you through the snow. If you try to escape, I'll kill you. If I ever see you again, I'll kill you. You'd best go as far away as you can and you don't ever come back."

The crackling inside grew as the fire spread. It was beyond anything the three men could extinguish now. Anything they had inside—clothes, guns, gear, food, drugs—would be lost in the flames.

Ragus turned his back on the men and returned to his horse. In the glowing flames, he looked at Conor and Barb, bundled in heavy winter clothes, weapons leveled on the drug dealers. They were his family. He slung the rifle on his shoulder and mounted his horse.

Conor leaned forward to pat him on the shoulder. "You did good, son."

Ragus found he could not reply. So much of what was dammed inside him had been breaking loose lately and a chunk of it was stuck in his throat right now. This was the last piece of an old puzzle. He could now lay it to rest with a lot of other things that haunted him. Life was different now. Ragus was different too.

There seemed to be understanding amongst the three. Barb and Conor expected no words from him. They understood and rode in silence, three abreast on a cold, dark night with the smell of wood smoke in the air, three sheepdogs of the apocalypse. They followed the freezing men to the boundary of their territory and waited until they disappeared into the night.

"Do you think they'll come back?" Ragus asked.

"Probably," Conor said. "Some folks never learn."

"You'll end up killing them eventually," Barb pointed out.

Everyone understood that was probably the truth. It was a fight for another day though. They turned their horses and began the long ride home.

"Sugar," Barb said to no one in particular. "Your mother named you after sugar." It was as if the memory of this confession hit her again and she felt compelled to bring it up.

"Yes, and yours named you Barb."

ABOUT THE AUTHOR

Franklin Horton lives and writes in the mountains of Southwestern Virginia. He is the author of the bestselling post-apocalyptic series *The Borrowed World* and *Locker Nine*, as well as the thriller *Random Acts*. You can follow him on his website at franklinhorton.com. Please sign up for the mailing list for special offers and the latest updates.

ALSO BY FRANKLIN HORTON

The Borrowed World

Ashes of the Unspeakable

Legion of Despair

No Time For Mourning

Valley of Vengeance

Switched On

Locker Nine

Grace Under Fire

Random Acts

Please Enjoy This Sample From

RANDOM ACTS
By
Franklin Horton

RANDOM ACTS - CHAPTER ONE

The thick hood over his head prevented Mohammed Karwan from seeing anything, but the dank smell reaching his nose convinced him he was standing on the earthen floor of one of Frankfurt's ancient buildings. He suspected his two other roommates were there with him but when he tried to ask in the back of the van he had been struck in the head with a fist. Although not an injurious blow, it was substantial enough to clarify that conversation would not be tolerated. He would have to wait as patiently as a hooded man could wait to see what fate lay ahead of them.

Mohammed and his roommates each received a text message several hours ago asking them to be at their flat by eight P.M. Fifteen minutes after the appointed time, a man they did not know arrived at the flat and instructed them to be at the mosque in thirty minutes. There was no confusion as to which mosque. There was only one mosque to which they were ever summoned.

"Do you think something is wrong?" Machmud asked. He was the most high-strung and nervous of the roommates, always concerned that he was in peril. Perhaps he was not cut out for this business of theirs, but that was irrelevant. This was their life. This was where they found themselves.

Mohammed, the senior of the men, shook his head at Machmud's question. "I don't know, my brother. I assume we will find out in due time." He was the stoic one, his fatalistic attitude the result of a life filled with brutality and violence.

Machmud did not speak again. The men filed onto the street and loaded into the used Renault Megane they shared when a vehicle was required. When they reach the mosque, they parked in an alley and entered through a side door. They were met by four men who gestured for them to turn around and face away from them. These were strong, menacing men dressed as laborers. They were not men to be argued with.

The laborers placed a hood roughly over each man's head. Mohammed was startled.

Machmud tried to twist away and face the laborers. "But why?"

The man attempting to place the hood on Machmud's head twisted his mouth in anger. He let loose with a powerful jab that sent Machmud staggering into the wall. The man twisted Machmud's stunned body and shoved him face-first into the wall.

"That was not a request," he growled.

The man made another attempt with the hood and this time Machmud did not protest. Mohammed was grabbed roughly from behind, his wrists clamped together by a strong hand before being bound with flex-cuffs. From the ratcheting sounds surrounding him, he could tell the other roommates were being cuffed also. Mohammed knew he'd done nothing wrong, but he still found the circumstances to be terrifying. He was also painfully aware that innocence was no guarantee he would return home this night. People in his line of work disappeared all the time and no one ever asked questions.

They were marched out the back door and shoved into the rear compartment of a windowless work van. Mohammed heard Machmud protest again. It was followed by the dull thud of a physical reprimand and the accompanying cry of pain.

Mohammed apparently failed to learn from Machmud's treatment. "Is everyone okay?" he asked. "Are you all here?"

He was rewarded with a blow to the head that rattled his brain and made his eyes water.

Mohammed chose to remain silent from that point and focus on the right and left turns. He was familiar enough with this area that, for a while, he was able to keep track of their direction of travel. It became clear the driver was attempting to confuse them, and he eventually succeeded.

The drove aimlessly for hours before Mohammed found himself standing on the packed dirt floor somewhere in the city. He assumed the location to be an abandoned factory or warehouse. The city was full of them. All he could tell with his senses muted by the hood and the noise of the van was they'd entered through a pair of rolling doors and parked inside the structure. When the engine was turned off, the van doors were opened and they were shoved out into a heap.

When the hoods were yanked from their heads, the roommates found themselves staring at six robed men seated in folding chairs. Propane lanterns were scattered around the room, providing a bright yellowish light that created long shadows and did nothing to reduce the grave appearance of the seated men. Mohammed recognized two of them. One was their handler, the man who came to the roommates for progress reports and updates. He was the man who brought them their instructions, the man he assumed carried news of their progress–or lack of it–to the leaders of their organization. If he were a betting man, Mohammed would assume these unfamiliar men in front of him were part of that senior leadership, fellow Syrians from back home.

The other man he recognized was the Imam, the prayer leader from the local mosque. Dressed in traditional robes and with a long gray beard, the Imam kept his hands folded in his lap, his eyes moving between the faces of the roommates. To the side of the seated men was a crude wooden table. A cast iron kettle sat atop a small stove, flames spilling out around it as the kettle heated. Mohammed did not expect they were going to offer him a cup of tea.

A man Mohammed had not met before addressed him. "Do you know who I am?"

Mohammed nodded, a slight bow of deferral. "We have not met, but I think I recognize you." He thought the man was a leader within his organization. Perhaps a man named Miran.

"Do you know why I am here?" Miran asked.

Mohammed shook his head.

Miran stood. He appeared to be in his forties, beginning to gray but still dangerously strong. He moved like a soldier, efficient and powerful. He walked to the wooden table and lifted the wire bail from the lid of the kettle, peering inside. He appeared to be satisfied with what he found as it brought a slight smile to his face. He looked from the kettle to Mohammed.

"Did you know an apartment with four of our brothers was raided yesterday?"

Mohammed nodded. "I saw the story on the news."

Miran left the table and stood directly in front of him. Mohammed didn't feel as if he'd done anything wrong but this man made him question that. This was a man who would not hesitate to kill someone who had failed him.

"Their arrest makes you our most senior group in the field. That's unfortunate for us because you've not produced any fruitful results. It's unfortunate for you since the pressure of a successful mission now lays upon *your* shoulders."

Mohammed did not know how to respond.

"We do not have the deep pockets some organizations have," Miran said. "We cannot support people living in expensive city apartments and not producing results. Many men work hard to allow you to live this life in the city, to allow you to work with computers instead of stone and concrete."

"We are working hard too," Mohammed said. "Work is all we do. Exactly as we were instructed. As we were trained."

Miran tilted his shoulders in a gesture that indicated he thought the sincerity of the statement was questionable. He gave Mohammed a disbelieving look. "Well, I think not *all* of you work as you should."

"We do," Mohammed assured him.

"Are you willing to stake our life on that?" Miran asked.

Mohammed looked down. "I assume it to be so. I do not look over every shoulder."

"Wise decision, not staking your life on it," Miran said. "Your fellow man will disappoint you as often as he will impress you."

A pop from the kettle drew everyone's attention. Miran smiled at Mohammed and rubbed his hands together. "Ah, it's ready. Finally."

Miran went back to the table, peering into the top of the kettle again. He reached into a pocket of his robe and drew out a potato. From a sheath on his belt he drew a traditional dagger, its point curved and wicked. He placed the potato on the table and cut it into slices. All eyes were on him, some curious, some terrified.

Miran stabbed the tip of the dagger into one round slice of the potato and dropped it into the kettle. There was a hiss and pop.

"Oil," he explained. "If you thought I invited you over for tea, you are to be sadly disappointed."

Miran walked back around the table and faced the three roommates. "Which of you is Machmud?"

"Why do you ask! I've done nothing!" Machmud burst out.

Mohammed turned and regarded his roommate. Why was the man so agitated?

Miran approached Machmud and smiled broadly. "Why are you so upset, my brother?"

"I feel like I'm being accused," Machmud sputtered. "I've done nothing."

"Perhaps that feeling is the jagged edge of your guilt sawing against your guts?" Miran said, leaning close to Machmud. "Perhaps your body betrays what the mind tries to cover up?"

Miran walked back to the table and used the blade of his dagger to fish the potato slice from the oil. It was browned to a crisp. Miran looked past the roommates to the silent row of laborers who'd delivered them here.

"Bring him to me."

There was no hesitation on their part. Instantly, a man was at each side and they dragged Machmud forward. He protested and kicked at the men. This was not well-received. One laborer stomped his heavy steel-toed boot sadistically across Machmud's calf, forcing a scream from the man.

"I've done nothing!" Machmud sobbed.

Miran ignored the protests. He walked around the table. "Stand him up!" he ordered.

The men pulled Machmud to his feet but his injured leg would not support his weight. He was weaving and leaning onto his captors.

"Where were you when you received our text message tonight?" Miran asked. "Where were you when we asked you to return to the apartment?"

"I was with a contact," Machmud said urgently. He was sweating profusely and tears cut paths through the dust caked on his face. "I was cultivating a relationship."

"What type of relationship?" Miran persisted.

"A contact. That's all."

Miran grabbed Machmud by the hair and raised the dagger to his throat. "Do you think we are so stupid as to turn you loose with no way to monitor you? Did you not realize you were always on a virtual leash? That we tracked all your movements both in the city and on the internet? That we know every website you go to and every message you send?"

Machmud's panic rose another notch and he tried to protest. "I've...done...nothing...wrong."

"Your job was to make inroads we could exploit. Your goal was to cultivate relationships and nurture those relationships into assets we could manipulate. Instead, all you've done is pursue your own *deviant* pleasure." Miran drew the word deviant out, relishing the way it sounded on his tongue.

"I did nothing."

"Do I need to read the transcripts out loud?" Miran yelled, getting in Machmud's face. "Do you I need to read the messages aloud? Do I need to show the pictures you exchanged?"

Machmud sobbed and went limp. The men supporting him allowed him to drop to the ground. His hands still flex-cuffed, he curled up and sobbed. "I am sorry. She tempted me and I could not resist."

"Did she tell you things you liked to hear?" Miran mocked. "Was she a temptress?"

Machmud moaned. "Yes. Yes!"

"Then we will make certain you do not hear things that tempt you again," Miran spat. "Hold him down!"

The men at Machmud's side slid on thick leather welding gloves which they used hold Machmud down. One of them, a thick man with arms like tree trunks, placed one on Machmud's neck and another on his forehead, crushing his cheek into the dirt floor. Miran went to the kettle of boiling oil and returned with it. He crouched over Machmud's ear.

Machmud whimpered and cried, still not completely certain what was about to take place. He could not see what Mohammed saw. He struggled but he could not gain ground against the strong arms holding him. Miran tipped the kettle to Machmud's ear.

Machmud screamed. He kicked and fought like an animal, but Miran continued pouring until the ear was full.

"Flip him over," Miran ordered.

The gloved men did as they were told. As they rolled him over, Mohammed could see Machmud's eyes wide with pain, shock, and terror. He tried to scream again but no scream could release the explosion of pain inside his head.

Once rolled to his other side Miran leaned over Machmud and whispered into his ear. "Remember my voice. It is the last you'll ever hear."

Then he poured the other ear full of the burning oil, deep frying everything within the canal. Miran returned to the table and placed the kettle beside the burner. "Take him away!"

The gloved men grabbed Machmud by his arms and dragged him away into the darkness. Mohammed wondered what would become of him. Would they kill him? Would they return him home? When Mohammed returned his eyes from Machmud to Miran he found the man staring at him.

"Have I made myself clear?" Miran asked. "Are you aware now of how serious and how urgent our mission is?"

"We understand," Mohammed replied.

"I will return in two weeks. You have that long to develop an actionable plan. Should you have nothing for me, what you saw tonight will look like the easy way out."

"We will not disappoint you," Mohammed said.

Miran's look indicated he was not convinced. "Get them out of here," he hissed.

The hood was thrown back over Mohammed's head and he was shoved from the room. He felt a sickness deep inside that made him want to throw up, though to do so with the hood on his head would only increase his suffering. He had not known Machmud well and had not known of his activities on the computer.

He also had not known they were being monitored so closely. That concerned him. There were times he watched a stupid video to blow off steam and relax. One thing was certain; he would type each word now with the understanding that he might one day have to stand before Miran and explain it. He would type each word with the understanding his life may one day depend on it.

W2

Made in the USA
Monee, IL
21 May 2020